MURDER
at
HAMMOND CASTLE

THE SECOND ANNIE QUITNOT MYSTERY

Gunilla Caulfield

GUNILLA CAULFIELD

ISBN: 1452853738
ISBN-13: 9781452853734
LCCN: 2010906584

Also by Gunilla Caulfield:

The Wave: A Novel in the Time of Global Warming
The Bookseller and Other Stories

• • •

Murder on Bearskin Neck
(The first Annie Quitnot mystery)

DEDICATION

For John Pettibone, the real life curator at the Hammond Castle Museum. A great caretaker of the beautiful castle, and a man of erudition with a deep knowledge of Hammond and his inventions, John Pettibone has many anecdotes to tell and does so at many of the events at the castle.

For Bob and Mabel Cooney, who took me under their wings when I moved into Rockport, and who introduced me to my husband.

For my earliest Rockport friends, Jim and Stephanie Cole.

For my friend Linda Johnson at the Cape Ann Museum, who advises me frequently on local history. (Any mistakes are my own.)

With a special thank you to the owners of the historic Hannah Jumper House for allowing me to use it as Annie Quitnot's abode.

And for Tom, always, with love.

. . .

PROLOGUE

"That is my home of love: if I have rang'd,
Like him that travels, I returne againe."
(Shakespeare, "Sonnet 109")

When the real murderer is found and all charges are finally dropped against Rockport reference librarian Annie Quitnot in the killing of her former lover, Carlo Valenti, Annie's brother Justin suggests that she fly down to New Mexico with him to get away from it all.

By the end of summer, Annie feels it is time to return to Massachusetts, despite the fact that she is suffering from a growing case of stage fright. Going back to her desk at the library seems a daunting prospect, especially after the front-page exposé of her former love life and the shocking murder charge. In a small Cape Ann town, it can be hard to live things like that down—especially that part about the love life. People will talk about that long after the murder is forgotten. According to local convention, once your reputation has come into question, some people will never look at you quite the same way again.

Annie misses her home, the snug old Hannah Jumper House with its view of the harbor, as well as her beloved Shakespeare collection and the comfortably worn easy chair by the fireplace. And—oh yes—she misses Augustus, her elderly dachshund. While Annie is away, Gussie is staying with

Duncan Langmuir, director of the library as well as a long-time friend. Duncan, another lover of Shakespeare and the arts, is a kindred spirit. Embarrassing as it seemed afterwards, he was also someone she had in a hysterical moment suspected of murdering Carlo. Undaunted by Annie's lack of trust in him, Langmuir had remained her loyal supporter. Before she left for New Mexico with Justin, the director had hinted ever so gently at a wish for a more "interesting" relationship, but Annie hadn't been ready yet. The loss of Carlo—and the shock of all that followed—had been too overwhelming. Still, life cannot be postponed forever, and Annie is reaching an age when spinsterhood looms as a distinct possibility.

• • •

CHAPTER ONE

"A woman's time of opportunity is short,
And if she doesn't seize it, no one wants to marry her,
And she sits waiting for omens."
(Aristophanes, Lysistrata)

When Annie returns to the library, she finds on her desk an arrangement of roses of such obscene beauty and overpoweringly sweet scent that she has to sit down. She knows they are not from Esa, the janitor, who frequently leaves a small, oddly put-together bouquet on her desk; and it's very unlikely that it has come from the trustees, who had not been forthcoming with any great show of confidence—or even courteous support, for that matter—during her ordeal. So, who, then? Well, who else?

Annie marches up to the director's office, a little annoyed. She had hoped to be allowed a low-key return, to simply melt back into normal library routines without drama. Now, several patrons have already passed by her desk while regarding this ludicrous and ostentatious bouquet with wary interest and stealing a curious look at the reference librarian cowering behind it. Annie turns left at the top of the stairs, finds the door open as usual, and walks into the director's office without knocking. And here is Duncan Langmuir, sitting at his desk grinning like the Cheshire Cat, hands braided behind his neck.

It's quite disarming, really. She had forgotten the warm, sympathetic feeling emanating from him. And, strangely enough, she suddenly doesn't feel all that annoyed—or even, in truth, compelled to fight the attraction any longer. There is nothing standing in the way now—at least nothing living. Duncan's grin is starting to look strained, and she takes pity on him.

"Oh, Dunc, you shouldn't have," she says, shaking her head.

"Ah, men that hazard all do it in hope of fair advantages..." he says, giving her a Shakespeare quote. Annie's love of Shakespeare borders on obsession, and Duncan is also a devoted fan, something that creates a significant bond between them.

Back at her desk she buries her face in the roses and takes a deep breath before going back to work. *Bring on that "interesting relationship," and we shall see,* she thinks.

• • •

Of course, once it starts, there are moments of hesitation and stumbling. Duncan's scholarly conversation, his polite, gentle manner and quiet humor, contrast greatly with Carlo's artistic, impulsive personality and his way of romancing a woman. How can she help making comparisons? How can she help seeing Carlo, larger than life, her Hemingway hero, standing there next to this ascetic-looking Englishman, so soft-spoken in private that she sometimes has to lean forward to hear what he is saying? And is it really possible, after having loved Carlo, to love someone who seems in every way his opposite?

There are other questions, too, the obvious one being, *Can one love again so soon?* Well, technically Annie's period of mourning has been five years, since that was when Carlo had left for Europe. But of course, that wouldn't be the way the townies would see it. Earlier this year, the whole town had devoured the daily newsprint about Annie and Carlo, reveling in the salacious descriptions of their once-secret love affair and Carlo's murder. They will surely be keeping a weather eye on Annie at all times.

There is so much Annie doesn't know about Duncan. She knows that he was born in Iowa to an American mother and an English father—a traveling don from some vaunted London University, she remembers. The father had gone back to England before the child was born, despite honorably giving the boy his name and sending funds for his support. When the mother died in a car accident, he sent for the boy— Duncan was ten at the time—and brought him up, sent him to school, and paid his way through college.

In middle age—although at forty, Annie is reluctant to consider herself already at what she considers a *highly* arbitrary halfway mark—a whirlwind courtship is often advisable. In this case, it doesn't really mean wining and dining or anything of that nature. It simply means having the courage to let go of the past, to try to avoid the useless comparisons that continue to plague her, and to be willing to accept a being as full of quirks and faults and impossible expectations as she is herself. Following these rules, it doesn't take Annie and Duncan long to decide to throw caution to the wind, disregard those local wagging tongues, and be seen together out of the library. While Duncan may be reticent and private, he draws the line at secrecy, and when he and Annie go out together it is in full view of the local spectators. Naturally, tongues start wagging and eyes begin rolling, but Duncan simply smiles benignly.

• • •

Late one evening, while slouching into her chair and sipping at a glass of wine, Annie turns on her home computer. As usual, Shakespeare's face appears on the screen, giving her that intense stare that penetrates right into the soul. It's her current favorite among the many portraits of the bard, a rather obscure one called the Ely portrait. "Well?" she says, staring back at him."Come on, Willie. Help me out, here."

Was that a wink she saw? She rubs her eyes. Willie's smile appears a shade wider, she thinks. *Ridiculous.* The phone rings, and she runs out to the kitchen to answer.

"How about dinner at Passports? Actually, you have to say yes. I already reserved a table." Duncan hums tunelessly while waiting for an answer.

Of course she has to say yes—although with a little trepidation, due to that wink she just got from Willie. Is this the moment? It sounded like a formal invitation, not the usual "Let's go grab a bite."

Duncan picks her up in his car. He is neatly dressed as always, in shirt and tie, tweed jacket, and pants with a crease. They drive into Gloucester and find a parking spot on Main Street, not far from the restaurant.

The hostess shows them to their table, hands them their menus, and recites the day's specials. After studying the menu, Annie orders *Sister's Haddock*, pan roasted filet with a hazelnut crust, and Duncan settles on *Chicken Roquefort,* cutlets with apples, bleu cheese and leeks, finished with white wine, butter and toasted almonds.

They eat in comfortable silence, enjoying the unique mix of flavors. After the plates are removed, Annie begins to feel restless and shakes her head to the waiter's offer of dessert, even though the menu lists several of her favorites. Had she guessed wrong about Duncan's invitation? He seems affable and relaxed, sipping at his coffee while looking around and pointing out new art works on the walls.

"Want to take a walk on the Boulevard?" he asks casually as they step outside. The Boulevard is a long, tree-lined boardwalk along the waterfront, with a view straight out to sea.

"A bit chilly, don't you think? It'll be windy there," Annie says, pulling her jacket tightly around her. She is wearing a long linen skirt with her favorite stand-by for a dressy occasion, an emerald green silk shirt, and leaving her usual comfortably wrinkled linen pant suits in the closet. The dark green corduroy jacket is a bit careworn, but it's an old favorite.

"Well, let's go home then," he says, and heads toward the car. He seems disappointed, she thinks, as he strides briskly a few steps ahead of her.

"How about walking at the end of the boardwalk instead, up along Stage Fort Park? The trees will give us shelter," she tries.

He turns around and waits for her to catch up. "Good idea," he says.

The sun has set, but there is still some light left in the sky, a creamy pink that may foreshadow a storm. They walk along the bay, climbing the rocky path carefully. Annie points to some odd decorations on the boulders along the trail. Artful mosaics created from bits of glass and shells adorn the rock walls along the side of path, and Annie and Duncan stop to admire the most creative ones.

"Too bad the walls are so overgrown with weeds. In the winter you can see many more of them," Annie says.

They continue along the trail past Halfmoon Beach, then uphill, climbing the steep boulder trail around the point and over to Tablet Rock. Down below on the right lies Cresseys Beach, then the western end of Gloucester Harbor takes over, past Freshwater Cove, Dollivers Neck and Mussel Point. Hidden beyond lies Norman's Woe, a small rock of an island, not far outside the famous Hammond Castle. The light is fading and the harbor is quiet, no ships or small boats are seeking harbor. The lights at Ten Pound Island and the end of Dog Bar Breakwater are blinking in vain. While the woods along the bay protect Annie and Duncan from the strong wind, even the breeze is turning chilly, and Annie shivers slightly. That's when Duncan takes her hand.

"Are we there yet?" he asks, looking into her eyes. It's a bit odd for a proposal, but Annie senses that's what it is. Duncan has been waiting patiently, and now he is asking if she is ready. It's not a Shakespeare quote, which is what she may have expected, but it's said gently, and he encloses her hand tightly between his two.

Annie nods. "I'm ready, Duncan."

And then he lets go of her hand and pulls out the ring. It's a simple gold band wreathed with tiny rosebuds. Annie notices lettering inside, and holds the ring close to see what it says. *MND A IV S I.* Whose initials are those? Is it a mistake? But then it strikes her. It's a code. And of course, the key must be Shakespeare.

"MND...Midsummer Night's Dream?" Annie frowns. "Act IV Scene I...let me think..." she mumbles, shaking her head while trying to think.

" O how I love thee! How I dote on thee," they suddenly burst out in unison. When Annie stops giggling, she slides the ring onto her finger and holds it up into the fading light. A kiss high up here on Tablet Rock may be hazardous, but turns out to be quite successful. A little extra vertigo just adds excitement and makes it more memorable. When they recover their balance, they start the trek back down to the Boulevard, Duncan gallantly leading the way in the growing darkness.

• • •

CHAPTER TWO

"Let us crown ourselves with rosebuds,
Before they be all withered."
(Apocrypha, Wisdom of Solomon)

The wedding guests are assembling in the Great Hall of
Hammond Castle. The medieval-style building, complete with tower and drawbridge, was built in the late nine-
teen-twenties by John Hays Hammond, Jr. It is located on the
western shore of Gloucester harbor, only a twenty minute ride
from Annie's house. Sitting on a steep slope, with a narrow
sliver of lawn and garden between itself and the rocky shore,
the castle overlooks Gloucester Bay and the entrance to the
Atlantic, which lies glimmering outside the half-mile long
Dog Bar Breakwater. The breakwater is an extension of the
point of land that ends at the Eastern Point Lighthouse, just
opposite the castle.

Museum apprentice Vinnie Santos, who is dressed in
chain mail for the occasion, receives the guests at the entrance
and points the way to the hall, where none other than John
Hays Hammond, Jr., himself—or a reasonable facsimile,
since the original is dead—greets them. Hammond's part is
ably played by assistant curator Ethan Haskell, John Hays
Hammond's young cousin by the third buttonhole—in other
words, distantly related to the famous man. Ethan, dressed in
a sepia-tone suit that makes him look as though he stepped

out of one of the many photographs on the castle walls, welcomes the guests and takes them around for a brief tour before herding them back to the Great Hall.

Ethan has worked in the museum over the summer, without pay, taking on the position for a lark. Hammond family money has already given him a privileged upbringing, including an Ivy League education. While he is deciding which call appeals to him the most, he is immersing himself in a mixed bag of postgraduate studies in Europe in fields such as literature, drama, and art history, along with some forays into the hi-tech field. A well-rounded education, to be sure. Ethan is due to leave for London tomorrow night.

. . .

The guests have all arrived. Duncan—taller and even more ascetic-looking than usual in tails and sporting a green brocade cummerbund—and his best man, library trustee Charlie Field, stand somewhat nervously waiting in the Side Chapel, located a couple of steps up from the Great Hall. The bride is late. Nothing worrisome yet, but still. A lock of auburn hair falls across Duncan's forehead, and he combs it back in place with his fingers, smoothing the silvery gray temples while he's at it. To relieve their uneasiness, the two men now and then turn to peer out through the leaded windows that overlook a sparkling Gloucester Bay.

Hammond Castle was a bridal gift from Jack Hammond to his wife, Irene Fenton. Unlike many of the wealthy of his day, whose opulent mansions were only used as "summer cottages," Jack built his castle to be a home, christening it *Abbadia Mare*, or *Abbey by the Sea*. The interior, with its gothic arches and stained glass windows, does evoke a feeling of a medieval abbey. In 1929 the couple moved in permanently.

At his death in 1965, Jack was buried on the castle grounds together with his cat ("who," Annie says, "was hopefully dead at the time"). Following a stipulation in Hammond's will, the grave was surrounded by poison ivy, so that no one could go near him—something Annie considers a strange request from such an open and gregarious man. However, someone did just that—come close to the body. To retrieve it, it was suggested, and hold it for ransom. Hammond's body has since been moved (along with that of his cat) and now rests in a secure place in the garden, walled and gated and with round-the-clock security.

Finally, a hush announces the arrival of the bride, and then the thunder of Hammond's ten thousand–pipe organ fills the Great Hall. Annie appears, wearing a dress of emerald green brocade laced across creamy white silk. Her curly red hair has been forced into dozens of intertwined braids to form a crown, which is surrounded by a circlet of small white roses. The picture of a medieval queen, in other words. She is escorted by the venerable Judge Bradley, who is giving her away. Judge (everyone simply calls him "Judge," as though it were his name) and Josie Mandel had turned out to be closely related to the recently murdered Carlo Valenti. They have treated Annie as a member of the family since Carlo's murder, and despite the fact that she is not marrying Carlo—as they, and at one time she, might have hoped—they consider themselves "family." When Annie was arrested for the murder of Carlo, Judge confidently stepped in to act as her counsel until she was found innocent, and he feels a great deal of satisfaction at now escorting her to the altar.

Annie and Judge are followed by Annie's best friend Sally, the matron of honor, who is wearing a flowing blue chiffon gown. Sally had been worried about the dress not "coordinating" with the bridal couple's outfits, which Annie, a habitually uncoordinated dresser, had simply laughed off.

Two small girls in white dresses follow slowly behind, littering the floor with rose petals, which they carefully toss down one petal at a time. The guests, some decked out in medieval garb, others in ordinary finery, touch hands to form an archway through the Great Hall for the bridal entourage to pass through. The Hall is hung with rows of colorful heraldic banners, and long refectory tables are laid out for the dinner.

Duncan has left the inviting up to Annie, who is the more sociable of the two, and only made sure that Geri, his able assistant, and Judge and Josie were on the list. Among the other guests are Annie's brother Justin and his wife Melanie, Sally and her husband Matt, and Annie's fisherman friend Tommy Cameron and his wife Annette. Sally's teenage sons, Ben and Brad, serve as ushers. Clare, the library cataloger and Annie's friend since school days, is there, too, looking like a Greek goddess, her slender figure draped in a foot-length dress of some soft, pale yellow material. Annie notices that Clare now and then casts a stealthy glance at Charlie Field, blushing slightly if he catches her eye.

Marie, Hedwig, and a very happy-looking Esa—the aforementioned flower-presenting library janitor, who makes up in cheerful attitude for what he lacks in brainpower —form the rest of the library contingent. Esa is wearing a slightly too large and very outdated suit, strutting about proudly, fingering his tie.

Charlie Field is the only representative from the Library Board of Trustees, and had been Annie's lone supporter on the board in the aftermath of Carlo's murder. Annie had once been friendly enough with Laura Swernow, one of the other two trustees, but Annie's suspension during the murder investigation had put a strain on the relationship. Nothing that time wouldn't heal maybe, but Laura was not invited. Douglas Matthews, the third trustee, is a close friend of Stuart Cogswell, the snide and supercilious children's librarian who seems to have been born with a permanently curled upper lip. Well, there's no accounting for people's tastes. Needless to say, neither Douglas nor Stuart made the guest list.

A few local artists, potters, and poets, all old friends of Annie's, make up the rest of the guests. As soon as Annie steps up into the small chapel area, she takes Duncan's hand and the ceremony begins. The wedding ring, to match the rosebuds on the engagement ring, has tiny open roses all around the band. Annie recognizes the work of Peter Russell, her favorite silversmith on Bearskin Neck. Peter gave her many valuable lessons in jewelry making when she had her own shop on the neck. Duncan slides the ring on her finger, she returns the favor, and Duncan takes another stab at giving Annie an attack of vertigo.

Vows exchanged, Duncan and Annie step down into the Great Hall to join their friends for the feast, giving the thousand pipes another chance at an airing.

• • •

CHAPTER THREE

*"A man hath no better thing under the sun,
Than to eat, and to drink, and to be merry."*
(Bible, Ecclesiastes 8:15)

"This is a great day in the annals of the Rockport Library," Charlie says at the end of his little speech. "Must be a first. Could be the beginning of a library dynasty!" General laughter follows, although some of the guests might be a little dubious on this point. After all, these newlyweds are no spring chickens.

"To the bride and groom!" Charlie lifts his glass to them then glances at Clare, and Annie notices a warm glow in his eyes. Everyone stands to toast the couple. After clinking and sipping some of the bubbly, they all sit back down and resume eating, drinking, and being merry. When Charlie puts his hand down on the table his fingers accidentally graze Clare's, and he places his hand over hers and leaves it there, without looking at her. Clare sits motionless. *A seated marble Aphrodite,* Annie thinks, noticing with interest this little scene before Charlie removes his hand to adjust his bow tie. Then Clare puts her hand in her lap and covers it with the other, as if to retain his warmth.

Duncan sees Ethan walk by and grabs his arm, and Ethan pulls up a chair and joins the newlyweds. When Ethan arrived, early in the season, Charlie saw the small notice in the paper about Ethan Haskell, Hammond family member, volunteering as assistant curator at the castle. Charlie called Spofford-Braxton and offered to take the young man on a tour of Cape Ann, and later Ethan came along on one of Charlie's and Duncan's antiquarian forays around the north shore. Duncan enjoyed the ride, chatting with Ethan about his favorite London haunts of days past. Now Ethan wipes away a few drops of sweat from his forehead with a silk handkerchief fished out of his breast pocket.

"Warm in here. Or is it me?" he says laughing, while casting an appreciative glance at Annie, winking insolently.

"Like a summer's day," Annie agrees.

"Well now, Ethan, when you return to London you'll have to look up some friends of mine," Duncan says. "I'm sure they'll help you get into a lot more mischief than you'd manage to dream up yourself. Call me tomorrow, and I'll give you a few names. And then we must get together in late spring, when Annie and I are coming to England for our honeymoon. We're planning to be in Stratford-upon-Avon during the Shakespeare festival, you know," he adds.

Charlie, who's been listening in, raises his hands in mock panic. "Oh, no! You two can't possibly take time off together! It would cause a major power outage at the library! Oh, well, I guess we'll have to draft Jean again"—at which Annie rolls her eyes. *Poor Jean.* "And, while I think of it," Charlie continues, directing his comments to any guest within hearing range, "it's too bad Duncan and Annie couldn't share a desk. After all, we could fit a whole bank of new computers into the reference area! As everyone knows, computers are the wave of the future and will soon make reference librarians obsolete anyway." Charlie winks at Annie, who doesn't think this is at all funny—especially since she knows it is probably true, at least when it comes to public libraries. She's had enough of this line of palaver from Stuart lately. But today is her wedding day, and she just crosses her eyes and sticks out her tongue at Charlie before smiling blithely.

After a while Charlie gets up and walks out through the courtyard and into the Renaissance Dining Room, where extra supplies are kept, to make sure there is enough champagne on ice. Charlie insisted on providing the champagne, and has bought the best. Ethan waves to Vinnie, who brings him a glass.

Ethan turns to Annie and Duncan.

"So, you two are Shakespeare fans? Well, here's to... whom should I say? Name me a lovely Shakespeare heroine who had a happy ending! Ah yes, I know...in *Winter's Tale*... Perdita! In fact, there's that Sandys's portrait of her, where she looks just like Annie does today, a redheaded beauty with little white flowers in her hair. Well, here's to Perdita, William Shakespeare's own Annie!" Ethan says, lifting his glass, his golden brown eyes looking deep into Annie's. Duncan smiles indulgently and joins in the toast.

"By the way, my dear Perdita, Duncan told me that he proposed to you on Tablet Rock. Now, what do you know of that monument? Apart from the fact that the rock has a large iron tablet dedicated to the earliest settlers, I mean. Do you know who the chief promoter of the monument was?"

"Who?" Annie says, actually puzzled. "I have no idea, Ethan."

"Uncle Jack, that's who. And he was here on the day it was dedicated, in 1907. His sister, Aunt Natalie, unveiled the tablet. And at the time it was the largest tablet ever cast in the United States. Well, I never thought I'd stump a reference librarian!"

Annie smiles indulgently. Still, what an extraordinary coincidence, she thinks.

When his glass is empty, Ethan gets up. He sweeps his hair back with affected vanity, buttons his jacket despite the heat, and pulls the shirtsleeves down to show a proper amount of cuff, acting the dandy. Then he gives Annie a swift, roguish kiss on the cheek, and barely escapes Duncan's admonishing slap before running off to entertain other guests.

While Charlie is gone, the blare of trumpets announces a parade of waiters carrying great trays held up high. Henry Spofford-Braxton, the castle curator, walks around like an anxious old hen, making sure that food and wine does not get spilled on any of the artifacts in the Hall. He also instructs Vinnie to mop up any accidental spills on the floor to prevent people from slipping and suing. When champagne corks start popping in the Renaissance Dining Room, Vinnie goes to mop the tile floor there as well. Charlie returns to his seat just as the tables are laden with platters, filled according to a menu posted by the entrance to the Great Hall:

PORWEAUNSE FOR THE FEASTE:
SWANNES ROSTYD
(the "swans" are actually capons)
VENESOUN
(venison—the real McCoy)
PYGGYS ROSTYD
(genuine suckling pig)
DATYS IN COMPASTE
(dates in relish)
PLOUERYS ROSTYD
(the plovers being Cornish hens)
GRETE CROSTUDE
(large custard tart)
SOTELTEYS
(subtleties—food disguised to look like something else, in this case, pink lobster meat elegantly wrapped in lettuce leaves to form small bouquets,

and small pastries filled with white lobster meat to simulate eel
pasties.
The lobster has been provided by Tommy Cameron)
FRETOWRYS
(fritters, apple or cheese)
VYOLETTE
(candied violets)

The guests gorge themselves, as one should at a medieval feast. Occasionally they get up and walk about to allow the food to sink and make room for more.

Sally Babson is fanning herself with a napkin. Her blue gown, which had appeared diaphanous and ethereal when she arrived, is now limp and speckled with food drippings. *How did medieval ladies ever clean their gowns after a feast?* Sally wonders. Her cheeks have taken on a high color after all the champagne, and the curls she spent hours on taming lie pasted to her face and neck. Finally, she just has to get away from the heat and noise around the table. She steps up into the Side Chapel, where a faint ocean breeze is sifting in. Out on the bay a small boat is moving toward the shoreline, and Sally follows its progress, idly at first, then with rising consternation. When it nears the reef just off the shore, Sally starts screaming.

• • •

CHAPTER FOUR

"Christ save us all from a death like this,
On the reef of Norman's Woe!"
(Henry Wadsworth Longfellow, "Wreck of the Hesperus")

"Oh my God, he'll go aground! Why isn't he turning?" Sally stands by the long wall of leaded windows, shouting and flailing her arms, making the blue chiffon sleeves flutter like the sails of a windmill. She is trying to catch the eye of the boatman, now only a few hundred yards away out in Gloucester Bay. The small motorboat, with a man dimly seen at the helm, is headed for certain disaster. It is speeding recklessly toward Norman's Woe, a rocky isle already of ill repute, having been the cause of many disasters.

The wedding guests in the Great Hall rise and flock to the windows, drawn by Sally's screams. They bob their heads up and down trying to see through the old wavy glass panes, and watch in horror as the boat crashes on the rocks and is blown to smithereens. The hull of a small boat doesn't stand a chance against formidable Cape Ann granite. Whoever the skipper is, he probably doesn't stand much of a chance either. Norman's Woe is a mere guano-covered islet, and waves often break over it at high tide. If the man was injured and thrown into the water, he'll surely drown before help gets there.

A small rescue party is quickly organized, while someone calls the authorities. Black tailcoats flying, a group of men run down to the dock, untie the two skiffs, and make wild zigzag bids for the rock, which lies not far from shore. Maybe the men are not mariners...or could it be the champagne? When they reach the island they scramble around, looking ridiculously like a flock of waddling penguins on an ice floe. The crowd watches anxiously from the castle windows. Now the penguins are throwing their arms about in distress, obviously not finding anyone to rescue. Streams of small vessels—lobster boats, pleasure craft, and even a couple of sailboats—are making their way toward Norman's Woe.

Suddenly the Coast Guard cutter arrives, followed by the harbor police launch and fireboat. The small craft are waved off. The penguins are shooed away—*"Back into the skiffs with you"*—and row disconsolately back toward the castle dock. People spill out from the castle onto the lawn to meet them, asking anxious questions to which there are no happy answers.

Annie has stayed inside and remains stone-faced in her seat. Duncan takes her hand and holds it between his two. Annie has told him how her parents died, drowning in a gale off Cape Ann after their small boat went down. Their bodies weren't found for several days, during which Annie had wandered the Headlands, hoping against hope. She finally gives Duncan a wan smile.

"I'm fine, Duncan. Just a shock. A bad memory, that's all." She gets up, and they step over to the chapel area just as the party moves back inside. The celebrants try to pick up where they left off. Now and then a wavering eye turns toward the bay. Esa, unable to stay in his seat, stands guard by the window. Divers have gone into the water; up and down they go, and finally, suddenly, there is a lot of activity, and the boats crowd together in a circle. Esa jumps up and down in agitation.

"Something is happening," he shouts, but when they all rush up to the windows they can't see just what. A Coast

Guard helicopter appears on the scene, and a basket is lowered, a load is lashed on, and the basket is hoisted back up. A communal sigh is drawn inside the Great Hall, with an equally communal wish that what they are witnessing is a rescue. As it turns out, it is not.

• • •

CHAPTER FIVE

"Lord, Lord! Methought, what pain it was to drown!
What dreadful noise of waters in mine ears!
What ugly sights of death within mine eyes!"
(Shakespeare, Richard III)

Once the Coast Guard helicopter disappears with its load, the wedding guests try to rekindle the spirit of celebration. However, the appetite is gone, the *fretowrys* and *vyolettes* remain untouched, and the champagne has lost its power to infuse them with happiness. They get up and mill about and finally gather in the glass-roofed courtyard. Despite a multitude of wrought-iron candelabras, a gloomy dusk hangs over the courtyard and the pool, which is surrounded by lush greenery and flowering hibiscus and bougainvillea. The walls around the yard are graced with arched doorways that lead to various parts of the castle: the Renaissance Dining Room; the library; the Inventions Room; and then, behind them now, there is the broad entrance and the stone steps that lead back down into the Great Hall.

At the far end of the courtyard there is a narrow stairway to a bridge that leads to the Gothic Bedroom, where the bride and groom are to spend the night. The enclosed bridge has a wall of arches that open out over the pool. When Jack Hammond was alive, he had the water in the pool treated with a special dye to make it look like a Roman *impluvium*—a shallow pool used to collect rainwater. Then he would astound and frighten his guests by diving from the bridge into water that looks shallow but in reality is a perfectly safe diving depth.

A small child's sarcophagus stands at the Great Hall end of the pool. On the lid is the sculpted stone image, worn with age, of a reclining child. *A sad reminder of the absence of children in Jack's life?* Annie wonders. The gloom in the courtyard is relieved when lanterns and hidden spotlights are turned on. The wedding guests look around, enchanted, suddenly transported from oppressive gloom to a feeling of expectancy. A medieval city square surrounds them. Original fifteenth-century shop fronts and house facades, shipped here during Hammond's forays in Europe, make up the perimeter of the yard, and in a corner stands a great fieldstone fireplace that would lend comfort on a wintry night. Music wafts up from the Great Hall, recorded music now, madrigals and lays.

Suddenly a shadow appears in one of the arches of the bridge. A figure clambers across the stone railing and stands crouched in the low space, lit by a single spotlight. It is Jack Hammond's double, Ethan, dressed in a twenties' style swimsuit held up by narrow shoulder straps. He looks around until he locates Annie, flashes a smile at her, and teeters slightly before aiming his hands down and diving into the pool, neatly, without making a splash. The underwater lights in the pool go on just as Ethan hits the water, illuminating the lithe, suntanned body.

Everyone cheers and applauds…but something is wrong. Ethan comes to the surface in obvious distress, his body contorting horribly. He seems unable to get himself over to the side of the pool, and Annie's brother Justin runs over to help him. When he can't reach Ethan, he climbs up onto the stone wall to jump in, but is interrupted by loud shouts from the curator, Spofford-Braxton.

"No! Stop! Don't jump! Don't anyone touch the water! Albert, go shut off the power! Hurry, for God's sake! Everyone, please stand back!"

The custodian, Albert Grover, turns pale and runs off to the utility room. The lights in the pool have gone out. Moments later, all the lights in the courtyard go out. In the remaining candle light they can see that Ethan's body has stopped twitching. The curator grabs a medieval stake from a wall display and uses it to pull the body to the side so it can be hauled out of the water.

"Albert, call an ambulance! Anyone here who can do CPR?" Spofford-Braxton shouts, looking around in desperation. Beads of sweat trickle down the curator's neck and stain his pink silk shirt. Sally, who used to be lifeguard on the Rockport beaches, nods nervously, and everyone makes way for her. She kneels next to the lifeless body. The blue chiffon drags in the pooled water, but Sally ignores it and starts the procedure with silent determination. Ethan's paleness is underscored by the wet, dark hair that lies slick across his forehead. The lids are closed over those large, expressive eyes that only moments ago so playfully caught Annie's. Annie rests her head on Duncan's chest. Her sobs are silent, but he feels her body heaving.

A police cruiser shows up moments before the ambulance arrives. When they wheel Ethan away on a gurney, after heroic and agonizing efforts at resuscitation, there seems to be little hope left. Sally shakes her head anxiously. While one officer interviews and takes down the names of the guests, the other takes a perfunctory look around. Shortly afterward the guests are ushered down into the Great Hall, while the officers string yellow tape around the pool and across the entrance to the bridge. They speak to Spofford-Braxton, taking more notes, and then a ghastly white Albert leads them down to the electrical room.

The wedding guests are eventually allowed to disperse, and most of them leave. Annie and Duncan sit disconsolately on one of the great carved benches in the Hall. Annie's eyes are red-rimmed, and now and then another spasm shakes her body. Duncan holds her hand tightly. Annie's brother Justin and his wife Melanie, who have come up from New Mexico for the wedding, remain behind with them, as do Josie and Judge, along with a few other guests who stay to lend their support. The power in the Great Hall is suddenly turned back on, and the madrigals start up again, echoing shrilly in the eight-story-high open space until the curator hurriedly shuts them off. Spofford-Braxton rubs his chin fretfully as he comes up to them.

"What a terrible tragedy…and I am so awfully sorry about the wedding…quite spoiled, I'm afraid. We'll make adjustments, naturally, no charge from our end. Can't do much about the catering, of course, and all your other expenses…"

"We won't hear of it," Judge says. Charlie arranged the event, and Judge is paying for it. Jack Hammond has long been one of Annie's favorite local characters, which was the reason Judge had arranged for her wedding at the castle. "Wasn't any of your fault, Henry. In fact, your quick reaction probably saved Justin's life. It is a great tragedy, of course. Hope that young man pulls through, but it doesn't look good, does it?"

Spofford-Braxton shakes his head. "The sad thing is that we have scheduled for the electricians to come and update all our wiring as soon as we close for the season. It never occurred to us that there might be any urgency about it, as I was explaining to the officers. Everything's been functioning well, but we're planning to add new displays and some electronic office equipment that would need extra power.

To think this horrible thing might have been avoided..." The curator puts his head in his hands, quite distraught.

"No way you could have known, Henry," Judge says. "The pool's been safe for swimming all these years, after all. You know, Jack Hammond was a friend of my father's, and I used to come along with Dad on his visits here. Went swimming in that pool myself many times back then. Jack would lift me up and toss me in from up there," he says, pointing up to the bridge. They all turn to look. The courtyard is still lit only by candles, but they can see the bridge in the glow, and the reflections from the water glimmer playfully on the walls of the yard. It all looks too peaceful to have been the scene of such a terrible accident. Now that the power in the rest of the castle has been turned back on, the darkness outside seems absolute. When Annie looks toward the windows, she shudders.

"And that poor man in the boat. I wonder if he made it."

Duncan rises and takes Annie by the hand.

"I think we could all use some coffee," he says. "Let's go to my house...er, our house...and I'll make a pot. How about it?" Under the circumstances, spending the night at the castle is obviously out of the question, and they might as well go home. A few of the remaining guests seem to appreciate the invitation, and they all hurry off, leaving the curator and custodian with the sad task of closing up. Albert is mopping the floor near where the water had pooled around Ethan's body, careful not to cross into the taped-off area. Now and then he stops and looks up at the bridge, then down into the pool, and shakes his head. He avoids getting too close to the edge of the pool, as though fearing that the water might still be electrified and somehow able to reach out for him. Vinnie, the apprentice, has changed out of his chain mail into jeans and a T-shirt and is helping sort the trash and gather boxes of empty champagne bottles from the dining room. Esa has been lending his janitorial expertise, too, but now Hedwig gets a stern hold of him.

"Do you want to ride back with me, Esa, or are you planning to walk home?" she asks. Esa smiles an apology to Vinnie and insists on at least holding the door open while the last of the wedding guests file out. Annie's train of silk and brocade trails behind her across the broad stone steps up to the parking lot, sweeping back and forth like a great, soft broom until Sally picks it up and carries it. The rest of the bridal party falls in behind them, and suddenly it all looks very formal. All that is lacking to make the getaway appear a festive part of a proper medieval wedding is a trumpet voluntary. However, the mood of the participants is somber, not festive.

•   •   •

CHAPTER SIX

"Past hope, past cure, past help!"
(Shakespeare, Romeo and Juliet)

The mood in Duncan's living room turns from somber to mournful after Judge makes a brief phone call and comes back to report that Ethan has been pronounced dead at the hospital. Annie starts to sob all over again, and Duncan holds her tightly, stroking her braided hair until the rosebuds begin to fall out. Josie and Sally join in with Annie, and tears that should have been of joy flow in abundant grief.

The weeping finally abates, but Annie knows that the accident will mar her memories of the wedding forever. It will even cast a melancholy shadow over the honeymoon in England next spring, when she and Duncan will not be meeting with Ethan. She had thought that the wedding would be a time of joy, and that it would wipe out the sadness and grief after the loss of Carlo. Is she destined to never be allowed to be happy? And to be always reminded of the drowning of her parents?

In the gloom that follows the phone call, the guests depart, and Justin and Melanie retire to Duncan's upstairs guest room. Annie and Duncan are left alone to try to dispel the overwhelming feeling of sadness. The expected nuptial joy will have to be kept at bay, somehow unseemly after such a sad event. They get out of their wedding finery and clear the dishes, then sit down together on the sofa. Duncan gets up and starts a fire in the fireplace, and as soon he sits down again, the phone rings.

"Just talked to the Coast Guard," Judge says. "The body in the boat...it was a *dummy*. Would you believe it? Had an old ID card of Jack Hammond's stuck in a jacket pocket. Genuine. Probably stolen from the museum at some point. And the head—wait until you hear this—the head was a human skull crammed into a sock, which was pinned to the collar.

"I'd bet you anything it's the one that's usually on display in the Great Hall, the one that supposedly belonged to a member of Columbus's crew. The skull was given to Hammond by the governor of Santo Domingo. Well, you know how Hammond admired and emulated Columbus, even duplicated some of his voyages in the West Indies. Loved adventure. Member of The Explorers' Club and all that.

"Anyway, I suppose someone put the dummy in the boat, jammed the wheel, and aimed it at the reef...odd, isn't it? Why, one would have to ask? And now you have to wonder about Ethan. Is it possible that his death wasn't an accident? I mean, two dead doubles for Jack Hammond in one day seems a bit too coincidental. Apparently, the police think so, too. They're looking into it, I understand."

Duncan can only shake his head and hold up a shushing hand when Annie mumbles questions throughout the conversation. When it is over and he gives her the gist of it, she sighs. Then they go to bed, agreeing forlornly that the joys of wedlock really do have to be postponed.

• • •

CHAPTER SEVEN

"Ye Gods, annihilate but space and time
And make two lovers happy."
(Alexander Pope, Martinus Scriblerus on the Art of Sinking in
Poetry)

The sun strikes the sleepers. Annie stirs and wakes up, smiling. The joint-tenant bed had been inhabited and enjoyed many times before the wedding night, as nearly always happens in this fast-forward time. Last night kind nature intervened, put all sorrows on hold, and true marital pleasures were enjoyed despite the shattering events of the previous day, which is what's causing the current silly smile on Annie's face. The smile is matched by Duncan's when he wakes up a few minutes later.

Although the honeymoon has been postponed until spring, they have arranged to take a couple of days off after the wedding. Still, they both have work that must be done and plan to go to the library today.

Annie's brother Justin is taking Melanie into Boston for a day or two of museums, shopping, and theater in order to give the newlyweds some time for privacy (and, Annie thinks, no doubt to show Melanie that the Northeast isn't just filled with "crusty, monosyllabic people who live in gray little cottages," which she had once suggested.)

After dropping them off at the train, Duncan and Annie prepare a picnic breakfast. Duncan fixes eggs Benedict, while Annie practices her skill at making coffee in Duncan's vacuum pot, which she thinks should be returned to whatever lab it must have been nicked from. With the food and Gussie secured in separate baskets on the back seat, they drive over to Halibut Point for an "al fresco" breakfast.

They go to their favorite picnic spot up at the high point near the watchtower, which was made to look like a church spire in order to fool the German submariners during the war. There they set their baskets down among a group of granite blocks.

The boulders are perched on a steep ledge overlooking Babson's Quarry, where long ago granite was quarried. The large stone blocks were pulled down to the water's edge and loaded into stone sloops to be shipped to distant and often foreign ports. Many a street in Europe was paved with Rockport cobblestones.

Beyond the ledge, on the opposite side of the quarry, which is overgrown with low brush and slender trees, the ocean stretches out to the horizon, but on a much lower level. To their right, on the northeast side of Halibut Point, lies the great heath with its maze of trails among blueberry bush and brambles, poison ivy and catbrier. As they near the water, the plants get lower and more stunted until all there is left is a thin, mossy mat and some stiff grasses, and then begins the stark bareness of the wave-swept rocks and ledges.

Gussie, who still snubs Annie after her summer-long desertion, reserves his fond glances for Duncan. The old dachshund barks at a squirrel, which retreats and chatters back at him from the safety of a high branch. Gussie proudly climbs back into his basket and gets a biscuit as a reward. Annie and Duncan enjoy their breakfast, served on Duncan's fine china plates, while looking down into the deep, clear water in the quarry below them. Annie looks idly for the "sea monster" that has been spotted in the quarry a few times. In reality, it's likely to be a very large eel, but Cape Anners like to keep the old legend of a local sea monster alive. Some people insist the monster *could* have swum through underground cracks from the ocean into the quarry. However, the sea monster is not showing up today.

"You know, Duncan, I'd like to go back to Hammond Castle this morning," Annie says suddenly.

"What on earth for, Annie?" Duncan gives her a startled look.

"I don't know. Laying ghosts to rest, maybe. It's not as though we can forget what happened yesterday, even though all seems so unreal. And I'd like to know what *actually* happened. I mean, Judge's ramblings may be just that, ramblings and speculation. Maybe it *was* only a prank and an accident that coincided, and not murder. Doesn't make it any less sad, of course. But I think seeing the place in plain daylight will chase away some of my nightmares. Want to come?"

Duncan shakes his head, dreading this hint of Annie's growing suspicions. Judge's idea has indeed taken root in Annie's brain, and now she can't shake free of it.

"I have to plan the agenda for the directors' meeting tomorrow, remember?" he says, his eyes following the coast northward up to Maine. It is a brilliantly clear day, with the water azure in the shallows along the shore and turning a dark marine blue farther out along the horizon, which stretches sharp around the island in a semicircle from north to south, where the sun's reflections make it too blinding to continue.

"Oh...sorry, Dunc, I forgot all about the meeting. I'll print copies for you as soon as I get back."

"Don't decorate them with wedding bells, now," he says.

"How about grim reapers?" she retorts.

"I didn't know you were so morbid," he says, meaning to be funny, but realizing too late her implication. Suddenly they look at each other and a mood of sorrow returns, spoiling the brief bantering.

• • •

CHAPTER EIGHT

"Come, Watson, come! The game is afoot."
(Sir Arthur Conan Doyle, The Return of Sherlock Holmes)

A phone message from Judge awaits them at home: "Spofford-Braxton's story checks out. He had the electrician lined up. Ethan's death is listed as an accident in a small notice on the inside pages of today's *Chronicle*. The dummy is actually getting more press. There's a picture on the front page of the Coast Guard's 'rescue attempt,' and the whole thing is treated as a joke."

Annie, still set on her mission, walks down to the Hannah Jumper House—her own home until she married Duncan—to retrieve her car. The house is part of local history, having been the home of Rockport's own temperance queen, Hannah Jumper, who made the town dry by hacking asunder all the kegs of rum and other liquor she and her gang of marauding women could discover.

Staying in Duncan's Victorian house is a trial balloon. After having decided that keeping both houses is an impossible luxury, they have agreed to spend one month in each house before choosing which one to settle in permanently. They are each adamantly and emotionally attached to their own home and equally reluctant to give it up. Duncan does not want to exchange his bright, roomy kitchen for Annie's cramped galley, nor does he want to dispose of any of his books—and Annie's shelves are already full to bursting. She, in turn, doesn't want to give up the home where she has lived most of her life, nor the salty air, the view of the harbor, or the cool evening breezes—nor still her studio and work-shop. Nor, for that matter, any of *her* books, and Duncan's shelves are just as full as hers. Furthermore, there's Augustus to consider. After all, Gussie has lived his whole life in the Hannah Jumper House. True, he didn't seem to suffer at all from staying in Duncan's house, but that was simply due to the fact that Duncan had spoiled and bribed him shamelessly. *So much for loyalty,* Annie thinks. At the time of the wedding, negotiations about where to settle were ongoing, and so the trial started.

Returning to the business at hand, Annie decides to give Sally a call. Sal is observant, and her lively, curious eye might catch something Annie misses—if, indeed, there is anything to catch. Annie is again disturbed by a feeling that her imagi-nation may be running away with her. What if her "hunch" is all wrong, and she will be casting suspicion on innocent people, or even causing trouble for the castle?

What makes her think it wasn't an accident? Well, there was the crash of the dummy on Norman's Woe, obviously dressed up to be Jack Hammond. On its own, she might have considered that a prank. But could it have been meant as a message? If so, there is no way she can accept that Ethan's death, following almost immediately upon that crash, was simply a coincidental accident. Too close in time and, to her way of thinking, to people in the same family. The two events simply have to be related. She can't think of a motive for either action, but she knows she can't give up yet. If no one else is looking into it, she must. She feels she owes it to Ethan. Meanwhile, Sally's cheerful presence would help dispel the chill of what happened at the wedding. The wedding, which has become overshadowed by the tragedy of Ethan's death.

"Want to go for a ride? I'm driving over to the castle."

"The *castle?* What one earth for? No way, Annie!" Sally has no interest in the morbid.

"I think it would help me deal with what happened yesterday...but I understand if you don't want to come." Annie tries to elicit a little sympathy, but to no avail.

"Too spooky for me," Sally says. Annie thinks she can even hear her friend shudder. Well, she'll try another tack and settle for second best.

"Want to meet when I get out of there instead? I'd like to go to Rafe's Chasm, just sit and listen to the waves beat against the shore. There are some good swells out there today. We can meet at the Lone Gull for coffee and go for a walk on Singing Beach afterwards. How about it?" An adventure is just the thing to tempt Sally with, Annie knows. Sally loves to have fun.

"Oh, okay. I'll meet you inside the Lone Gull. Whoever comes first grabs the seats. If I leave around two, will that give you enough time?"

"That'll be perfect. If we have a quick coffee, we'll get to the chasm just at high tide. See ya!"

Ned Mazzarini, Annie's favorite local carpenter, has fixed the garage door so that she can drive out without scraping any more paint off the roof of the car. "Now Annie, ah ya ready faw me to do them windahs yet? Wintah's comin'," he asked, but she deferred once again. Maybe she won't be keeping the house, after all. She looks out through the living room window as she walks by, feeling a small lump in her throat. How can she give up this view...or this house? It's a part of her.

The old blue Chevy starts reluctantly. She hasn't used it for a while. Is it sulking again? It often does when it feels neglected. Once on the road, though, it perks up, happy to escape confinement. Twenty minutes later, Annie gives it a little pat on the dashboard as she parks it in the Hammond Castle parking lot.

Annie walks into the museum shop to buy her ticket, and stops to chat with Vinnie. Vinnie is a student at the local high school. Among all his other duties at the castle he helps man the cash register afternoons and weekends to let Ruth, the shop manager, get a little time off. Whenever he has a few hours free during a school day, he'll often show up and do odd chores. Sometimes he helps Albert; other times he spends time out in the shop by himself, cleaning and repairing some of the museum's artifacts.

When Vinnie was helping out at the wedding, he had worn chain mail over ribbed black tights and had his hair slicked down and waved in a short Prince Valiant pageboy. Today he is back to "normal." His black hair is spiked, his ears mutilated by safety pins and other nasty looking objects, and colorful tattoos of dragons are exposed on his forearms.

The museum shop carries a multitude of dragon items, from cheap little toys to more expensive pieces with semiprecious stones, and children are fascinated by Vinnie's dragon tattoos. Parents have been known to complain about his *punk* look, but Vinnie, amazingly, is a sweet and good-natured young man, and the kids love him.

It's eleven o'clock, opening time, and Annie is the first visitor. Later, once the local paper comes out, there will probably be a crowd of gawkers.

"So, Vinnie, how are things?" Annie asks.

"Okay, I guess. Except for yesterday, I mean. That was pretty bad. Didn't know if we were gonna open today even. Called Spoff, he said to come in, so here I am."

"How's the curator today? He was pretty shook up yesterday."

"Still is. Walks around mumblin' to himself. He's been a bit off anyways, since he got a notice about, like, an audit or whatever. I've heard him and Ruth talkin' about it a few times. But this thing with Ethan really, like, did him in."

"He'll really miss Ethan, won't he? I mean, I'm sure Ethan helped out a lot this summer?"

"Oh, yeah," Vinnie stifles a giggle, "I mean, a lot of people liked talkin' to Ethan better than to old Spoffie. Ethan was real friendly, like he was always yakkin' about the Hammonds, personal family stuff, '*Uncle Jack said or did this-and-that,*' you know, that kinda stuff. Ethan was, like, you know, real popular with the crowds. Said he loved workin' here. In fact, he told old Spoff to watch out, said that when he's through with school he may come back here and, like, take over the family business."

"And what did Spofford say to that?"

"Nothin'. Just looked kinda glum and walked out."

"You think Ethan was serious?"

"Jeez, no. Soon as Spoffie was out the door, Ethan started laughin'. He had, like, totally other plans."

"Like what, Vinnie?" Annie leans casually over the glass counter as if admiring some faux medieval jewelry.

"Travel, for starters. Wanted to see a lot of places before the world got to be all the same everywhere, he said. Guess he was a Hammond that way. Like, that's how his Uncle Jack ended up with this castle and all the stuff that's in it, wasn't it? He was a travelin' man, was Uncle Jack. *Ack*-shally, Ethan liked living in England. Said he might even move there. Maybe live in a 'real' castle. He said they're, like, *cheap* over there. Anyway, he wasn't gonna get stuck in some small New England town for the rest of his life."

Annie shudders. That's just what Carlo had often said, before he made good and moved to Italy.

They hear approaching footsteps, and Vinnie starts shuffling paper behind the register, lining up piles of pamphlets and price lists, looking busy. Annie smiles and moves over to the book rack.

Spofford-Braxton looks startled when he walks in and sees Annie, but she smiles reassuringly. She explains quickly that it will make her feel better to walk through the castle in the sunlight. The curator seems relieved and lets her in without charging her for a ticket.

"Would you like me to accompany you?" he asks with a look of concern. Is he worried about her or about what she might find? Annie wonders suddenly.

"Oh, no, I'm just going to amble through. I'd like to relive my wedding, I guess, but without the traumatic parts. Just walk through the rooms in peace and quiet with the sun shining in." Spofford-Braxton nods and ushers her to the doorway of a little anteroom that leads to the complicated maze of corridors between chambers and halls and tower stairways. There he lets her go, looking a little anxiously after her.

"It's okay, really it is. I know my way," Annie says, with a little wave.

• • •

CHAPTER NINE

"Facts are stubborn things; and whatever may be our wishes, our inclinations, or the dictates of our passions, they cannot alter the state of facts and evidence."
(John Adams, Defense of the British soldiers on trial for the Boston Massacre)

Annie goes downstairs and into the Great Hall, which has been immaculately cleaned. No evidence of the wedding remains, not a single rose petal on the floor. It gives her an eerie feeling, as if the event had never taken place. Annie shivers in the massive, chill space. Her footsteps echo on the freshly polished stone floor. She looks around idly, turns her head up toward the great, round, stained-glass window and the forest of organ pipes. Some say there are only 8200, not 10000. Well, whatever the true number is…Maybe someday she'll count them. She squints up at the clerestory windows, high up on the other side of the hall, on the back wall of the balcony.

Climbing the stone stairs, she continues out into the glass-roofed courtyard. The pool is still blocked off with yellow tape; otherwise there are no signs of last night's event. Annie closes her eyes, remembering that last playful smile from Ethan. She can't face walking up to the pool and goes into the Inventions Room instead. Jack Hammond looks down at her from one of the wall photographs. There is something very intense about the way he looks at her. She feels his presence. *"Okay, Jack. I'll find out what happened to Ethan,"* she mumbles.

The room is filled with examples of Hammond's inventions, some reminiscent of the large-scale early computers that people now laugh about, along with various memorabilia: notebooks and sketches, blueprints and articles, certificates of patents, legal briefs, testimonials with famous signatures, and yellowed newspaper clippings.

On the walls are photographs of Jack in the company of many of the greats of his time. Annie looks at a photo of Hammond, taken in his younger days, and is struck by the likeness between Jack Hammond and Ethan. *Both so handsome. Regular Gatsbys. Would Ethan have followed in Uncle Jack's footsteps and become successful and famous? Very likely,* Annie thinks. If his death really wasn't an accident, as Judge suggested, who on earth would want to kill Ethan? He seemed the kind of person who wouldn't have an enemy in the world.

There is a photograph of Jack Hammond with his famous father, "a Croesus of a man, cohort of Cecil Rhodes in South Africa," as he was described by Joe Garland, a popular Gloucester historian.

John Hays Hammond, Sr., who made a fortune in diamonds, was also one of the "Gang of 4" led by Rhodes in a raid on Johannesburg. Hammond was caught and put in jail for treason, and given a life sentence. He was fortuitously visited by Mark Twain, who came to see him in jail while on a speaking engagement in South Africa. Twain notified people back home, and Hammond's ransomed release was organized. Then Twain sailed for America, where on arrival he was met with the news that his beloved daughter Susy had died just a few hours earlier.

For a time, the senior Hammond was also on the Guggenheim family payroll to the tune of a million dollars a year, then a rather fabulous sum. According to rumor, Jack's parents did not approve of their son's choice of a wife-to-be, and this was why Jack decided to build a bigger home than the one his father owned next door on Lookout Hill. Annie thinks that the photos of Jack's wife, the lovely-looking Irene Fenton, show a woman it would be hard to dislike. Perhaps the explanation was simply that the Hammonds were staunch Catholics, and Irene Fenton was a divorcée.

Hammond Senior's estate was used only as a summer cottage, in the manner of the wealthy of his generation. He left it in his will to the Roman Catholic Archdiocese of Boston, and the mansion soon became known as the "Cardinal Cushing Villa." It was used as a religious retreat house, and for a while as a convalescence and retirement home.

At the time of Cardinal Cushing's death, the Villa was in the hands of the Daughters of Mary of the Immaculate Conception, an order of nuns with a motherhouse in New Britain, Connecticut. When new public safety regulations prevented the further use of the structure as a nursing home, the few caretaker nuns were left to wander the cold, echoing rooms of the immense Tudor-style mansion alone. The stately building sits on acres of oceanfront that lie wide open to New England's famous Nor'easters, and to the Daughters of Mary it was now nothing but a grand but useless possession. The nuns hastily sold it off and hightailed themselves back to New Britain.

The Cardinal Cushing Villa was purchased by a second party—a "straw," in legal jargon—who immediately turned it over to the Korean reverend Sun Myung Moon and his "Moonies," as members of Reverend Moon's Unification Church are commonly called. It is still owned by the Unification Church. At the time, Moon's church members had already established themselves in the lobstering business in Gloucester, to the dismay of many of the locals.

The Gloucester Moonies were soon accused of everything from taking the fishing business away from the local fishermen to enticing, and even brainwashing, the town's youth into joining their cult. It was rumored that people working for Moon were paid only with bed and board. And, the townspeople said, everyone had *known* that the Unification Church had for some time had their eyes on the Cardinal's Villa, since the Moonies not long before had purchased some acreage along the Freshwater Cove waterfront nearby. Public prayers and novenas had even been said at Masses in town to keep the Moonies from getting their hands on the Villa—though, obviously, to no avail.

Be that as it may, many Gloucesterites also blamed the Archdiocese, which has, in what some think equally underhanded ways, sold off other local properties to the hue and cry of Gloucester residents. The sale of St. Peter's Catholic High School, for instance, which was suddenly presented as a fait-accompli, caused quite a furor. The Archdiocese is even now, in the aftermath of the recent nation-wide scandals, in the process of divesting itself of a number of Cape Ann churches, some of which will no doubt be turned into luxurious condos.

Not knowing what the distant future would hold, and continuing to follow in his famous father's footsteps, Jack Hammond had also willed *his* castle, *Abbey by the Sea,* to Cardinal Cushing and the Roman Catholic Archdiocese of Boston. Just as had happened with Lookout Hill, *Abbey by the Sea* was soon sold off by the Archdiocese.

Annie knows that the Abbadia Mare, now known as the Hammond Castle, is managed by a private museum trust these days. But what if the trust were running out of funds? What if that audit that Vinnie had mentioned spelled trouble, not for Spofford-Braxton but for the museum? Could Hammond Castle be in difficult financial straits?

Suddenly the room seems to close in on Annie. *The Moonies?* Could they have had a hand in what happened, in order to force a sale of the museum? Were they still trying to buy up sections of Gloucester waterfront? Times are hard for small countryside museums these days, and a scandal may just be the last straw. If the museum foundered, would the Moonies be able to lay their hands on the property through a second party, the way they had gotten the senior Hammond's property at Lookout Hill? Are they still in the money? The Moonies have been out of the news in Gloucester for some time. Are they lying low, staying out of the limelight, waiting to pounce on a "loaves and fishes" shore front property? It's a chilling thought.

Annie decides to leave the castle and come back later. That will give her time for a quick check on the Internet before meeting with Sally.

• • •

CHAPTER TEN

*"I want to establish something permanent in Gloucester, so
I recently bought a big estate there, which used to belong to the
Catholic Church. I would like to have that house prepared to
welcome people from all over the world. I see this house as an
essential base for diplomacy."*
(Reverend Sun Myung Moon, Sermons)

When Annie gets out to the car and starts a search on her laptop by punching in "Moonies" as a subject, it yields over four hundred thousand instant hits, and she begins to thread her way through the maze. It seems Moon had some difficulties in his early days in Gloucester.

In a speech at the Villa, Moon told his followers that he wished to build a marine college in Gloucester, and that was why he had bought the land. But the people of Gloucester had been scared. They said that the Catholic Church had been okay, but the Unification Church—oh no!

The Villa was closed for four years before people had been allowed in. "Is there any other nation in the world, which has freedom of religion like the United States?" Moon asked. When all the legal matters were finally settled, Moon said in one of his sermons, "Now we have a marina, plus a dock and an estate, so Gloucester is almost a Moonie town now!"

A different Web site states that Moon has been in jail at least six times, one of them in the United States after a conviction of tax evasion, when he was sent to Danbury. Moon was forbidden entry into European countries, according to the terms of the Schengen Treaty; and he was barred from entering Japan, where some of his followers were said to have been convicted of defrauding elderly of their life savings.

Next, Annie happens on more recent articles, one of them describing Reverend Sun Myung Moon's "Coronation" in the Dirksen Senate Office Building on Capitol Hill, which took place in June of 2004. The event was attended by a number of high-ranking U.S. lawmakers and religious leaders. Moon, who considers himself the second Messiah, appeared in a floor-length robe, together with his fourth wife, Hak Ja Han Moon. A U.S. congressman wearing white gloves placed the ornate, bejeweled gold crown on Moon's head. Mrs. Moon was crowned as well, in this ceremony that dubbed the former felon and his wife "the King and Queen of Peace." The *New York Times* made some reference to *Caligula,* and in numerous articles and blogs immediately following the coronation, questions were raised about whether this was "proper use of a taxpayer supported facility."

Sites abound listing Moon and the Unification Church as the owner or power behind hundreds of companies worldwide. It is an astonishing and varied mix of properties, including the *Washington Times, World Media Association* and *News World Communications,* which owns UPI. (Which, it is noted, gives the Moonies a press seat on board Air Force One.)

Annie looks out the window. The museum will be busy today; a number of cars have parked since she came out. Only a month is left before the Hammond Castle is shut for the winter, but there are still some events left, the most popular being the Halloween celebrations.

Annie goes back to her research. Also on the list of Moonie-owned companies are a large number of corporations including the International Oceanic Enterprises, with its many subsidiaries. One of them is True World Seafoods, which has an operation in Gloucester, and which also operates fishing vessels and an at-sea factory processor in Alaska. Annie scrolls down page after page of foundations, educational institutions, political groups, media organizations, businesses, and religious organizations that are affiliated with Moon and his church. Well, it is quite obvious that the money is there, and furthermore that Moon's organizations are still active.

On the next hit she runs into the Unification Church's supposed beliefs and teachings, and things begin to sound a bit extreme. For instance, there were allegations of an early purification ceremony known as "blood separation." Perhaps, the report offers, it was Moon's effort to continue his own royal line, to duplicate what some ancient and secret societies suggest the original Messiah had done. Truth or scurrilous rumor? There was no way to tell, which Annie has found to be the most serious problem with Internet searches.

And of course, there are the much publicized mass marriage ceremonies, where Moon blessed thirty-five thousand to fifty thousand couples at a time, with all the couples chanting, *Mansei, Mansei, Mansei.* Most of the future spouses had never met each other. The marriages are said to have been arranged by Moon himself after matching the partners by photographs. The arrangement fees alone are said to have brought the church vast amounts of money, counted in the billions.

Moonie couples, it is said, are commonly separated and assigned to distant locations, the children taken to be raised in Moon's nurseries, where they are taught to speak Korean— an important part of becoming a Moonie. Most Americans (including the Yankees, Sicilians, and Italians that live in Gloucester) would probably balk at this requirement, and the Korean immigrants Annie knows on Cape Ann work hard to adopt their new language—English. Books on ESL, English as a Second Language, are frequently requested at the library.

What did the Moonies really want in Gloucester? A waterfront for their fishing fleet, along with the establishment of a marine college? An international diplomacy conference center? An out-of-the-way place to build a vast political empire? An impressive and inviting home location for the Unification Church? Whatever it was, they had obviously been both willing and able to go after it. To what lengths would they go?

• • •

CHAPTER ELEVEN

"Pleas'd with the danger, when the waves went high"
(John Dryden, Absalom and Achitophel, pt. I)

Annie, whose mind by now is seriously boggled, suddenly remembers that she is supposed to meet Sally at two o'clock. She shuts off the computer and tries to reach her friend, but Sally has left the house already and is not answering her cell phone. Annie speeds over to downtown Gloucester. No parking to be had on Main Street, of course. She turns down onto Rogers Street and parks in the public lot next to the Gloucester House Restaurant. When she gets to the Lone Gull, Sally is there waiting already, smiling triumphantly. She has managed to snag the leather sofa by the window, the Lone Gull's most coveted seat.

"Sorry I'm late, Sal, got carried away…" Annie says, out of breath after her run from the car.

They get their coffees and share a huge brownie bulging with walnuts. While munching, they appraise the new show on the walls—the Lone Gull has a rotating show of art works. This month they are photographs, large local images printed on canvas. Annie looks at her watch.

"Hey, we have to go. Almost high tide! Your car or mine?"

Sally doesn't much care for riding in Annie's car. Annie often drives on fumes, and the passenger seat is permanently stuck in an upright position fit only for a yogi. Also, the car has been making loud, rumbling noises lately, and Sally is convinced that Annie's muffler is about to fall off. Besides, Sally prefers her own CD collection of country music (while Annie shudders at the thought of having to listen to some cowboy crying in his beer) to the odd assortment of jazz, opera, and Gregorian chant that Annie usually sticks into her tape deck.

"We'll take mine, thank you," Sally says. "Just got the tank filled. So, are you feeling any better now that you've been there in broad daylight? And where's your car parked?"

"Had to park it down on Rogers Street. I put enough in the meter to last until we get back. Do you know your way to the chasm? Just a mile or so past the castle, it's on the left. There's a long red fence by the parking lot..."

"I know, Annie, I know. C'mon, you're not at work now. Quit handing out information."

They park and walk through the woods to the rocky shore. Halfway there they hear the roar of the waves, and soon, between the thinning numbers of gnarled tree trunks, they see the spray of water against sea and sky. With Annie leading the way they climb along the rocky ledge above gullies and ravines that slope down toward the roiling water. Remnants of a fence warn them not to get too close to the chasm, which has claimed a number of lives over the years.

"I'm staying here!" Sally yells over the roaring noise. Annie nods with a condescending smile, and continues over to the next ledge. When a huge breaker nears shore, she nimbly hops back up to where Sally is standing. The wave roars into the chasm, causing a thunderous noise as it hits the hollow at the back, and slurps back out again, swirling over the ledge that Annie just vacated. Sally screams, and Annie laughs uproariously.

"That was a real *whoppah!*" she shouts. They climb up to a higher and safer location and watch from there. Waves come crashing in, sometimes met by the outgoing wave and tempered by it. Then all of a sudden the conditions are just right, and a monster wave rolls in, booming. The ground shakes, and Sally squeezes her eyes shut and covers her ears. Finally, when they become inured to fear and their hearts resume a normal rate, Annie pulls Sally along the ledge back to the woods trail.

"Wasn't that exhilarating?" Annie asks. Sally nods, with far less enthusiasm.

"What's the matter? Where's your spirit of adventure, Sal? You live for excitement, you always say."

"I never said I have a death wish," Sally retorts, and they both laugh.

"So, Sal, where do you want to go? I'm ready for another cup of coffee," Annie says, panting like a thirsty dog. Annie is always ready for another cup of coffee.

"I brought a thermos. That way we can walk on Singing Beach and have a cup there, if you want," Sally says.

Annie has suspected as much. Sally is always thoughtful that way. And as it turns out, she's brought goodies, too. They get in the car and drive down to Manchester (or Manchester-by-the-Sea, as the inhabitants there like it to be known), past the railroad station, and amazingly manage to slip into a parking spot that has just been vacated on Beach Street. Sally hefts her backpack out of the trunk. They make their way across Masconomo Street and soon pass the kid in the beach chair who spends his summer, sitting in the shade of an immense tree, collecting fees for the twenty-dollars-per-car parking lot unless the car has a town sticker. Once on the beach they take their shoes off, leaving them with everyone else's at the dry upper edge of the beach, and walk out onto hot sand that is so fine that it sings when you walk on it. *Twing, twing, twing.* Singing Beach at dusk is a lovely place to be, with slanting, peachy sun rays hitting the craggy islands out there in the bay. A good place to forget your worries.

• • •

CHAPTER TWELVE

"Genius is one percent inspiration and ninety-nine percent perspiration."
(Thomas Alva Edison)

L ater, after picking up her car in the lot and waving good-bye to Sally, Annie returns to the castle. She waves to Vinnie and walks back up to the sunlit courtyard. Albert is wheeling his cleaning cart around, dusting, mopping, and reaching over the tape to water the tropical plants.

"Hello, Albert," Annie says.

"Oh, hi there, didn't I see you here earlier today? Been here all this time?" Albert looks a little confused.

"No, I just got back. How are you doing today, Albert? Oh, it looks so strange here, with the pool drained." Annie looks over at the empty pool, dismayed.

"Don't think it'll be filled now until after we've rewired," he says, matter-of-factly. "May be a while. Hope not. Depressing, seeing people in here gawking."

When Albert leaves the courtyard, Annie sits down on a bench, letting the sun that shines in through the glass roof warm her. She closes her eyes and tries to sum up what she remembers about Jack Hammond.

Ethan Haskell's "Uncle Jack," John Hays Hammond, Jr., was the most prolific American inventor after Edison, it's been said. Hammond, who was nicknamed "Jack" after his grandfather, the explorer Jack Hays, was the son of the perhaps even more famous John Hays Hammond, Sr., a diamond mining magnate often seen in the company of presidents Grant, Hayes, Taft, Roosevelt, and Coolidge.

Jack Hammond grew up in South Africa, where his father hobnobbed with Cecil Rhodes and others of the wealthier set. That was when Hammond Senior landed in jail. Sometime after his rescue by Mark Twain, the Hammond family moved to England (where Jack's love for castles was born) before they finally settled in Washington, D.C.

Among the family's friends—beside the presidents—were the Wright brothers, Thomas Edison, and Nicola Tesla. As a young inventor Jack met Thomas Edison, who taught him his most valuable lesson: "Patent everything!" Edison later introduced him to Alexander Graham Bell, who helped the young man further. For three years, Jack worked as a clerk in the U.S. Patent Office under Bell's guidance.

In 1911, at the age of twenty-three, Jack started his own company, the Hammond Radio Research Corporation. By his death, he was credited with hundreds of inventions and patents. Jack's inventions covered everything from the sublime to the ridiculous—from electronics and guided missiles to a hypodermic meat baster, a magnetic bottle cap remover, smoke-eating ashtrays, and musical instruments, including the ten thousand– pipe organ right down behind her in the Great Hall. (When looking up "Hammond Organ" for a library patron once, Annie had learned that Jack Hammond's organ was not the well-known electric organ by that name— the one heard in old movie theaters and ballparks—which was invented by a totally unrelated Hammond.) Jack Hammond also sold one hundred patents to the U.S. War Department, and became known as "The Father of Remote Radio Control."

Annie opens her eyes, coming out of her reverie. She slips into the Renaissance Dining Room, which has a view of the bay. Across the water lies Eastern Point, with its castles and mansions. Many are well hidden from gawkers by trees and high stone walls, but they are quite visible here, from the seaside. The lighthouse sits out on the rocky, wind-beaten point, right after the Audubon Sanctuary, and the Dog Bar breakwater extends from the point out across Gloucester Bay. These days there is no need for the lighthouse keeper to walk the half mile out to the end of the breakwater in order to light the beacon, something that must have been a daunting task on a stormy winter night. Waves frequently break over the massive granite jetty, waves so strong that the stone blocks, which weigh twelve or thirteen tons each, sometimes get dislodged as easily as teeth in an old man's mouth.

Today is a lazy day for sailors out on the water. Swells are coming in through the gap at the entrance of the harbor, but there is very little wind. A windsurfer over by Niles Beach tries to catch whatever breeze there is, but keeps flopping over, and Annie turns away from the window.

The floor in the dining room is covered by tiles with a nearly endless variety of motifs. Some of the tiles are original and some are copies, but Annie has long since decided that after years of wear, it is impossible to tell the difference. Glass-fronted cupboards are filled with hand painted china and glass, and tables and glass-topped cases around the room hold trenchers and large bowls, old books, and photographs, along with assorted other items.

One of Hammond's inventions rests casually on the windowsill, next to a forgotten, half-empty champagne bottle, and a narrow refectory table holds the last of the flowers from her wedding—white roses, with a sprig of mimosa tucked in at an odd angle. Annie suddenly laughs out loud, thinking it looks like one of Esa's nosegays. Seeing the champagne bottle and the bouquet comforts her. *It did happen. We were married. Maybe the rest was only a dream.* But it hadn't been.

She goes back down the steps into the Great Hall. The Hall is crammed with medieval and Renaissance artifacts and oddities collected by Hammond. Annie smiles at the sight of the bishop's chair, which has a seat designed to automatically flop down if the bishop should try to actually *sit* on it instead of merely rest his tired derrière against it. Suffering is good—even for bishops, apparently.

She passes the Chickering Grand Piano that Gershwin used to play when he visited. It contains one of Hammond's inventions: the tonal pedal system, which allows the player to make the piano louder or softer by opening and closing a series of louvered shutters mounted on either side of the strings.

As Annie continues around the room, she makes a discovery. The niche that usually holds the skull of Columbus's crewman is empty. Judge was right.

•   •   •

CHAPTER THIRTEEN

"To unmask falsehood and bring truth to light."
(Shakespeare, Romeo and Juliet)

Annie feels restless and looks at her watch. Why did she come here? There are no real answers to be found in the castle. Jack Hammond died a long time ago, who would want to "kill" him again? Everything here is ancient history, and none of it seems to have anything to do with Ethan. She goes back into the courtyard and is met by the curator, who still looks a little apprehensive.

"It's a sad day, isn't it?" Spofford-Braxton asks. He looks pale and drawn, and dabs his forehead with a handkerchief. Annie nods.

"Tragic. I'm trying to understand what happened, Mr. Spofford-Braxton. But it's still incomprehensible to me."

"Please call me Henry, Miss...aah, Mrs. Langmuir," he says, grabbing her name out of his disturbed brain at the last moment.

"I'm keeping Quitnot as my last name, but please, just call me Annie. I'm stunned, Henry. I can't even imagine it. Who would want to kill Ethan?"

Spofford-Braxton's eyebrows rise almost up to his hairline, and his eyes bulge.

"What on earth makes you suggest that?" he asks, and she can hear panic rising in his voice. "It was an *accident,* at least that's what I was told, and that's what the paper says," he sputters, and applies the handkerchief to his forehead again, more vigorously now.

"Well, I heard that they may have be keeping the investigation open. Haven't they called you yet?" Annie asks innocently, intrigued by his agitation.

"No. But it simply can't be true. I won't believe it! It must be just routine procedure, to cover all the bases, as they say. I can see no possible reason for anyone to murder Ethan, none at all. He didn't have a mean bone in his body, did he? No, the boy was just full of enthusiasm and good will, and such a hard worker." Little drops of spittle have collected in the corners of his mouth, but he appears oblivious to it.

Annie remembers her conversation with Vinnie. Spofford-Braxton seems sincere enough, but Annie decides to press him a little.

"Must have been nice to have Ethan around. I mean, the personal touch, the connection to the family. Did he ever tell you anything about the Hammonds that you didn't know?" she asks. Altering the course of the conversation actually seems to have a calming effect on the curator.

"Well, he recounted old family legends and such... although he may have exaggerated a little, I believe. The boy never met Jack Hammond, so he didn't have any firsthand memories, of course, and I don't really think the old families got together that often. Ethan grew up in Washington, you know. And Jack Hammond wasn't actually Ethan's uncle. They were a little more distantly related. Jack would have been Ethan's great uncle, I guess. Ethan's mother was a Hammond, of course, before she married Haskell, and there was obviously more than enough Hammond money to go around..." The curator's voice trails off.

Trying to elicit some impulsive, emotional response, Annie says, "It's all too sad. He might have become a permanent fixture at the castle, joined the board or something, don't you think? I mean, he seemed so enthusiastic, just like you said."

Spofford-Braxton's small mouth becomes even smaller, turning into a tight line underneath the thin, bristly moustache. He takes off his wire-rimmed glasses and rubs them vigorously with the handkerchief. "Very sad. Yes. Very sad indeed." He puts the glasses back on, adjusting the wires behind the ears, and mops his brow again.

"Did anyone call his parents?" Annie asks with a start. Why hadn't she thought of this earlier? Because yesterday had been her wedding day, that's why.

"Ethan's father passed away some years ago, but I think Charlie got hold of the mother. I don't envy him that phone call, must have been a tough one to make." He shakes his head while noisily sucking in a breath between clenched teeth.

"Do you know where the funeral will be?" Annie is relentless.

"No, but again, I'm sure Charlie will be able to tell you that." The curator steps aside and gestures to let her pass and, it seems, disappear and leave him alone in his misery.

"Of course, Henry. Thank you." Annie wonders why the curator wasn't the one making the call. Just as well, maybe. Charlie has a more compassionate manner and would handle it much better than the doleful Spofford-Braxton. And Charlie, as best man, had arranged the wedding program and taken care of all the details—obviously with Ethan's help, since Ethan had a big part to play.

Spofford-Braxton looks at his watch, and this time gestures for Annie to precede him through a doorway.

"I just made some tea, would you like a cup? It's lovely out on the lawn...you should go out and sit in the sun; it would do you good. You look a little pale, Annie."

Annie nods. It sounds tempting. She follows the curator into the museum shop, where he removes his tweed jacket and drapes it, a little pedantically, over a wire hanger which he hooks onto the wainscoting. The lining of the jacket is in tatters and darkened by sweat. Then he walks over to a small table below the window and pours tea from a proper china teapot kept under a tea cozy.

"Darjeeling, my favorite. Now take your cup and go on outside," he urges her, herding her out of the shop as if she were a reluctant goat. Annie takes the tea and a couple of cookies the curator presses into her hand. Taking her elbow, he leads her through the workshop that used to be Hammond's lab and out onto the back lawn, where screeching seagulls are fighting about a paper bag someone has left behind. Limp french fries and a tattered lot of lobster shells fall out of it and are soon carried aloft, where the fight continues. Some of the seagulls take their bounty out to Norman's Woe, where other gulls join in the fracas among small bits of wreckage from the boat that went aground there yesterday. In a day or two, tides, winds, and waves will have swept away most of the debris. Annie reclines in a lawn chair and sips her tea. The curator was right, she feels better out here. She closes her eyes. The sun feels warm on her skin.

A while later she wakes with a start, realizing suddenly that time has flown, and heads back inside to return her teacup. Spofford-Braxton is nowhere to be seen, and she waves a hurried good-bye to Vinnie, who is showing a miniature castle to an entranced youngster.

"Tell Spoffie thanks, got to go," she calls to him.

· · ·

CHAPTER FOURTEEN

"In early July I spoke in five cities around Korea at rallies held by the Women's Federation for World Peace. There, I declared that my wife, WFWP President Hak Ja Han Moon, and I are the True Parents of all Humanity. I declared that we are the Savior, the Lord of the Second Advent, the Messiah."
(Reverend Sun Myung Moon, quote from Unification News, August 24, 1992)

Annie has just a little left time before she has to go and meet Duncan, so she gets back to her Internet search, picking up where she left off.

Jim Munn, a well known writer for the local paper, wrote in one of his columns: "Over the years this city has demonstrated a remarkable capacity to accommodate a wide range of people, including those who dare to be different or simply come here that way. Gloucester has greeted the arrival of the Unification Church perhaps more rudely than what one might have expected. I doubt, however, that this community will turn its back on its own rich heritage.

"Gloucester has survived too many storms to feel threatened by those who are misguided enough to seriously suggest that within twenty years everyone here will be speaking Korean. Hell, most of us are still having a hard enough time just trying to get a handle on the King's English."

Munn's column probably referred to one of Moon's lectures that had riled people in Gloucester. The lecture had included the following statement: *"You need to learn Korean before you go to the spiritual world, because your ancestors will be upset with you. I know this reality very well. If you don't believe me, then tonight you can pass away and find out for yourself."* What a challenge! Moon had declared that everyone needed to learn Korean by 1980, because after that the Messiah would no longer speak in English.

That threat had not intimidated Gloucesterites, who on the whole are an independent lot. For instance, they would rather let the whole waterfront lie unused—the shacks rot, the wharves fall in and the empty lots grow rank with weeds— than let fancy hotels or condos be built there. "The fish may yet come back," they say, "and then we'll be ready." Maybe it's a sign of the desperate optimism that prevails in fishing towns these days. And in Gloucester, at least, Korean has not displaced the King's English, nor has it taken the place of the Portuguese and Sicilián that is still spoken there.

Annie soon notices that something called "Principle of Indemnity" is hammered home frequently by Moon. Apparently, this is how people earn their salvation, by paying for their sins and past mistakes. Annie finds articles reporting that Moon and his followers insist that the Jews called the Holocaust down upon themselves, since, the Moonies claim, the Jews were responsible for Jesus' death.

Moon claims to have spoken, "in the spirit world," with every deceased American president as well as with John the Baptist, Jesus, Moses, and Mohammed. Moon's spiritual manifesto, the "Divine Principle and its Application" (created by Moon, and considered the "Moonie Bible," which Moon claims was revealed to him directly by Jesus Christ), is considered by the followers to be the "Third Testament," and superior to the Bible.

According to Moon, "The hostages were symbolic in dispensational history, and through their suffering of 444 days, indemnity was paid for America's dividing Korea at the end of World War II, and for her standing by while the free world became weak and communism expanded. To indemnify the failures of America as a Christian nation, 52 Americans suffered as hostages." Thus the United States, as a nation, apparently paid indemnity for its sins.

In his 2004 speech at the "Coronation Ceremony" in the Capitol, Moon made this pronouncement: "The founders of five great religions and many other leaders, including… dictators such as Hitler and Stalin, have found strength in my teachings, mended their ways, and been reborn as new persons." Moon claims that he has saved their souls, and that Hitler and Stalin have reformed and vouched for him from the "spirit world," calling him "none other than humanity's Savior, Messiah, Returning Lord and True Parent." In response to these and other controversial teachings, Israel's Knesset and the French Parliament, among others, have classified the Unification Church as a cult.

Annie yawns. There is just too much information to slog through. While all this talk about indemnity and reformed dictators may be both shocking and interesting, Annie has as yet found nothing specific to connect the Moonies with any violent "Mafia" tactics, nor anything much on the more recent history of the Moonies in Gloucester. Is she far afield here? Does any of what she has found point to an effort to undermine the Hammond Castle, to put it out of business so that they can acquire it? Cause a scandal, harm its reputation, and force it into bankruptcy so that it would have to be put up for sale? Well, for now, she has run out of time.

• • •

CHAPTER FIFTEEN

"My conclusions have cost me some labor from the want of
coincidence between accounts of the same occurrences by different
eyewitnesses, arising sometimes from imperfect memory, sometimes
from undue partiality for one side or the other."
(Thucydides, The History of the Peloponnesian War)

Annie parks the Chevy in the garage and walks into her house. The kitchen smells a little musty, and when she pulls out a chair to sit down, the wooden backrest feels cold and clammy. She turns the heat on to dry things out. Moisture from long stretches of humid weather or recurring fogs always linger in homes along the shore long after the weather has turned. Annie goes into the living room to start a fire. That is when she suddenly remembers that she doesn't live here anymore. She looks around disconsolately, walks over to the bookshelves and caresses the leather spines of her collection of Shakespeare books. They feel sticky, too, and she worries about them. "Willie" is her most trusted companion, after all, and has seen her through many hard times. Then she remembers her other "companion"—her husband...and dinner... and having to go to the library to help prepare for tomorrow's meeting.

She leaves the heat on and hurries home—home to *Duncan's* house, that is—on foot. Duncan hasn't arrived yet, and Annie breathes a deep sigh of relief. She looks around, something she doesn't always feel comfortable doing with Duncan present. Will she ever be able to think of this as her home? It's a masculine place, neat and organized, with leather furniture, elegant mahogany chests and tables that look very English but are surely copies, and handsomely framed images of Duncan's favorite frescoes. Even the fireplace is neat and clean, ashes swept away and wood stacked neatly in a wood box that doesn't leak dust and bits of bark all over the floor. For a moment she misses her own comfortably messy house. Then she shakes it off and starts preparing one of her half-hour specials: spicy Andouille sausages sautéed with mushrooms and onions, to be served with a bowl of five-minute couscous and a Romaine salad topped with olives and capers.

"Mm, smells terrific," Duncan says, husbandly, as he walks in the door.

"How was your day?" she returns, wifely. They both laugh and sit down to eat.

"My day was long. How about yours? You and Sally have a good time on the beach?"

"Great. Oh, and my visit to the castle was interesting, too. Talked to Spofford, who hadn't heard that the police are still looking into Ethan's death. Seemed pretty upset when I mentioned it," she says and puts a forkful of sausage and mushrooms into her mouth.

"I don't blame him," Duncan says, before coughing sharply and taking a quick sip of wine. The sausages are very hot indeed, and a small piece of jalapeño has glued itself to the back of his tongue. Annie whacks him on the back, and after taking another sip of wine Duncan nods that he's fine.

"And Vinnie—you know, the apprentice—told me that 'Spoffie,' which is what he calls him, hadn't even called the trustees to tell them about what happened."

Duncan carefully chews a piece of sausage and swallows it down with wine before answering.

"Well, Annie, Henry did seem very shaken. It's understandable, don't you think? But I agree, the trustees should have been informed…"

"Oh, Charlie told them. By the way, Dunc, Judge was right. Columbus's crewman's skull is gone. And Vinnie mentioned that he had overheard Spofford and Ruth talking… they were saying something about an audit…and then he told me that Ethan had threatened Spoffie with the idea that he might come back and take over the *family business,* as he called it, when he was through with school." Annie tosses the salad with balsamic vinegar and olive oil and sprinkles some feta cheese and sunflower seeds over the top.

"Aha. And now you have a suspect?" Duncan puts down his fork and knife. After having lived most of his life in London, he eats European style, fork in left hand and knife in the right, using the left hand to bring the food to his mouth, which Annie thinks looks very quaint. Duncan helps himself to some salad while waiting for Annie to respond.

"Well, apparently old Spoffie seemed upset by the idea," she says lamely.

"I see." Duncan rather pointedly changes the subject. "Delicious dinner, wife. Shall we save coffee for later? I'd love to finish up at the office. Still game to come in and help?"

"Of course! I'll even leave the dishes," Annie says gallantly.

They amble over to the library, walking down Main Street, where the dark expanse of Sandy Bay is visible between the houses. It is a balmy evening with a mild sea breeze. The quiet is broken by the measured whooshing of swells striking the shore, and the clattering of pebbles and rumbling of boulders that rock and roll back and forth. The half-moon-shaped Front Beach is sandy, but as it curves outward toward Old Harbor and Bearskin Neck, the sand turns to shingle and rocks, especially during the winter season.

The library is dark and quiet, and they leave the lights off and continue upstairs, guided only by the emergency light—this to avoid a visit from the local constabulary to check for prowlers. People in town are always on the watch for unusual goings-on, and are quick to call in their suspicions.

Duncan hands her the pages to be copied, collated, and stapled, one for each library director who is to attend the meeting. Esa has set up the tables in the Friends' Room, and Annie places a copy of the agenda by each seat, while Duncan sets out china and napkins on a side table. The freshly polished coffee urns are in place, and in the morning Duncan will stop at the coffee shop for the platter of Nisu and Norwegian coffee bread he has ordered.

Too bad I'm not wifely enough to bake something myself, Annie thinks ruefully.

· · ·

CHAPTER SIXTEEN

"The fog comes
On little cat feet.
It sits looking
Over the harbor and city
On silent haunches
And then moves on."
(Carl Sandburg, "Fog")

A dense sea fog has covered the island for days. The seagulls screech forlornly. The remaining tourists, and even the natives, are getting restless. It's the time of year when islanders expect those clear, crisp days when they own the island again, and the *summah people* are gone. But in the usual order of things, busloads of *golden aygahs* and *furrinahs* will arrive next for the leaf-peeping tours. And then, before winter sets in, many of Rockport's own seniors—*snowbirds,* in local parlance, recognizable by their white plumage—will migrate to their winter homes in Florida, most of them heading for Bonita Springs, Punta Gorda, or Marco Island. Only then will the streets echo with the footsteps of the diehard Rockporter.

Annie drives along deserted roads, following the shoreline. She is on a brief mission before getting ready for library duty, and has set off early in the morning. Many of the homes and cottages along the roads and lanes are boarded up for the winter. Precious shrubs and hedges have been covered with tightly belted burlap coats against snow and wind, and garden plants hibernate in comfort under evergreen branches or salt hay.

Apart from the occasional *day-trippahs*, the tourists that remain after Labor Day are mainly *Nuh Yawkahs*. On foggy days they wake up, get into their mist-laden landaulettes and go "across the cut" to North America, from where the fog looks like a great woolly cap covering the island. As soon as they reach the mainland, the autumn sun instantly prickles on the backs of their necks. They spend the day prowling the other small coastal villages, antiquing, and swilling down amazing amounts of *chowdah*. At the end of the day they return to their fog-bound cottages or B&Bs on the island. Halfway across the Piatt Andrew Bridge, they are again shrouded in mist.

But Annie isn't interested in going "ovah the bridge," another euphemism for leaving the island (as in, *You mean you had to go ovah the bridge to find a job?*) Her goal this morning is Eastern Point—the "Newport" of Cape Ann, though the *"cottages"* may be a little more modest. When looking up Spofford-Braxton in the phone book, she was puzzled when she found that he was listed as living on Eastern Point. She still cannot imagine how the meek and threadbare curator could possibly afford such a fancy address.

The mitten-shaped island of Cape Ann, with Eastern Point as a woolly tassel at the wrist (although the Eastern Pointers would probably prefer their exclusive enclave referred to as a *silk* tassel), sticks out into the Atlantic, attached to the mainland by three bridges, all spanning the Annisquam River. Two are old drawbridges: the Railroad Bridge and the Blynman Bridge. The Blynman is known simply as "the Cut," as that is where the isthmus was cut to join Massachusetts Bay with Ipswich Bay. This is also what changed Cape Ann from a cape to an island. This water bypass, the Annisquam River, made the often hazardous passage around the Cape unnecessary.

The largest and most recent connection to the mainland is the Piatt Andrew Bridge, rising in a graceful arc high above the Annisquam River.

Annie heads out along the Atlantic shore road from Rockport over toward Gloucester. The outermost road around the island measures just about the same distance as a Marathon run, and is used as such by practicing local runners. Totally unperturbed by irate honkers, many would-be marathoners, along with other less ambitious duffers, brave the traffic every day, especially at dawn and dusk, when they are most difficult for drivers to spot. Bravely they run on the pavement, since there are few stretches of sidewalk or even shoulder on the island roads.

Driving along Rockport's Cape Hedge and Long Beach, Annie continues past Gloucester's Good Harbor Beach. She sees people dimly outlined in the fog, walking across the long wooden bridge that spans the creek. This morning most of them choose to go strolling just beneath the dunes in lee of the wind. Dogs roam happily in packs now that fall is here and they are allowed on the beach again.

The next stretch of the island is known locally as the Back Shore, which confuses many, as it is the ocean front. It includes Bass Rocks, though how one would know whether the bass are running is anyone's guess, as most of the rocky shore is well marked with *Private* and *No Trespassing* signs. The signs, typical wherever the McMansion Society has bought itself a foothold, spoil the grand view, but Annie supposes they give the owners that satisfied sense of "validation." Hotels and inns sit thigh-to-thigh with great faux mansions (and a few real ones) on the inland side of the road. In storms, great boulders are often coughed up onto the road by the angry sea, and some even pile up on the front lawns of the properties.

Wild breakers crashing over Table Rock is a favorite motif of seascape painters, but it is a subject heard rather than seen today. The swells rumble against the coastline, scattering cormorants off the rocks and throwing a mist of yellow sulphur-smelling froth across the road. When Annie gets to the corner by Niles' Beach, she makes a left turn onto Eastern Point and drives through stone gates with bold signs declaring the area PRIVATE. But no one guards the gates in the off-season. On the right-hand side of the road is a long stretch of private sandy beach, on the left some of the great homes. Right now she is passing the old Clarence Birdseye Estate, the Birdseye of the frozen foods. From the address she scribbled on a note Annie can tell that Spofford lives somewhere on the right, which is the Gloucester Harbor side of Eastern Point.

On the way there, she passes a few of the more imposing old homes, visible high up on the north side of the road. Ornate Victorian stone or brick mansions, grandiose villas, and more understated colonial clapboards sit at the back of the properties, with their multi-windowed facades eyeing the bay. Fieldstone walls and wrought-iron gates line the road. Other grand estates, including substantial castles of gray granite, remain completely hidden behind tall stone walls and pillared gateways, the domiciles visible only from the water.

Suddenly she sees a mailbox with the right number. There is no name on the box and no house to be seen, only a tree-lined dirt road leading down toward the water. Annie hesitates, as parking is not allowed along the road on Eastern Point—after all, one must keep "the great unwashed" from roaming around here—and she is not about to drive down the private lane. Instead, she drives out to the end of Eastern Point and parks her car in the Lighthouse parking lot before making her way back on foot.

She stops by the mailbox and looks around to make sure she is not observed. The dirt lane curves between large boulders and stands of gnarled old cedars. Skillfully built free-stone walls, undulating gently to follow the natural lay of the land, separate the property from its neighbors.

As she gets farther down the lane, a building suddenly looms in the mist. It's a castle-like granite structure similar to others on Eastern Point, though this one is not quite as stately, with a round, slate-roofed tower at each end. In the center of the main building there is an archway entrance leading into an atrium courtyard. There is no car parked at the end of the driveway. Annie assumes that Spofford must be off somewhere, maybe out for coffee or a morning paper.

It's a pretty dilapidated old place, to be sure, but still... could this really be Spofford's home? The lot alone would be worth a fortune. Location, location, location, as they say in the real estate trade. The building itself looks to be in need of a lot of work. Piles of cut granite overgrown with weeds lie along the sides of the yard, remnants of some unfinished project. Gargoyles guard the property from the eaves, each one with a malevolent face of its own. One has fallen and lies on the ground below, looking like an old dragon's tooth waiting for the tooth fairy.

Annie tiptoes carefully around to the back of the building. The shrubs are neatly pruned, some of them cut topiary fashion into spirals and balls. She turns and looks up at the house. The interior is hidden by lace curtains, and there is no sign of anyone being at home. No visible light is on inside; no motion-sensitive floodlights come on when she moves closer. A stone patio holds wrought-iron furniture, and built onto the outside of the house is a granite fireplace with some half-burned logs in it. The fireplace is not as big as the one in the Hammond Castle Courtyard, but it is certainly reminiscent of it. Faces and shields are cut into some of the stones.

Annie continues on, driven by curiosity. As she rounds the second tower, she walks by a curtain-less window and peeks in to see a round, well-stocked library, furnished with odd pieces of furniture and topped with a cupola ceiling. Paintings line the walls above and between the bookshelves—old master oils, Persian miniatures, and a painting that appears partly gold-leafed, much like a Russian icon.

When she gets back around to the arched entrance Annie hesitates before stepping into the courtyard. She reads the inscription carved on the keystone of the arch: *FINISTERRE*. Land's End. The small atrium courtyard is glassed over, and niches and ledges in the walls hold a myriad of stone and bronze sculptures, wrought-iron candleholders, and clay urns overflowing with wilted plants. An ancient-looking carved wooden bench next to the door has a pair of rubber boots under it along with an umbrella and an old galvanized watering can.

She slips out again and heads down toward the water. The path meanders through a stand of locust trees with slender, spiked branches reaching out from sinuous trunks. Farther down, on a wide ledge above the rocks, a wall of familiar-looking gothic arches frames the misty bay. Annie, amazed, walks around the arches and down some stone steps to the water, where a small pontoon landing bobs and clucks on the wavelets. There are mooring rings and rubber bumpers along the sides, but no boat is moored there.

The fog is too thick to see across the bay, but Annie guesses that she must be standing diagonally across from Hammond Castle. To think that she had stood over there, looking across the water, without ever noticing these sister arches. Over to her left there is a boat shed with a ramp leading up into it from the water. She walks over and puts her nose against the windowpane, only to find that someone is standing right on the other side of the window, looking back at her. A wide, pale face with shaggy bangs hanging down over deep-set eyes. A lopsided grin, probably caused by the scar that runs from the temple down to the mouth, splits the strange, flat moon-face in half.

Suddenly the figure moves and Annie, who feels like screaming but can't utter a sound, stands paralyzed. After a moment she hears him crashing down onto the shingle below the ramp, roaring wordlessly. Scared stiff, she finally regains her ability to move and starts running up the path. When she gets near the house she hears a car approaching. It hasn't made it all the way down the driveway yet, and Annie races for cover behind some boulders.

Spofford-Braxton pulls in and steps out of his old green Valiant, carrying a grocery bag and a newspaper. Without glancing around he walks into the house. As the door slams, the figure from the boatshed comes lumbering around the corner tower. He is carrying a collection of heavy tools, axes and augers and other menacing-looking objects, which he drops in the courtyard.

The clanging gets Spofford's attention, and Annie hears an outburst of loud voices but doesn't stay to listen. Alternately crawling and running, she weaves her way back up to the road and then half runs out to the lighthouse and the safety of her car. When she reaches it she is trembling and barely able to unlock the door. Fortunately the car starts without trouble and she drives carefully along the road. After she passes Spofford's driveway, Annie inhales deeply and steers for Rockport.

. . .

CHAPTER SEVENTEEN

"It takes a heap o' livin' in a house t' make it home,
A heap o' sun an' shadder, an' ye sometimes have t' roam
Afore ye really 'preciate the things ye lef' behind,
An' hunger fer 'em somehow, with 'em allus on yer mind."
(Edgar Albert Guest, "Home")

On the way back Annie stops in at her own house. A sigh of relief always escapes her when she steps inside the door. A little reluctantly, she has brought a few of her favorite pieces of furniture to Duncan's house, for instance a comfortable chair that is not too ratty looking, and a bureau to hold her folded clothing. Duncan has given up half a closet in the bedroom for her "library outfits," but she still keeps most of her clothes down here. Where would she ever put all her favorite stuff in his house?

She sits by the kitchen window, looking out into the fog, wondering about Spofford-Braxton and his castle. What does it all mean? How can he afford a castle on Eastern Point, small though it may be? Maybe there's some kind of family money. She remembers the tattered lining of Spoffie's jacket. People with "old wealth" often dress down and drive clunky old cars, after all. But what about this "audit" that Vinnie mentioned? Why would Spofford-Braxton have to worry about a thing like that, then? And where have all those old artifacts on his property come from? What about the stone arches down by the bay, and all the paintings and objects she glimpsed inside? She tries not to give in to the obvious suspicion that Spofford might be creating a castle for himself by lifting items from Hammond's collection. And who was that alarming figure in the boat shed? A gardener? Or a hired killer?

She is still trembling from the morning's experience, but it's time to get going. Annie makes this daily stop-in to check on her house, anxious to keep the dust off Willie's books. Also, to make sure no unwanted critters have found their way in; and to air things out, since the weather has been more than usually damp lately. Annie is an islander and enjoys every kind of weather, but after several days of fog she is beginning to wish for a change. This morning she even ironed her linen pant-suit—not to make it look good, just to take the dampness out of it. Annie is not generally an advocate of ironing; however, today it actually wouldn't *hurt* to look good. It will be her first day back at the reference desk after the wedding, and she is likely to be scrutinized by townies as well as colleagues, and also by the library trustees, should they happen to drop by. After all, she has been gone for two months, and despite Duncan's assurances she has some anxiety about whether she has a job to come back to. She knows she has Charlie Field on her side, but what about the other two trustees? *Well, time will tell.*

Annie glances in the mirror on her way out, forcing her obstinate red hair into a twirled knot at the nape of the neck. No makeup is necessary—freckles and green eyes provide enough color and interest, and the fine lines around her eyes have appeared slowly enough over the years that she doesn't even notice them herself. She rarely wears jewelry to work except for earrings of her own making, big dangling ones mostly. Today's are not too outrageous. She intends to keep a low profile until people get used to her being back.

Knowing that the library will have a busy day, Annie feels extra jittery. In bad weather (anything but full-sun, blue-sky, beach-bag weather is bad weather in the eyes of the Summer People) the readers come out in droves. The Rockport Public Library, being one of the few in the region to be open on Sundays, has two comfortable reading rooms: Franz's and Luisita's. Annie especially likes Franz's Room, with its dark brown leather-covered wing chairs and permission for "quiet conversation."

The library, which is the central point in town for important local news, is not known for its hushed circumambience—in fact; new patrons are often mystified by the amount of hubbub in the building. It goes far beyond the normal white noise of hushed footsteps and whispered directions usually heard in libraries. Luisita's Room is the only exception, being the official Quiet Reading Room. Well, almost. A lot of paper rustling goes on in there by patrons who stand in line outside the library to be the first to get their hands on the daily onslaught of news before anyone else messes up the paper.

When Annie steps out through the kitchen door—as usual she leaves the back way—she sees the sun, moonlike in its pallor, through the fog. She shudders, no doubt from a combination of the damp chill and the morning's strange experience. By noon the fog has burned off and the horizon is finally visible again, crisp and blue, far out beyond the breakwater.

• • •

CHAPTER EIGHTEEN

"It's them that take advantage that get advantage i' this world."
(George Eliot, Adam Bede)

Jean, who has substituted at the reference desk, greets Annie at the door, grinning ecstatically.

"Annie, welcome back, and congratulations!" Annie even gets a brief hug from the usually shy and retiring library assistant, which she takes as a clue that her own position is secure. Jean, who normally works at the main circulation desk, took on the reference desk with some eagerness during Annie's absence after Carlo's murder. Annie was actually surprised, knowing that Jean is painfully timid when speaking to patrons and quite insecure when it comes to learning new systems or taking on added responsibilities. But Annie, after some initial hesitation, took it as an encouraging sign that Jean might be feeling more self-assured. However, Jean seemed a little more reluctant when asked to continue for the duration of Annie's trip to New Mexico. Perhaps the reference desk turned out to be more challenging than she expected.

Marie, head of Circulation, comes up from the dungeon, (the affectionate term for the downstairs staff room,) and Annie waves to her before she walks over to her desk. There, one of Esa's flower arrangements greets her. This time, it consists of sprigs of wild purple asters surrounding one red rose. Esa, a Finnish boy—well, he seems still a boy though he is in his late thirties—is a true blithe spirit, born with a slow mind but a sunny nature. He kept her desk decorated with odd assortments of cut flowers while she was suspended as the main suspect in Carlo's murder, confident that Annie was innocent. A perennial innocent himself, Esa had whispered to her right from the start, "I know you didn't do it, Miss Annie." Seeing this latest posy, Annie smiles gratefully and sinks into her comfortable leather chair, feeling safe at last.

Charlie stops by Annie's desk to welcome her back. The fact that Charlie is a close friend of Duncan's no doubt has something to do with the visit. Charlie and Duncan often go book hunting together, following a route that stakes out their favorite antiquarian bookshops along the seaboard. On one of these jaunts Charlie found a couple of rare Shakespeare volumes that he gave Annie for Christmas that year.

Charlie and Duncan have many things in common besides the love of old books, one being a traumatic childhood. According to Duncan, Charlie's grandfather killed himself after a business failure, leaving the family in poverty. Eventually the children, a somewhat dysfunctional group, each sibling marked by the tragic loss, split up and took off for various parts of the country, as if they reminded one another of the tragedy. Charlie's father was the only one that remained in the area. Marrying late in life and struggling to make a living, he had only the one child—Charlie. The traumatic past had finally come to claim Charlie's father, who drank himself to death. Charlie's mother worked hard to help put her son through school but died the week before his college graduation.

Charlie stubbornly worked his way through graduate school, and finally started his own small publishing company. To Annie, Charlie seems a nice and easygoing enough fellow, someone who would make a lovely husband and a good father. She has noticed the budding relationship between Charlie and

Clare, and hopes it will bear fruit. Clare and Charlie are both thoughtful and sensitive people, similar in nature, and would probably make a good couple. Of course, small publishing houses are struggling in the sluggish economy, and Duncan has hinted that Charlie's company is languishing. If it fails, it might subdue Charlie's ardor. Annie hopes a business failure won't send him into the doldrums that claimed his father and grandfather. But today Charlie, affable and good-natured as always, shows no outward signs of stress.

"You've been missed, Annie. Good to have you back. Anybody gives you any trouble, just come straight to me," he says, loudly enough for nearby patrons to hear. He gives her a vigorous thumbs-up sign and smiles broadly. Annie cringes slightly, hoping he isn't going to overdo the staunch supporter act.

"Thank you, Mr. Field," she says, respectfully using his last name rather than the too familiar *Charlie*, which she uses only in private. Despite being embarrassed she can't help feeling buoyed by his kindness, and attacks a sticky reference question with renewed vigor.

Later in the afternoon, the two other trustees, Douglas Matthews and Laura Swernow, come by to welcome her back and to assure her that of course they *personally* believed in her innocence. Unfortunately, they felt obliged to suspend her until her name had been officially cleared.

"I know you understand, Annie, that it was just a formality, a way to keep the library out of any possible legal trouble," Swernow says. Matthews mumbles some similar sentiment. Would they have felt it necessary to explain themselves to her if she hadn't just married the director? Annie has to force herself to keep from telling them how she really feels—which is that they acted cowardly in not supporting her—and nods with what she hopes is a reassuring smile.

"Of course. We must always keep the library out of any bad publicity. Just glad it's over," she says, and to signal that they don't need to embarrass themselves any further, she opens her desk drawer and pretends to search for a file.

Task accomplished, Matthews and Swernow walk up the stairs to the director's office, presumably to inform Duncan that they have discharged their responsibility and mended fences. But Duncan is not in, and moments later the two trustees leave by the back door. Swernow looks irritated, her face flushed. Douglas Matthews was the driving force behind the suspension, convinced that Annie was "guilty as sin," and Swernow is embarrassed at having gone along—especially after all the phone calls she received afterwards from upset patrons asking, "Whatever happened to innocent until proven guilty?"

· · ·

Early library patrons are beginning to line up at the main desk. One of them, Mrs. Davis, waits for Jean to be free before plunking down her stack of five books. Jean scans the patron card and starts checking out the books. At the third one she hesitates.

"Is this for the high school project, Mrs. Davis? You know the limit is two books per student on the subject of the current essay, to make sure there's enough for everyone. Wait, let me check…yes, 'American Inventors' is the subject…so, I'm sorry, but you'll have to pick just two of these."

Mrs. Davis leans across the desk, tilting her head with an ingratiating smile, and whispers:

"Oh, Jean, it's for my Timmy. He's trying to get a scholarship so he can go to college. You know, we couldn't afford to send him otherwise…"

Jean buckles quickly under pressure, which is exactly what Mrs. Davis has counted on—that's why she chose to wait in Jean's line. When the stack has been scanned, Mrs. Davis remembers something else.

"Oh, and I have some inter library loans waiting. Got a call just this morning." She cranes her neck and squints at the ILL trolley behind Jean to see if she can find her name on the little yellow slips sticking up at the top of the books.

Jean turns to the trolley, and there she finds four more books on American inventors. She checks them out without comment. ILL books are not included in the local rule...*but still,* she thinks. Mrs. Davis bags her loot in a capacious and dingy canvas bag with the library logo, and leaves looking well pleased with herself. Jean, feeling more than a little used, looks up Mrs. Davis's checkout record on the computer and finds that the woman had already checked books out on Edison and Bell last week. When she checks Timmy's record there are four more, checked out on his card. Jean ponders whether to tell the director. Or should she let it go? She would have to admit to breaking the rule. She goes and checks on what is left on the science and biography shelves and sees that there are still a fair number, so she decides to let the matter drop. However, by the end of the afternoon the supply of books on inventors has dropped drastically, and when yet another student comes looking, Jean has to send him to the reference desk for help. Annie shakes her head at the nearly empty shelves.

"Well, Jared, I know I'll have something for you in the vertical files. Just follow me." She leads the way to the cabinets behind her desk and goes to the section where she keeps local biographies. She flips through them, but when she gets to "Hammond, John Hays, Jr." she finds the file empty. The thin, worn book on Hammond and all the pamphlets and papers on his inventions are missing.

Annie feels a mixture of sadness and vexation. Hammond is a well-known and romantic figure in the annals of local history on the North Shore, and over the years Annie has carefully collected and filed interesting bits of information on the inventor.

"How odd," she says now. Not many patrons use the vertical files, and Annie normally knows what has gone out. Of course, she's been away for a while. "Well, Jared, I'll take a look down in the Rockport Room, I know there's more stuff there. Just wait by the main desk while I check." She points to a spot where she expects him to stand until she returns. Jared sighs and rolls his eyes when Annie turns her back. The afternoon is fleeting, and Jared has other plans.

Annie finds the Hammond biography and files to be missing downstairs, too, which now really perplexes and annoys her. Only in unusual circumstances do books and papers go out on loan from the downstairs "Local History" collection. If the Board of Selectmen are studying a proposal, for instance, or some reputable author or historian is working on a paper and needs prime source material, they will get special dispensation to sign items out.

Jared, who has been waiting impatiently, says he has to leave and Annie promises to call if she finds something for him. Jared smiles, thinking maybe he's in luck. He can blame the library if he is unable to turn his essay in on time.

Annie goes up to the second floor and checks with Clare in cataloging.

"Any new books on science to be catalogued?" she asks. Clare checks the list. It turns out there are a few, and she says she'll get right on it. Annie asks her to put a reserve slip in one of them for Jared (who is surely going to be disappointed) before going back down to her desk, where she soon gets caught up in a new flurry of reference requests.

• • •

CHAPTER NINETEEN

"Beware of all enterprises that require new clothes."
(Henry Thoreau, Walden)

After work Annie walks over to the Hannah Jumper House to change into something a little more romantic than what she is wearing, which is one of her favorite, comfortably wrinkled library linen suits, this one moss green. Then she ambles up to Duncan's house. *Home*, she tries to force herself to think. Well, maybe in time, if that's the way it has to be. She steps into Duncan's spacious and rather grand living room with its high ceiling, large windows, and walls of bookshelves, and sinks down in one of Duncan's admittedly comfortable chairs. Would she dare to put her favorite lumpy chair in this room?

Gussie, who has stayed truculently hidden behind the sofa, finally sticks his nose out and eyes Annie sourly. Annie bends forward in her chair and stretches her hands out toward him. Since she returned from New Mexico, Gussie has steadfastly refused to forgive her for deserting him. Maybe he doesn't recognize her? Maybe he's getting old and forgetful? That would be understandable today. She doesn't usually wear dressy clothes, and the long black skirt topped by a shimmering ivory silk blouse has been hiding at the back of her closet since God knows when. Since Carlo's days, to be sure.

"Aw, come on Gussie. You know I love you." When this does not yield a result, she gets down on her knees and slaps her thighs. Gussie wiggles his head a little, half shutting his black-marble eyes as though he's still not quite sure. Then, with a sudden wild yip, he catapults himself forward and ends up nose to kneecap with Annie. Annie picks him up and dances around the room with him, her skirt billowing, and a lot of nuzzling and licking takes place. She has been forgiven.

Finally she lets him down, and Gussie stalks over to the wing chair, sits down on his haunches in front of it, and turns his head toward her with an imperious look. Just then Duncan walks in and, seeing the situation, gives Annie a guilty look. He lifts Gussie up and puts him in the chair. Gussie nods, satisfied, and immediately closes his eyes.

"I see," Annie says. "So this is what I'm faced with now?" Then she chuckles, and Duncan looks relieved.

"Dinner's on," he says, and leads the way to the dining room where candles and steaming plates of food await.

"Don't try to tell me *this* fell out of your fridge," Annie laughs. That is what she usually offers hungry people at her house: *"You'll get whatever falls out of the fridge."*

"Well now, what fell out of mine would probably have frightened you away forever," Duncan answers.

"Why? I love kippers and black and white pudding and all those peculiar things you Brits eat!" Annie says. She is adventurous when it comes to food and enjoys foreign cooking, the spicier and more unusual the better.

When Duncan's father sent for him, seeing him through school and university years in England, Duncan adopted the customs and habits of his new country, including the cooking style of the English. As time went on, he began his career by teaching at Oxford (no doubt with a little help from his father) before eventually returning to the States years later as a librarian. Now he is hoping that the directorship at the Rockport Public Library will last until his retirement, which is some distance away as he is still in that somewhat murky stage of middle age. While his preference for English cooking is still strong, he also has a weakness for ethnic food, especially northern Italian cooking. They sit down, and then Duncan gets up again immediately to pour the wine. Annie slices into the meat, which is grilled to a rosy pink, and tender.

"And the steak isn't boiled, either," she says, jokingly.

Duncan frowns. "Now Annie, that's unfair. That was only true during the war, when meat was rationed and tough as shoe leather besides. You *had* to boil it before doing anything else to it, or it would have been inedible."

"Well, *you* would know about that, I guess. *I* wasn't born then," Annie says with a devilish glint in her eye.

Duncan coughs sharply, pretending to be wildly insulted. "Neither was I, actually," he says half under his breath—but then, Annie knows that already.

"This is really good, Duncan. I didn't know you could cook. I mean, other than muffins and tea bread." This is what the librarians usually serve when they get together for coffee on Library Night, taking turns as host every Thursday evening. Library Night is a long standing tradition at the library, started by Duncan. The regular staff members get together to discuss library problems of any kind, community needs, book purchases, poetry readings or other upcoming events, and any news from the consortium about programs or system improvements. At first they met at Duncan's every other week, but soon they started taking turns and changed to meet every week, enjoying both the conversation and the goodie table.

Duncan has recovered from the cough attack and sits back and studies Annie pointedly.

"I'm sure there's a lot I still don't know about you, either," he says, still huffy about her hint at his advanced age.

Annie decides to stick to the subject of cooking, which is something Duncan enjoys. He is actually an excellent cook, and Annie is looking forward to sharing this chore.

"Well, I'm no cook, as you well know. I have my moments, but my general rule is that supper can't take more than half an hour from grocery bag to table."

"Ah. That leaves out a lot..."

"Afraid so. No bouillabaisse, no boeuf bourguignon, paella, osso bucco, or even a homely meatloaf...but I do lobsters and crab cakes and I make a great salad. And the best leftover soup ever, with everything in the fridge thrown in, including the salad."

Duncan shudders and pretends to look frightened.

"Remind me to check whether it's 'leftover day' when it's your turn to cook dinner," he says. "Anyway, I'm sure we'll survive. There's always takeout. Oh, speaking of takeout... I had a chat with Hedwig today. The missing Hammond material hasn't turned up yet."

"Oh? I'd almost forgotten about that. Oh, now that I think of it—could the disappearance of those materials could have something to do with the...ahem, you know, what happened at the castle?"

Duncan is royally sorry that he brought the subject up. He looks at her silently, knowing, not without a certain dread, what is in her mind. Choosing not to comment, he just shrugs his shoulders and gets up to refill their wine glasses.

When they have finished eating, Duncan suggests they take their coffee in the living room, and Annie helps bring the dishes over to the sink. Duncan's kitchen isn't the neat-as-a-pin place Annie once imagined. She can tell that it's his favorite place in the house. Cooking pots fill the sink and counter, choppings from the salad have spilled from the cutting board onto the floor, and there's hardly any free space left to put the dishes down.

Judging by the lack of machines—there's not a blender or food processor in sight—Duncan likes to do everything by hand. Hanging on racks above the counter are various choppers and other dangerous-looking implements to reinforce this assumption. High up on top of the cupboards that surround the kitchen is a collection of beautiful bowls, crocks, and baskets. Some of the baskets hold plants that spill their lush foliage in cascades all around the room: emerald green asparagus ferns; fragrant, trailing geraniums with tiny pink flowers; ivy with little heart-shaped leaves.

The lighting, except for the fluorescent lights under the cupboards, is sunny and incandescently friendly. A small desk in a corner holds a computer, hinting that Duncan spends a lot of time in his kitchen. The screen saver is a continuously revolving show of one of his many interests: Italian frescoes.

Duncan makes espresso in one of those little octagonal Italian pots directly on the stove. No electric coffee maker lives in this kitchen. On Library Night he makes coffee in the large glass vacuum pot that Annie still distrusts. With the espresso Duncan brings a small plate of chocolates and a bowl of plums in Madeira, with whipped cream to go on top.

He pours the coffee and waves a bottle of brandy questioningly in front of her, and Annie nods and holds up thumb and index finger to indicate a small amount. Duncan hands her a glass with an etched design of small stars and sits down in a leather easy chair, leaning back and crossing his legs. They sip the brandy, and Annie bites a thin leaf of dark chocolate in half before she tries her espresso.

So far the evening has been relaxed and chatty, but in a slightly uncomfortable silence that she doesn't know how to break she feels anxious. Everything in her life now seems too sudden. She can't believe she is sitting in this grand living room—surrounded by leather furniture and mahogany chests, pictures in gold leaf frames, gleaming wooden floors, and lamps with white shades that look freshly dusted—sipping espresso with a *husband.* Her little demitasse cup rattles against the saucer. As if he has sensed her change of mood, Duncan gets up and turns on some music. He stays on his feet and walks over to check on Gussie, who is sleeping noisily.

"Don't be afraid of me, Annie," he says, with his back turned. That just about puts her over the edge. Duncan sits back down and closes his eyes, listening to the music, tapping his feet lightly and sipping his coffee. Annie sits stonily looking at the sleeping Augustus, wondering if she could just rise, pick the dog up, and walk out the door. What is she doing here, all dressed up in fancy clothes and feeling completely out of place in what is supposed to be her new life?

• • •

CHAPTER TWENTY

"Everyone can master a grief but he that has it."
(Shakespeare, Much Ado About Nothing)

Duncan gets up and goes out to the kitchen. Annie hears the clanking of pots and water running. She should get up and help, obviously, but leans back and closes her eyes instead. She needs to calm down, to slow down time. She thinks back to the time of Carlo's death and all that followed. The upheaval, the scandal, and then the trip to New Mexico to recover.

During her first weeks in the desert, Annie reveled in the constant sun, feeling the warm silence restore her soul. Wandering through the curious hills and stone formations that once inspired Georgia O'Keeffe, she pushed away all thought of the ordeal she had just lived through.

Memories of Carlo crept in, of course. It had been several years since Carlo had left her and moved to Europe. Annie had been shocked by the return she had somehow always hoped for, but before she had even had time to plumb the depth of her current feelings for him, Carlo had been murdered— stabbed, right outside his gallery on Bearskin Neck. Suddenly he was gone forever, and at forty, Annie had known that she finally had to get the grieving over with and start a new life. But grief has its own marching speed, and now Ethan's death has cruelly reopened the wound.

The only thing she can do now, Annie thinks, is *find out how it happened.* Did someone kill Ethan, and why? Annie feels in her bones that it was murder, but when she tries to imagine who and the reason why, the answer eludes her. There is something she is not seeing, some missing piece is floating about. Solving puzzles, giving her mind an occupation—while acknowledging that she can sometimes become a bit compulsive—is Annie's usual way of keeping sane. It was how she dealt with the loss of Carlo, by trying to solve his murder. Concentrating on finding the murderer helped her to avoid the abyss of loneliness and unbearable sorrow that threatened whenever she tried to step back from the task.

It is no longer a matter of Carlo. During her stay in New Mexico, she came to terms with the loss, a loss that had in reality taken place several years earlier, when Carlo had left her to go to Europe. When she thinks of Carlo now it's mostly with a certain nostalgic pleasure, remembering knowing and loving him as one remembers the loves of one's youth.

No, it isn't Carlo who is in the way at this moment; it isn't grief. To be honest she has to admit that it's a fear of starting the journey again, at her *advanced* age. Has she waited too long to embark on such a voyage? Will she be able to adjust to living with someone else, whose habits and quirks are so different from her own? Will she have to give up her admittedly bohemian lifestyle to suit someone who might be hardened into a more customary mold?

Regarding Duncan, there's also the fear of being judged by someone she admires and respects—someone she could lose as a friend, should things not work out right. Not to mention the fact that he is her superior, and what that might mean to the job that she loves. Several entirely different kinds of relationships will have to fight it out, and she certainly values her friendship and her job.

Love seems such a difficult and elusive thing. Has she been foolish to throw herself into the game, at the risk of losing… maybe everything? She knows that once she lets herself go, she will want no holds barred, from either side. Will Duncan, who is so correct, so *careful not to intrude,* be able to free himself enough for her liking? She'd rather live alone than in a *reserved* relationship, one in which she would feel that he was always trying to second-guess her or spare her feelings…by not talking about Carlo, for instance…*Oh, it's getting far too complicated, now,* Annie thinks. *I'm putting up obstacles.*

"Annie, you must be tired. I'll take Gussie for his evening promenade. Why don't you go on upstairs?" Duncan has finished with the dishes and appeared silently, bringing her back to the present with a jolt.

"Thanks, Dunc. Solicitous as always," she says, unable to keep a sudden bitter tinge out of her voice. Duncan's eyes darken.

"Annie," he says carefully, "I may be *solicitous,* I may be *considerate*…and I *will* be patient, but not forever. If you can't free yourself from the past enough to feel confident in our new relationship, then…well…it may sound harsh, but I would prefer to continue living alone to living in constant submission to your past." He gathers up the tray and walks off to the kitchen.

Annie sits motionless. She deserves the rebuff, after doing nothing to let him know what she honestly wants from him—yet, he has given it to her, has actually in a few spoken words told her everything she wants to know. The absolutely worst thing she can do at this moment is cry, and she groans angrily when her eyes begin to sting.

• • •

CHAPTER TWENTY-ONE

"My solitude grew more and more obese, like a pig."
(Mishima Yukio, Temple of the Golden Pavilion)

Annie scoops Gussie up and walks down to the Hannah Jumper House. After a while she calls Duncan. There is no answer, and she leaves a message: "I need some time alone, Duncan, so I'm staying at my house tonight. See you tomorrow." She remembers the old saying that one should never let the sun set on a quarrel—but something, most likely her pride, prevents her from going back to Duncan's house tonight. And yet, she is soon overcome by a growing sense of loneliness.

Annie has always been a believer in symbols. Not witchcraft or astrology or anything supernatural, she just likes concrete symbols of events or feelings. Planting a tree in memory of a friend, for instance. Picking up a rock on the beach and bringing it home to remind her of a perfect day. There's a small cairn in her backyard of "perfect days." *Oh, if I have to move into Duncan's house, can I take the cairn with me?* As a child she had pulled petals off daisies to read the future: *Loves-me, loves-me-not,* moaning if the last petal was a "not."

Trying to pull herself together, she goes out to her studio, stopping in the "smithy" section, where her jewelry-making corner has gathered dust for some time, and rummages through the boxes to see if she has what she needs for a suddenly inspired project. Green jeweler's wax, little scraps of gold and silver, plaster of Paris, various containers, a small clay crucible, a torch, and tools that look a lot like what a dentist might use. She selects a couple of small seed pearls from one of the jars of gleaming glass beads and gemstones that line the back of the desk.

She starts by drawing a design for the project. The life-sized outline of a cowslip appears on the page. The pencil-thin, gored skirt of the calyx will be made out of silver, while the scalloped slip of the corolla will be cast in gold. And from within, a little knobbly seed pearl will hang suspended. The earrings, when finished, will be the test used in tempting fate. Will Duncan pass the test? And does she want him to? How will she know?

Getting up early in the morning, she sits by the kitchen window, watching the harbor come alive. The coffee maker has long since stopped making its familiar and homey gurgling noises, and she goes to pour herself a cup. She brings it along out to the stone patio and flops down in one of the old weather-beaten Adirondack chairs her father made years ago. She has spent most of the night sleepless, painfully aware that it was her thin skin and not the lack of affection for Duncan that made her act rashly. She has always been too impulsive. The pain of Ethan's death has added to her unsettled state and made her jittery and over-sensitive. But now she feels lonelier than she ever felt before, lonelier even than after Carlo had left her.

On her way to work in the morning she hopes no one notices the fact that she and Duncan arrive separately and from different directions. When the intercom on her desk lights up, she cups her hand over the receiver and asks him quietly to come down to her house when the library closes.

• • •

They sit down by the window overlooking the harbor. Annie pours them each a small glass of Campari, the only offering in the cupboard with enough liquid left to serve two. Looking through the gap between Bearskin Neck and the Headlands, they can see all the way across the darkening bay out to the great Sandy Bay breakwater. A late sailor pulls into the harbor, catching the last of the evening breeze.

Clouds edged in gold by the setting sun make a display that is quite electrifying after the long siege of fog. The golden edge melts away quickly, however. The sky purples; the clouds lose their luminescence and turn a dull gray. A lone, high cloud remains pink, with a stubborn glimmer of gold at the edge, but finally it also gives in to the inevitable. They sit in silence for a while, sipping the bright red, bittersweet drink and watching as darkness settles over the harbor.

Duncan finally turns to Annie and bends forward a little, noticing the twinkling items suspended from her earlobes.

"And wild-scattered cowslips
Bedeck the green dale," he recites.

Annie feels a pang of disappointment. Duncan has failed the test. *I don't believe it! He quotes me Bobby Burns,* she thinks.

Her face must betray her reaction. Duncan gets up and walks over to the picture window, where he stays with his back turned to her. A thin moon has appeared and is reflected in the water. The harbor is beginning to look empty, with many of the boats already pulled for the winter. Come the first of October, the insurance cutoff point for most pleasure craft, only the lobster boats and fishing trawlers will remain.

Annie sits morosely in her chair, unwilling to join Duncan and reveal her disappointment, too tired to get up to clear away the glasses. Finally he turns and walks back to her. She half rises to walk him to the door, assuming this has all been a big mistake and he has decided to leave, but he sits down again in the chair next to hers.

"I must go seek some dew-drops here,
And hang a pearl in every cowslip's ear."

Duncan has finally offered the wished-for Shakespeare quote and passed the test. He reaches out and puts his index finger behind her earlobe and wiggles it back and forth to hear the soft tinkling of the pearl in the bell. "Is that what you wanted me to say? I felt your black looks, believe me." Then he bends forward and kisses her earlobe. Annie slowly turns her head to face him, and his lips drag along her cheek until they meet hers, to which they remain fastened for quite some time without any apparent objection on Annie's part. When they finally separate he looks at her.

"Did I pass the test? This was a test, wasn't it?" he says. Annie nods, blushing a little.

"Duncan, I'm so sorry. I don't know what came over me last night. You were just trying to be nice, and I was incredibly mean. Can you forgive me?" She stands, nervously twisting a curl of red hair between her fingers.

Duncan shakes his head ruefully, trying to disregard this unwittingly charming pose.

"Annie, I went overboard. I had no intention of pressuring you—at least not yet. I went way ahead of myself. I promised to be patient, and then I bullied you instead. Shall we call a truce?"

"Truce it is. And as soon as I can find my way around your kitchen, I'll cook you one of my fantastic half-hour dinners."

"As long as…"

"…it's not leftover day? Deal."

• • •

CHAPTER TWENTY-TWO

"Not a log in this buildin' but it memories has got,
And not a nail in this old floor but touches a tender spot."
(Will Carleton, "Out of the Old House, Nancy," st. 17)

They have decided to have this week's Library Night at Annie's house, and Duncan helps dust the furniture—and the lamp shades—while Annie makes coffee and putters in the kitchen. Just as they sit down by the picture window to wait for the crowd, there is a knock on the door, and Jean and Marie enter, followed by Maureen.

Annie gets up, and Duncan follows. They have to move to the upper part of the living room now, the only place where there are enough chairs to accommodate the group. Clare walks in without knocking, and Geri appears right behind her. Stuart may also turn up, even though he is still officially on leave from his position as children's librarian.

Clare and Stuart were both suspended for a time for their unwitting—at least on Clare's part, Annie is sure—involvement *after the fact* in Carlo's murder. Stuart, who is much too sharp to have been taken in so easily, should have known better. While Clare has returned to work as the library cataloguer, Stuart took this embarrassment harder and is now "on vacation," which presumably will be easier for him to return from.

Clare comes out to the kitchen to give Annie a hand.

"Seen much of Charlie lately?" Annie asks, with a significant sideways glance. Clare blushes.

"You've noticed."

"You have my blessings, kid. Charlie is a great guy." *Beats Stuart by a mile,* she thinks. Stuart had tried to ensnare Clare earlier in the year, and for a while Clare had seemed moved by whatever charm it was that she had detected in him, but in the aftermath of Carlo's murder, that had fortunately petered out.

"Well, Annie, there's absolutely nothing definite yet..."

"Keep me informed, won't you? I'll try not to wield my influence. I'm sure you want to do things in your own time."

"Thanks, Annie." Clare is embarrassed and turns to load the china tray.

Annie sets out mugs and coffee in a pump thermos, and since there was no Nisu to be had, a quickly put-together dessert: store-bought angel food cake filled with thawed raspberries and covered with a frosting of raspberry yogurt mixed with low-fat Cool Whip.

"Yummy," Geri pronounces.

"Thanks. Grandmother's secret French recipe," Annie assures her with a wink. Annie, as Geri well knows, has no French grandmother—her background is a mixture of Irish, English, and Italian, a fact she proffers to explain her red hair, love of Shakespeare, and impulsive temper.

Just as the general small talk begins to peter out, another knock on the door announces Stuart's arrival. He seems to have recovered all his former self-assurance and simply stalks by Annie with a slight nod. No one has the nerve to ask him how his "vacation" is going, and he takes the only seat that is empty, the one where Annie had been sitting, her beloved frayed and lumpy easy chair.

While Annie gets a wooden stool to sit on, Stuart squirms to make himself comfortable and finally puts his hands on his lap to avoid touching the armrests, which no doubt have little invisible critters crawling about on them. Annie pours his coffee ("a touch of cream, no sugar") and points to the cake, which Stuart eyes and declines with a noticeable shudder.

"Well! So what's on the agenda tonight?" Stuart asks. When no one seems willing to start, Annie introduces the topic of the puzzling missing material on John Hays Hammond, Jr. She has waited purposely for tonight's meeting so that nobody—especially Jean, who had been manning the reference desk at the time when things vanished from the vertical file—will feel singled out as accused of letting materials out of the library that normally have to be perused in the building.

"The book and papers from the vertical file could only have been checked out with one of the generic barcode cards we keep at the main desk in that little box—but I've been through them, and I didn't find anything there. And the books and files missing from the Rockport Room would have had to be itemized and signed for at Hedwig's desk, but I found nothing entered in her log," Annie says.

"Probably some kid who needed material for the high school essay—which is on 'American Inventors,' I understand. You know, someone who couldn't find their library card, or who owes a fine or something," Stuart volunteers, cynical as always.

Jean's face suddenly takes on a worried look. "Well, I don't know if this has anything to do with it, but I'd like to confess to something anyway," she says, and tells them about Mrs. Davis's underhanded acquisition of a large number of books on the school essay subject. "If I had known that she'd already taken some out—and her boy, too—I wouldn't have let her get away with it, but I only discovered that after she left," she says, looking down at her hands.

Marie shakes her head. "That woman. She does it all the time. You'll just have to harden yourself, dear. It really is unfair to the rest of the students. And the Davises could afford to *buy* the books for the boy, for that matter—that thing about being poor is just an act. But she's cheap as they come, that Mrs. Davis. Next time, tell her she has to get special permission from the head librarian." Marie looks at Duncan, who nods.

Annie sighs. Lorraine Davis is, unaccountably, a good friend of Sally's. Annie frankly can't see what Sally has in common with Lorraine—maybe it's simply that Sally's twins, Ben and Brad, are classmates and friends of Timmy Davis. Add that to the fact that the Davis and Babson families are neighbors—and Sally is about the neighborliest person anyone can imagine.

Annie, still unwilling to give up on the mystery of the lost files, continues worrying the subject. Duncan knows that Annie's present obsession with the Hammond files has to do with Ethan's murder, but decides not to interfere.

"It still doesn't solve the problem," Annie says. "It's easy enough to pilfer stuff out of the vertical files, I suppose, even though much of it has been outfitted with tattle strips, but from the Rockport Room? When it's open, it's never left without a monitor. How could someone remove something without 'Eagle-Eye Hedwig' noticing?"

They all nod. Hedwig is an energetic volunteer who comes in for the hours that the Rockport Room is open. She is a retired widow with a great deal of local knowledge and enthusiasm, an amateur historian who feels extremely possessive about the local history material. Hedwig would never let anything past her desk that wasn't signed for—and the desk is placed right by the door, with an unobstructed view of most of the shelves and files in the room. In fact, whenever a patron starts opening files to have a look, Hedwig immediately dons her white gloves, walks over with an authoritative smile, and says, "Let me help you—exactly what is it that you are looking for?"

Stuart says, "I don't see what the problem is. Just a few pamphlets gone missing. What's the big deal? I bet you can get all the information you want on the Internet." He gives Annie a glance—baiting her again, hoping she'll rise to the challenge.

Annie cringes and tries to stay calm, determined not to show her fury at another of Stuart's frequent hints that the Internet is about to make her redundant.

"Not just pamphlets, Stu. There were some books, too, including the bio, which is pretty hard to come by, and several old newspaper clippings and a folder full of papers regarding his patents. Some of it is material that's nearly impossible to replace, and Hammond is certainly a man of local interest and historical importance.

"Anyway, stealing from the library is a federal crime, as we all know. I hear other libraries have had problems with their special collections, too," Annie continues stubbornly, not letting anyone cut her off. "At our last reference meeting, one librarian told us how someone had managed to get away with a number of pages from one of the library's original genealogies. They're pretty sure they know who it was, but they can't prove it. Apparently the fellow had brought some wet string, which he slipped into the crease of the book. Then he waited until the paper had softened, and was able to tear out the pages without a sound. When it was discovered, the library closed the local history room to the public. Anything anyone wants there now, they have to make a request for and get a copy of, which they have to pay a fee for."

"Tragic," Marie says, "and the ironic thing is that ripped out of the book, the page is worthless as a source, anyway. But what's happened here seems to be a different story—I mean, we all know that people get a little fanatical in their genea-logical searches, but the Hammond thing? It doesn't fit. Unless it's just a coincidence, it sounds to me as though Stuart might be right about it being related to the school project. Let's ask Hedwig. Of course, we could call the school and find out if anyone is doing a project on Hammond..." Marie says.

Jean nods—what a clever idea. But Duncan shakes his head.

"Afraid not. That would be illegal—patron privacy, civil liberties, and all that. You know how *we* feel when the govern-ment wants to know what our patrons take out. They've been especially interested since the Patriot Act. To the government, everyone is a potential terrorist. So, with the new consortium changes, we can't even search our own patrons' past records. As soon as the book has been checked in, *that's it*, the record is gone. And as you know, we don't even tell the parents what books their children take out." They all nod immediately, remembering the rules.

"I miss the old card system, in a way," Marie says. "You could always tell a patron whether they'd read the book or not just by checking for their patron number on the card. You know how some of them come in and they're so forgetful."

Jean nods agreement. "But in this case, the Hammond material was never checked out anyway, so it wouldn't have helped much."

"Let's just see what Hedwig has to say, and then maybe give it a week or so and see if the materials are returned," Duncan says.

Annie says, "I'll go over to Hammond Castle tomorrow and see what they have on Jack Hammond in the gift shop. I'm sure they'll have some pamphlets at least, so we won't be completely without." The library is closed on Fridays, and Annie has planned to go for a ride along the shore while

Duncan is off at a meeting. Now she has another excuse to roam around in the castle.

Leaving other problem issues for the general staff meeting, they go on to discuss the state of the world—and eventually, of course, new books. Annie jots down a list of everyone's recommendations for the "Favorite Staff Selections" shelf, and another list of "woefully overrated" that she keeps for herself.

Maureen's list includes several new large print titles for the retired crowd that she serves. The outreach librarian has a new couple on her list, and made her first delivery to them earlier in the day.

"They're elderly, you know, and Mrs. Moore told me to just walk in and drop the books on the hall table so they wouldn't have to come down. She waved to me from the top of the stairs. Must be at least seventy-five, poor old thing," Maureen says. Everyone laughs at this, knowing Maureen to be at least ten years older than "the poor old thing."

Maureen looks a little startled. "Oh, dear. Yes, I always seem to forget how old I am. Must be the onset of senility!" She laughs, too, a high-pitched girlish titter, and rubs away a tear that creeps down her soft, pink cheek.

Marie, as usual, contributes with a few new biographies. Jean mentions a couple of garden books; and Geri, Duncan's peripatetic assistant, has a slew of new travel books to recommend.

Duncan takes out a note that lists the titles of several new novels, one especially, a debut by an Indian woman author. "Very beautiful," he comments. Annie wonders if he means the book or the author, and feels a sudden pang of jealousy. The realization makes her giggle, and the others look at her.

When they remain silently waiting, Annie realizes it's her turn to share ideas on new books. She grabs a note from the side table and reads off the names of a few Southwest poets she discovered on her trip, which the others dutifully nod to—Duncan somewhat more encouragingly than the rest. Poetry is not high on the list of priorities with most people, but Rockport has a solid core of lovers of verse—not to mention a number of reputable versifiers.

Clare, who has pointedly avoided looking at Stuart and not said a word all evening, finally suggests that maybe the library ought to have a few more books on American inventors, which draws chuckles.

Stuart has been unnaturally quiet. Perhaps he's been too busy to read? Normally he has a long list of weighty pronouncements, mostly negative, on recently published books in the field of politics, finance, and current events. Annie wonders whether he might be quietly putting out his résumé—is he perhaps looking for a position more suitable for a man of his erudition? She knows he always describes himself simply as a "librarian," omitting any reference to the children's desk.

Without contributing to the book list, Stuart soon is the first to excuse himself. Shortly afterward Marie and Jean leave. Maureen offers to help with the dishes, but Annie shakes her head, and Clare says she'll drive Maureen home.

Geri stays around, oblivious to the fact that the newlyweds may have other plans for the rest of the evening. Geri is one of those women in late middle age, usually thin and just beginning to go gray, who have taken to having their hair shorn to within half an inch of their scalp. An odd fashion, which Annie can't help associating with concentration camps. You have to have a face to go with this severe style, and Geri is fortunate to have great features—a Maria Callas nose and rather dramatic dark eyes. She is gaily chatting about her Florida trip when she suddenly appears to notice that she is doing all the talking, while Duncan and Annie sit listening politely, if somewhat distractedly. She gazes with sudden interest at the two of them, raises a dark, winglike eyebrow, and then checks her watch.

"Uh-oh, I didn't realize it got so late. Well, darlings, got to run. Miles to go, and all that. I'll see you both Saturday! So nice to have you back in the library, Annie!" she says, breezing toward the door.

Annie sinks into her easy chair, drinks in the last of the heat from the dying fire, and caresses every nook and cranny of the old place with her eyes.

"Well, Annie, time for us to go home, too," Duncan says.

But I am home, she thinks, before rising and turning to leave.

• • •

CHAPTER TWENTY-THREE

"The greatest invention of the nineteenth century was
the invention of the method of invention."
(Alfred North Whitehead, Science and the Modern World)

Annie and Duncan go to the library together in the morning. The visiting directors from the consortium have brought flowers and a present—a pair of bookends in the shape of Romeo and Juliet.

"Now, don't keep the poor lovers apart by putting too many books between them!" one of the directors says, jokingly.

The library is open. Annie hears laughter and loud conversation from downstairs, where the daily news is being shared. As soon as the directors' meeting starts, Annie gives her husband a chaste kiss on the cheek, which is returned, though less chastely and not on the cheek, and escapes out into the hall. She waves to Clare through the Tech Services window. Further down the corridor she notices that Stuart is back at the children's desk. As he has noticed her, she steps inside.

"Welcome back to the library, Stu!"

"Why, thank you. Didn't think I'd see you here today. What about the honeymoon?" He gives her a bland smile and makes great pretense at shoveling papers around on his desk.

"Postponed. We're going to England next spring."

"Well, well. Now, I'd better get busy trying to straighten this place out. I can see that it's going to take some effort. Just look at those stacks!" With a look of disgust he points to the shelves. "Somebody has let the pages slack off. Those kids don't do anything unless you keep after them."

Annie disagrees. The pages are hardworking high school kids, and the stacks look just fine to her, but she refuses to get into an argument with Stuart today.

She goes downstairs and stops by her desk. On an impulse, she opens the vertical file drawer and checks for the Hammond folder. She has to pry the tightly packed Pendaflex folders apart before she can read the tabs. The file is still empty— the thin book, the newsprint articles, the lists of patents and other materials she had kept there have not been returned. Should she leave the folder where it is? Someone might still come and return them. What if there *is* a connection to the murder? Could there be fingerprints on the folder? *Sure, of every patron and staff member that ever touched it.*

She can't ask Duncan for advice—Annie senses that her sleuthing is making him more than uneasy, even though he hasn't said so. She hasn't even mentioned the visit to Spofford-Braxton's castle on Eastern Point, or her continuing research on the Moonies. Annie can imagine how he would react. Nevertheless, she will check the Local History shelves downstairs for the missing Hammond files, and maybe have a quick look at old local newspaper accounts of the Moonie years on microfiche while she is down there.

The dehumidifier is going full tilt in the Local History room. Without it, the books and papers stored down there would start to rot, especially after the kind of weather they've been seeing lately. Annie walks over to the biography section, where she discovers, unsurprised, that the Hammond materials have not been returned down here, either. She must talk to Hedwig later. Just as she walks over to the microfiche corner to check for old newspaper articles on the Moonies, Charlie Field sticks his head in the door.

"What are you doing in the library today, Annie?" he asks, although he knows full well that the honeymoon is planned for next spring. Maybe he assumes that they would have taken some time off anyway.

"Oh, I was just helping Duncan get ready for the meeting, and then I had a quickie reference question I thought I'd sort out for someone," she says airily. Annie doesn't want Charlie to worry about what she is up to any more than she would want Duncan to. Charlie did everything in his power to protect her name during the aftermath of Carlo's murder, but he would probably appreciate it if she stayed out of the news for a while. She leaves the Local History room as quickly as she can without seeming impolite, as she doesn't really want to lie to him—either as a friend or a trustee.

• • •

CHAPTER TWENTY-FOUR

"I am interested in pipe organs. I needed more room."
(John Hays Hammond's answer when asked why he was building the castle)

She drives back over to the castle. Vinnie hasn't turned up after school yet, and Ruth greets her. The manager has been told by the curator to let Annie in without a ticket.

"Have you been busy?" Annie asks. "I mean, after the paper came out I suppose you must have been visited by curiosity seekers."

"Oh, yes. We've had plenty of gawkers here. Shouldn't complain, of course—sold a lot of tickets. I'd have been happier if it had been for a different reason."

"How's Henry doing? He was still very upset yesterday when I was here."

"He's out today. Nerves shot, I think. Maybe the trustees gave him a hard time—I heard they phoned him after the paper came out. Nobody had informed them of the accident, you see. Vinnie told me he asked Henry if they had been called, but apparently Henry shrugged it off and said he'd call them later. He was trying to avoid it, I think. He's already had a bit of a run-in with them on another issue recently." *She's referring to the audit Vinnie mentioned, no doubt,* Annie thinks.

They chat for a while, and then Annie goes through the Great Hall and back into the Inventions Room. Next to the framed patent for Hammond's "System for Radio Control of Moving Bodies" hangs a yellowed newspaper clipping from the Washington Gazette, showing the inventor standing bent over some unidentified project. The article is a brief life story, with a focus on the wealthy Hammonds and their illustrious friends, and describing Jack's recent success with a remote control system. It is surrounded by other news stories, most with the text cut off. Annie reads some of the headlines: *"Seaside Homes Damaged in Storm," "Automobile Accident on Lexington Ave"* (big news back then, probably), *"Suicide of Local Inventor"* (how ironic, right next to the report of Jack's success), and *"Opening of Geddy's School for the Blind."*

Hammond, who died in 1965, had been a prolific and ingenious experimenter. Annie studies the dynamic amplifier (what people now call a stereo) and various other table- or wall-sized communications and radiodynamic control boards that fill the room. As in a computer museum, everything seems oversized. Multitudes of notes and sketches of his pioneering inventions—ranging from radio and television to radar and frequency control and modulation—line the room. *Hammond would have been amazed to see what his inventions led to,* Annie thinks. *Depth sounding, satellite positioning, all sorts of war toys like guided missiles and drones—and how small their modern versions now are in comparison with his room-sized contrivances. Would Hammond have approved of these uses?*

But there were also inventions that saved or improved the lives of men at sea, and ideas for all sorts of practical household gadgets. Then, of course, there was Hammond's interest in musical instruments. And according to another article, Hammond helped install the radio system for the Vatican. *Now, how did he manage that?* Annie wonders. It was well known that Hammond was afraid of flying, and his preferred mode of travel when in the States was to ride in a comfortable mobile home, which he even had outfitted with a built-in salter-sander. *He would have gone to Italy by ship,* Annie concludes. Hammond was an avid mariner, after all, even following some of the very routes Columbus had taken.

Hammond's company, *Hammond Radio Research,* was housed right in the castle. His old lab overlooks the spot where Annie and Duncan planned to have their wedding photo taken. When visitors enter the castle grounds, they are met by a stunning view of the ever-shifting water of Gloucester Bay—from ethereal turquoise to deep ultramarine; at times calm as a pond, more often choppy—glimmering through the set of great, vine-covered stone arches that Hammond had brought back from Europe. The arches, as she knows now, that are so mysteriously matched across the bay on Spofford-Braxton's shorefront. Annie imagines that the view of the water through the arches must look just like a view somewhere along the Mediterranean. The wedding photo, sadly, was never taken. Maybe they can still come back and have it done? But no, she'll never go through that hairstyling session again.

Annie moves on to the library, which lies across the courtyard. The library is a circular room in one of the castle's many towers. A small stairway leads down from it to the round War Room, which is dedicated to Hammond's many military experiments and patents. Murals and paintings of war subjects surround the room, and more framed newspaper clippings rest on easels and against the walls. There is an article about Hammond's two wooden radio masts, at 360 feet the highest ever built at the time; another about the remotely operated U.S. Navy's Salamander, carrying 1200 pounds of explosives. One article tells how Hammond scared the daylights out of local fishermen with his pilot-less boat *Pioneer* racing around the harbor; yet another talks about his accidentally setting off an underwater detonating device and blowing a fisherman and his boat one hundred feet into the air.

The most famous report is perhaps the one about the radio controlled boat, outfitted with his "Gyrad" system, which Hammond sent on a 120-mile round trip to Boston and back with no one on board. This report attracted the attention of the United States military and led to protracted discussions, experiments, arguments, demonstrations, and then more meetings and arguments about rights and contracts that carried on all through the war years, when one would think the military might have benefited from many of these inventions. The differences were finally resolved, and the Navy settled and bought one hundred of Hammond's patents.

The article about the radio-controlled boat gives Annie pause for thought. What if the dummy had been traveling in a radio-controlled boat? *Come to think of it, how else could it have gone? By somebody manually setting it on its course, aiming it for Norman's Woe? That dummy surely couldn't have held the boat steady.* Since the matter had not yet been looked into, there were no answers. If it were radio controlled, the same questions that plague her in what she intuitively feels must be a murder still remain: from where, by whom, and why? From Spofford-Braxton's pontoon landing, conveniently located just across the bay, maybe by the strange moon-faced figure in the boat shed? But why?

It's getting late, and Annie remembers that she is married now, and that her husband will likely expect her to be home when he gets back from his meeting. Ruth waves to her when she passes the museum shop, apparently getting ready to leave. Annie glances into the woodworking shop as she goes by. The workshop is housed in the old lab, and inside she sees Vinnie working diligently on a project, lubricating gears, tightening screws, and polishing metal parts. He is helping restore a number of the museum's displays, Spofford-Braxton told her. A multitalented young man, apparently. Vinnie, sensing her presence, turns around and smiles at her, looking like a kid having fun with Dad's tools.

• • •

CHAPTER TWENTY-FIVE

"Do you not know I am a woman? When I think I must speak."
(Shakespeare, As You Like It)

Annie goes home and waits for Duncan to return from his meeting. She throws a load in the washing machine, empties the dishwasher, and gathers up clothes and papers in the living room, all in a valiant effort to appear a good housekeeper. When Duncan arrives, Gussie beats her to the door to greet his master and benefactor. Duncan is toting the Romeo and Juliet bookends under one arm and flowers under the other. Along with the fancy bouquet from the directors there is a smaller one, which consists of a red and a white rose surrounded by small yellow coreopsis that look suspiciously like the ones growing in the library flower bed. Annie smiles.

"From Esa?" she asks. Duncan nods.

"They were on your desk. Thought you'd want them, since we won't be in until later in the week. Esa looked pleased when I took them along. I'm telling you, that boy has a crush on you."

"Naw, I'm just like a big sister to him. Which reminds me, Justin called and asked if we felt like having dinner with them tonight, now that they're back in town." That wasn't quite how her brother had phrased it. *Are you lovebirds ready to behave in public yet?* was the way the invitation had been proffered. Annie had told him she'd call back when Duncan got home, and then brought Justin up to date on what little they knew about Ethan.

"Of course we'd like to," Duncan says. "Aren't they leaving soon? We still have tomorrow off, so let's plan to spend it with them."

"Thanks, Dunc."

"It'll do you good. You need some distraction." Duncan appears a little concerned. He noticed the map of the castle and the sheaf of notes on the hall table when he walked in, and he knows that when Annie puts her mind to something, she won't let go until she has the answer. It is a trait that makes her a good reference librarian, but he hopes it won't interfere too much in their private life. She got into serious trouble trying to solve Carlo's murder—but that was very personal. Can he keep her from getting as deeply involved in Ethan's case? Duncan unloads the bronze bookends on the hall table. Gussie is snuffling eagerly at his pant leg, not wanting to be ignored.

"Oh, did you happen to see Charlie today? I tried to call him about Ethan's funeral, but I wasn't able to reach him. Nobody seems to know when it is," she says, casually bringing up the subject that Duncan is striving so hard to avoid. *Too late to keep her from getting involved,* he thinks with a sigh. She's locked in on her target. *As if I had expected otherwise.* He bends down and gives Gussie a little pat. Disappointed, Gussie goes into the living room and lies down on the carpet, sulking.

"I called Charlie earlier," Duncan says. "He was on the way out of town, but he had talked to Ethan's mother. She said they'll set the date as soon as the initial investigation is concluded. The funeral will be in D.C." Duncan tries to report only the bare facts, then walks out to the kitchen where he sticks the big bouquet into a vase. He hands Esa's little arrangement to Annie, and she places it in a cobalt blue wine goblet on the breakfast table by the garden window. Gussie comes sauntering into the kitchen looking for a treat from Duncan, who finally pays attention and gives him his due. Annie frowns disapprovingly, but after Gussie gets the expected treat and gives her a smug look, she can't help laughing.

"So, where are we going to eat?" Duncan asks.

"Somewhere in town. I said we'd bring the wine—a bottle of red and a bottle of white."

Rockport is still a "dry" town, but you can bring your own wine to most restaurants. There's a move afoot again to call for a referendum on making "likker" legal. There have been several tries in the last few decades, and so far the "dry's" have won. Now the liquor question is up for a vote again. *Maybe the time has come,* some say. Annie shakes her head and leaves the question to ponder another day. Some people think the tide has turned, what with all the yuppies moving into town, the merchants and, naturally, the restaurant owners, campaigning heavily; and maybe they are right, maybe they've got the votes this time. *Then our town will be just like any other town,* Annie thinks.

"How about Brackett's?" she says. "I know Justin loves it there. He proposed to Melanie below the restaurant on Front Beach, so we could try to get a table with a view of the beach."

"I'll call and make reservations," Duncan says, happy that the subject has changed and the mood lightened.

• • •

CHAPTER TWENTY-SIX

"Luxurious lobster-nights, farewell,
For sober, studious days!"
(Alexander Pope, "A Farewell to London")

"Anything new about Ethan?" Justin asks, unaware of the struggle of wills between the newlyweds on this issue. Duncan's shoulders sag, but he pretends not to have heard the question and starts uncorking the wine. Annie hesitates, sensing the rising undercurrent of tension in her husband.

"No, Juss, nothing new. Judge left a message for us to call him later tonight—maybe he knows something. Now, tell us what you two did in Beantown," Annie says. Duncan gives her a grateful glance and the start of a pleased smile before the corkscrew slips off the lip of the bottle and gashes his thumb. He tries to take it like a man and be casual about it, but groans inwardly. Annie looks suitably concerned, but Duncan just shakes his head and smiles bravely.

"Boston is a beautiful city, at least the parts of it Justin showed me," Melanie says. "We went to see *The Lion King*, which was great. Yesterday we had breakfast at the Ritz and had to skip lunch to make up for it. Of course, we *had* to drive by Fenway Park. Then we went on a harbor cruise. The Mystic is one huge river! In the afternoon we got a takeout dinner which we ate on a swan boat ride in the Public Garden. And then we walked part of the Freedom Trail."

Duncan pours the wine. White for Justin and Annie, who have chosen surf, and red for Melanie and himself, who are opting for turf. Melanie looks apprehensive when Justin's lobster arrives.

"Are you sure it's safe? I mean, you hear all this about seafood and hepatitis and red tide and all that." Justin laughs and pulls the carapace off the lobster, squirting juice gleefully around the table before holding the lovely red lobster back upside down, as if it were a cup. He winks at Annie, who is the only other aficionado at the table. Duncan will eat lobster, but only lazy-man's style. Melanie, in self defense, covers as much of herself as possible with napkins, stealing a few from Justin's ample pile.

"Well, here's to the newlyweds," Justin says, and slurps the salty liquid right out of the carapace. The others modestly take a sip of their wine. Melanie looks around, a little embarrassed, but other patrons, being quite used to this sort of primitive eating behavior, are not paying any attention.

"Don't worry, Melanie, red tide doesn't affect finfish and lobsters and crabs and shrimp. Even scallops are safe, because you don't eat the stomach and intestines, only the muscle. It's only clams and mussels and periwinkles and snails that you have to stay away from," Annie explains, going into more detail than Melanie wants to hear. "Ohh, Justin, can I have your loblolly?" Annie begs. A forkful of chicken stops halfway to Melanie's mouth.

"Loblolly?" she says, puzzled.

"Sure, sis, it's all yours," Justin says, scraping the green stuff out of the lobster shell and plopping it onto Annie's plate.

"Ugh, what is that?" Melanie looks disgusted.

"That's the loblolly. Or tomalley. My favorite appetizer," Annie says gaily. She loves to perform this little act for the uninitiated. "Actually, if we did have a red tide right now, I wouldn't eat it, just to be sure. It's the lobster's liver, if you really want to know, and pollutants and poisons accumulate in the liver and stay there permanently, but I'll take my chances."

Melanie and Duncan take a sudden and intense interest in a lobster boat out on the bay. They watch, squinting in forced concentration, as the lobsterman hauls out a trap, pulls out the lobsters, measures them, bands the claws of the "keepers" and throws them into a plastic tub, and tosses the "shorts" back into the water. Then he puts fresh bait (*An oxymoron if there ever was one,* Annie thinks) into the bait pocket and slides the trap back into the water.

Finally, Annie clears her throat.

"Okay, you two, it's safe to look now. I'm all done," Annie says, licking her lips. Melanie shudders. The chicken and a lovely mound of butternut squash soon put her back to rights—and the wine helps, too.

"Are you sure you don't want white wine with your chicken?" Duncan asks.

"Oh, I hate white wine. Too sour. This red wine is delicious," Melanie says.

For dessert Annie suggests that Melanie try the "Rosette with Lingonberries and Whipped Cream."

"Rosette?"

"It's a thin, crispy, waffly sort of thing, pressed in a special iron. You should try it in honor of the Scandinavian stonecutters who came here and cut and drilled and blasted all those big holes in the ground. You know, the quarries, where Justin and I went swimming when we were kids," she says. Melanie nods. She's been to the quarries, but she stayed close to the edge after Justin assured her they were "bottomless."

She follows Annie's advice and orders the Rosette, and makes loud satisfied noises with every bite. The wine has loosened her inhibitions. Now it's Justin's turn to glance around, but no one is watching them.

They leave a good tip and walk down to the beach, where Justin takes Melanie out to the very spot where he proposed to her (in what the local kids call the Pigeon Coop, actually a granite gazebo on the rocky Observatory Point), and gets down on one knee. Melanie giggles. Duncan takes Annie's hand, and they stroll off along the water's edge. The night is getting chilly, and they soon start for home, quickening their pace when gusts of wind tug at their clothes.

As soon as they get back in the house Annie calls Judge. Duncan resigns himself to the inevitable. Dinner has been a brief reprieve. From now on, Annie will surely focus all her senses on Ethan's murder.

• • •

CHAPTER TWENTY-SEVEN

"In order to arrive at what you do not know
You must go by the way which is the way of ignorance."
(T.S. Eliot, Four Quartets)

"They're shipping Ethan home tomorrow," Judge says. "Cause of death was electrocution, and apparently there's nothing more to be learned from the body. The general investigation is ongoing, though. No hint so far about whether they seriously think it was foul play. It's the family name, I think. They just want to make sure they've been thorough. I did find out that even they consider the dummy in the boat more than a coincidence. To me, that's a pretty good indication of the direction in which things are going."

"Aha. Have they gone down to search the wreckage?" Annie asks.

The thought has also occurred to Judge. "They say that since no human being was harmed in that incident, they can't justify the expense. But I still thought something useful might have been learned from it."

"Me too. I had an idea, Judge. What if the boat was remotely controlled? I've been thinking about it, and I'm sure you were right when you said that the boat crash and Ethan's death seemed to be more than a coincidence. I don't know why, yet…"

But Judge interrupts her.

"Annie, don't do anything hasty now. Better not to involve yourself in something again. Remember what happened last time. You nearly got yourself killed. And if it *does* turn out to be foul play, the foul player is still on the loose. Josie and I don't want anything to happen to you. At least discuss your plans with me beforehand. Promise?"

Annie knows he is right, of course. Going after Carlo's murderer has put her in danger, and now she is involving herself again. But Ethan's murder took place *at her wedding,* and that she can neither ignore nor forgive.

"If I *personally* plan to get into something risky, I promise to talk to you first," Annie says, leaving herself a small window. Judge notices, but takes what he can get. Better than nothing, when it comes to Annie. The best he can hope for is that she will proceed with caution.

"You do that," he says.

"So, we still don't know when the funeral is?"

"I did speak to Mrs. Haskell earlier today. The poor woman is terribly distraught. She promised to call as soon as the arrangements have been made."

"I'd like to go, whether Duncan comes or not. Haven't mentioned that to him yet, he'll probably say he can't leave the library."

"I did tell Mrs. Haskell that I'd attend. If you want, you can travel with Josie and me. As long as this doesn't cause a problem between you and Duncan—I won't be a party to that. Charlie is going, too, of course, and Spofford-Braxton."

"Well, quite a contingent. Let me check with Dunc. Thanks, Judge."

As she has guessed, Duncan is less than enthusiastic about the idea.

"We really shouldn't both take any more time off. You've had the summer off already, don't forget. We don't want the townspeople to start grumbling." This is an important point for Duncan. Rockport library patrons are a generous lot, and Duncan frequently reminds staff of this. They must keep faith with the patrons and not risk losing their goodwill. "I suppose since Charlie is planning to go, he could square your going with the other trustees. But I think I'd better stay around—I don't want to fall too far behind. Pretty soon it'll be time to tackle the budget, and we also have to deal with our five-year inventory before the end of the year."

"Oops, I'd forgotten. Shouldn't be too bad, though. We've gotten used to the new computer system, finally. Anyway, it beats the way we did it in the old days, closing the library and getting volunteers to help us physically go through each and every book on the shelves and mark it 'present' with a date on the card. Of course, what we are doing now is only a sort of 'virtual' inventory in comparison, isn't it? Still, I think one of us should go to the funeral, don't you? It might seem unfeeling otherwise," Annie says with a certain note of finality that Duncan has come to recognize.

"Guess you're right. Well, you go then, wife," he says with a smile. "Only come right back. I don't want people to think you've grown tired of me already."

Annie instantly proves that she has not grown tired of him.

• • •

CHAPTER TWENTY-EIGHT

"To fish in troubled waters."
(Matthew Henry, Commentaries, Psalm 60)

Duncan tells Annie to take the day before the funeral off. A distracted reference librarian may do more harm than good, he figures, hoping that when she comes back from the funeral she'll concentrate on her reference tasks. As soon as Duncan leaves for the library in the morning, Annie calls her lobsterman friend, Tommy Cameron, who provided the lobster for her wedding.

"Hiya, Annie, how's my favorite liberian? Need some lobstahs today?" Tommy's Northshore-speak is thick but somewhat easier to follow than Ned Mazzarini's.

"Thanks, Tommy, not today. Actually, I have a strange favor to ask you," Annie says, "and please keep it quiet, because I wouldn't want anybody to know...especially Duncan," she adds, a little nervously.

"That don't sound real good, Annie mah deah, you just married and all. Whazzup, then?"

"You have your scuba gear in order?"

"Gettin' late in the ye-ah to go divin'."

"I know. I just wondered if you'd be willing...ah, to do a dive around Norman's Woe and check for some wreckage? There might be a clue to the, you know, to the things that happened at the castle."

"You mean the prank with the boat?"

"If it was a prank. Maybe it was a distraction. I don't know. Would you consider doing a dive?"

"A distraction? From what?"

"The murder, if it was murder."

"You mean Ethan? I thought they'd pretty much decided that it was an accident."

"Well, there are still some questions…"

"Boy, I'd have to think about it. I mean, if we're talkin' *muhdah* heah, the police and the Coast Guahd may have something to say about it."

"It's not illegal to dive in the harbor, is it? Couldn't you say you lost some gear or something?" Annie says.

"Lost some geah around Nahman's Woe? I don't know, Annie. Who'd believe me? I don't need trouble. Don't want to risk mah license. Besides, we've got some weathah comin', and I'm already in the middle o' pullin' all mah traps. Can't affawd to lose any moah, after that sudden stahm we had last fall. Got a whole mess of new wiyah ones since then, and they cost a bundle."

Annie wonders for a second what "wiyah" ones are before it comes to her. "Wire" traps.

"Oh," she says, disappointed, "I understand. And if that's the case, the storm will probably get rid of any important evidence among the wreckage, too," she says, trying to make it harder for him to refuse.

"Lemme see what I can do, Annie," Tommy says, softening. "I'm goin' back out raht now, and if it don't staht to blow too hahd, I should be able to get the rest of 'em in bah noontahm. If I do, then I'll give ya a call—unless the swells get so bad they'll pervent me from gettin' around the bend. It can get nasty out theah. You lookin' faw anything in pahticulah?"

"No, not really. You know, anything that seems unusual. Something to identify the boat, for instance, although it might have been stolen, of course. Some sign that it was aimed at Norman's Woe on purpose. It occurred to me that someone could have controlled it remotely, maybe. Well, anyway, whatever you can find. Got your underwater cam still?" Tommy has made some underwater videos of lobsters and schools of fish that he has given the library copies of.

"Shoah. But like I said, gotta get mah traps out fihst. Then I'll see. Not promisin' anythin', mahnd yah. I'll call ya latah."

"Thanks, Tommy. I don't want you taking any risks, so if the weather worsens, forget it. Nothing's worth your getting hurt."

• • •

Tommy calls her back a couple of hours later.

"All set, Annie," he says.

"Already? Did you get all your traps out safe?"

"Yup. Good thing, too. Some of the guys ah gonna take big losses, I heah. It's tuhning into one of those stahms that sweep along the sea bottom. Sucks the traps raht along, *kee-rash,* up on the rocks they go. Whatevah don't get washed ashoah ends up in such a tangle you maht at well just cut the lahns, except then the traps would lie theah on the bottom and collect moah visitahs than a Miami motel in February."

"Big dilemma."

"Not really, Annie. With wintah comin', theah'll be a lot of spayah time to repayah traps. Although I must admit it was moah fun fixin' th'old wooden ones. The wiyah mesh can do a job on yoah hands. Anyways, if we hurry, we maht get a coupla dives in ovah by Nahman's Woe befaw the stahm gets too bad. You do wanna come with me, raht?"

Annie looks at her watch.

"Would half an hour from now be too late? Duncan should be home for lunch any minute. He's just stopping by to pick up a sandwich I'm making for him, but I'd like to be here when he comes. I've barely talked to him lately."

"Oh, deah. Not on speakin' tehms already?"

"No, no, nothing like that. Just been busy."

"You enjoyin' married lahf?"

"Let's say I'm looking forward to it. I'll keep you posted."

"You do that. Pick you up in haff an houah, then. Maybe you and hubby can come ovah aftah faw coffee? We can show him what we got."

"Uh, yes, well…"

"Oh, come now, Annie. Don't tell me Duncan really doesn't know about yoah emulatin' Shuhlock Holmes?" He gives an elaborate sigh. "Well, suit yahself."

• • •

CHAPTER TWENTY-NINE

"Have I not walked without an upward look
Of caution under stars that very well
Might not have missed me when they shot and fell?
It was a risk I had to take — and took!"
(Robert Frost, "Bravado" from Five Nocturnes)

I must be insane, Annie thinks, as they round Straitsmouth Point and the waves sideswipe the boat. They are on their way from Rockport Harbor over toward Gloucester Harbor, following the rugged coastline. The engine races at the crest of each wave, and the boat dips and slides, careening sideways as much as making forward progress. She looks at Tommy, and he smirks at her. *Can you take this?* his look says. Well, if he can take it, she can. Fortunately, Annie does not get seasick, and she knows that Tommy is no daredevil. If it wasn't safe he'd turn around. *Wouldn't he?*

They alternately ride the crests forward and slide down in the ditch as they head farther out, and soon Thacher Island looms ahead. The Twin Lights appear, stark and gray sentinels in the mist. Somewhere farther out, far beyond any islands, is where her parents' boat went down, so long ago, now, leaving them to drown...

It has started to drizzle, and Annie pulls on one of the orange foul weather slicks that hang behind the cabin door. The shoreline becomes invisible as the rain increases. The wind forces the rain and spray to come at them nearly horizontally, and icy needles pelt their faces. Tommy whistles gaily and adjusts their course a little. Thacher Island is disappearing in the mist behind them, and now land is no longer visible. Out ahead to the southeast Annie notices a dark shadow. *Looks like another boat on a fool's errand,* she thinks. As they come closer they see that it is a gillnetter, and that the boat is not moving—at least not by its own steam. It's seems to be buffeted about by wind and waves, and Tommy changes course slightly to take a closer look just in case the fishermen are in trouble. When they get near enough to see clearly, the two men aboard signal an appeal for help. Tommy looks at Annie.

"Hope yah're ready fah this, Annie. Hold on, we gotta face the wind now," he yells. Annie nods and gets a good grip on the rail by the cabin door. When they get alongside the gillnetter, Tommy slows down, keeping just enough speed to keep steering control, and points to the back of the boat.

"See that rope?" he yells. "The one that's fahsened back theah, yeah, that one. Ya gotta throw it to them!" he shouts, with gestures so that she will understand. Annie nods. On her first try, the rope uncoils and lands in the water, far short of the other boat. Her second try is worse, as the rope gets caught by the wind and flies right back in her face. Stubbornly, she coils it again and, thinking of how her father taught her to toss the looped end of the rope around the dock piling, throws a perfect ringer. One of the men grabs it and scrambles up to the front of the boat and makes the rope fast on his end. Then he struggles back and hauls the sea anchor, which has kept their boat from drifting too far. Finally, he waves to Tommy. The engine groans unhappily at the extra load, but they slowly make their way landward, toward the wide bay that is Gloucester Harbor. The gillnetter is much larger than Tommy's boat, with an iron superstructure that holds the nets the fishermen had just hauled. The heavy "doors," used to weigh the nets down, hang over the side. Tommy's engine is laboring hard, and he begins to look concerned.

When they pass Hammond Castle, Annie notices the waves breaking over Norman's Woe. It had been sheer madness to go out. As the Dog Bar Breakwater appears faintly in the mist, Annie sees a vessel coming out of the harbor, nose rising high on each wave. She points at it. Tommy nods.

"Coast Guahd. Good thing, too," he yells. "We 'bout had it." Just then the engine coughs and stops. Tommy smiles. "We'll all need a tow now."

The Coast Guard lines them up like two ducklings behind the mother duck, and they get a tow into the harbor.

Tommy gets permission to tie up at the Coast Guard Station in Gloucester until he can get his engine going again, and they are offered a ride back to Rockport by the grateful gillnetters. As they walk through the station, Annie chats with one of the Coast Guardsmen.

"Were you on duty the other day—you know, the day that dummy went aground on Norman's Woe?" she asks. He laughs.

"As a matter of fact, I was. What a commotion. Happy ending, though," he says.

"Do you know if the divers found anything down there besides the dummy?"

"They did, they brought up a mess of stuff before they came up with what they thought was the body."

"What happened to the stuff? Did it go to the police?"

"We were going to hand it over, but the police aren't pursuing the case. Not enough manpower, and nobody dead or injured. And we've got too much to do on our end with protecting the lives of fishermen and foolhardy sailors to worry about some prankster. But we probably still have the bag around here somewhere. Why, what's your interest?"

"Well, you see, I was getting married in the castle right when the boat went aground, and so I was curious about it."

"Ah. That must have put a damper on the occasion. Well, wait here a minute, then," he says, and disappears. He returns with a big trash bag.

"Here, be my guest. We were just going to discard it anyway, so keep it. A wedding gift, you might say. Haha."

Triumphant, Annie runs after Tommy and the gillnetter, and Annie tells Tommy what she has.

"Will you keep the bag in your shed until I get home from the funeral? Right now I've got to get back to the house and get supper on before Duncan comes home. Oh, Tommy, you're a sweetheart. Hope you can get the engine going, I'd feel really guilty otherwise."

"Well, you know, the way I look at it is, it was probbly meant to be. Raht, Jack?" he says, patting the gillnetter on the back as they climb into to his fishy-smelling truck. Tommy is used to fishy-smelling trucks, of course, but Annie finds the odor a little overwhelming. It's been a long time since she rode in her father's truck, where he kept his fishing gear handy. Her father had a license for a single string of lobster pots, like many Cape Ann families do, and Annie sometimes went out with him to check the pots. Today the smell provokes equal parts of nostalgia and nausea.

"You betcha, Tommy. Weah sure grateful you tuhned up. And you, too, lady. You got a good throwin' ahm on ya. Wanna job fishin'?"

Annie laughs. The gillnetter drops her off first, and she hurries up the steps to get out of her soaked and smelly clothes before Duncan shows up. He has been remarkably patient, but this time she may have gone too far.

• • •

CHAPTER THIRTY

*"The effort really to see and really to represent is no idle business
in face of the constant force that makes for muddlement."
(Henry James, What Maisie Knew)*

Judge, Josie, and Annie leave Rockport on Sunday night,
traveling in Judge's big old Chrysler. They are staying at a
small and exclusive hotel that Annie could never afford, even
on *two* librarian's salaries, but Judge insists and has already
paid in advance.

"We should all stay together—it will make it so much
easier tomorrow," he says. Annie doesn't put up a fight,
knowing it to be futile. Judge is just as stubborn as she is.
Spofford-Braxton and Charlie Field are traveling separately
in Charlie's Mazda, but they will stay at the same hotel.
Tomorrow they will all travel together to the funeral in the
Chrysler.

Annie and Josie sit up late in Annie's room and remi-
nisce about Carlo. They both still feel the loss, and Josie
starts rooting through her pocketbook for a tissue. Annie
has laid in a supply for the funeral tomorrow, and hands a
wad to Josie. Carlo had been dear to Josie, not only as family
but also as her favorite among the artists she supports with
a legacy inherited from her first husband. Annie's own tears
over Carlo have dried up, and she feels no guilt or regret
about having "transferred" her feelings to Duncan. Her love

for Carlo remains, and always will. Her love for Duncan may be more sedate, but she's had her wild love. And, somehow, one love does not diminish the other. Annie tries to steer the conversation away from Carlo, as it seems to upset Josie excessively, no doubt aggravated by Ethan's murder. After a while the conversation changes to Ethan.

"Judge thinks the investigators are still leaning toward calling it an accident. They haven't turned up any evidence to prove otherwise, and they can't think of a motive," Josie says. "Yesterday, when Judge spoke to Eleanor Haskell, she insisted it must be an accident. 'Ethan had no enemies,' she said. Doesn't look like a crime of passion either, since if it was murder someone obviously would have had to plan it, set it up. Money issues don't seem to be involved—they just can't think of a reason to call it murder, I guess," Josie says.

"There are random killings and murder for reasons we don't understand until later," Annie offers lamely.

"Well. Still—it *could* have been an accident," Josie says.

Annie looks thoughtful. "Then, what about the dummy? And the missing material in the library? No, I have an odd feeling about this," she says.

"Yes. I have to admit that I do, too," Josie says.

"What are we missing, then? Why did it have to happen during my wedding, for God's sake? I resent that. Why did it take place at the castle? Is that important? What did the dummy have to do with it, if it was Ethan the murderer wanted to get rid of? Would *anyone* stand to gain by Ethan's death—financially for instance? Not his mother, that's for sure, she's very well off. What other motive could there be? If the same person is responsible for both the dummy's crash and Ethan's death, we could be dealing with some kind of psycho—someone who's playing a game with us. And it would take somebody pretty clever to rig both of those events, someone capable of setting them both up single-handed, so close together—unless he had an accomplice of course," Annie speculates. And when she says "psycho," she can't help thinking of that moon-face staring back at her from inside Spofford-Braxton's boat shed.

Even Annie finds the idea of a willing accomplice unlikely. It is hard enough to imagine *one* person wanting to kill Ethan, never mind two, so the accomplice would either have to be coerced or paid. But then it definitely begins to sound like a Mafia or gang-style slaying, and that seems preposterous. She thinks of the Moonies again. *But they are a religious group, after all,* she thinks. Even so, Annie will continue to check into the history of the Gloucester Moonies. *Leave no stones unturned.*

As for Spofford-Braxton—wasn't it strange how alert he had been, warning Justin not to jump into the pool before anyone else had come up with the thought? Both Annie and Josie noticed this. *As if he'd known.* But what would be his motive? Did the curator seriously feel that Ethan was a threat to his position just because of that silly "family business" comment? What if Ethan found out about the audit that Vinnie mentioned, and questioned the curator about it? Was it possible that Spofford-Braxton had something illegal or unethical to hide—some financial mismanagement, or absconding with museum artifacts, for instance? Maybe he has embezzled funds or sold off some valuable items over time to finance buying his home. And if so, would he go so far as to kill Ethan to hide it? Ruth knew about the audit—did that mean *she* could be in danger, too? *Or be in on the plot?*

Whoever killed Ethan thought it out, planned ahead, maybe even borrowed the Hammond files from the library to study the layout of the castle. Or went through the patent and invention papers and came up with the scheme of using a radio-controlled boat—but to what end? Why crash a dummy? And Spofford-Braxton certainly wouldn't have needed the library files; he had enough information to hand in the castle files and displays. Annie gets up and paces the floor impatiently. Were the missing files really important? Maybe they weren't connected at all. Annie sighs. Her thoughts travel around and around, and she is getting nowhere.

"What about those pilfered papers in the library? How do they fit into it? Are they part of it, or just a coincidence? What was someone looking for in those files?" Annie asks out loud, to see if Josie might have an idea. They both shake their heads. Josie tries to hide a yawn behind her hand. Just then Judge knocks and sticks his woolly head in the door.

"Are you ever coming to bed, woman?" he says gruffly. Josie titters like a young girl, and Annie makes a thumb-to-the-door sign.

Annie sleeps uneasily, dreaming of her wedding. Ethan appears on the bridge and dives off—but instead of ending up in the pool, he floats in the air. He whirrs about like a giant beetle, large shiny wings flapping, legs vibrating madly before getting caught in her bridal veil. Then he shrinks and starts crawling around among the rosebuds in her braids. Spofford-Braxton appears with a long stake and whacks her on the head, killing Ethan, who falls to the floor twitching all his little golden legs.

Annie wakes in a cold sweat and gets up and pours herself a glass of water. When she finally goes back to sleep she dreams of trees, of leaves rustling in a soft breeze, and then of the ocean, waves rolling against the shore. The rushing, rhythmical sound of the waves keeps her sleeping soundly until the alarm on the bedside table goes off.

CHAPTER THIRTY-ONE

"Born for success he seemed,
With grace to win, with heart to hold,
With shining gifts that took all eyes."
(Ralph Waldo Emerson, "In Memoriam E.B.E.")

After a substantial and leisurely breakfast, Annie goes back to her room to change into something more appropriate for the funeral. What she is wearing, one of her staple pantsuits, was hardly even suitable for the breakfast room of this elegant establishment. Charlie and Spofford-Braxton came dressed in dark suit and tie, obviously ready for the funeral, and Annie felt like going back up to change, but that was before Josie and Judge appeared. Judge wore what Annie thought of as his "Hemingway outfit," a multi-pocketed safari jacket and khakis, and to top it off, an Aussie hat (with one side of the brim snapped to the side of the crown), which he immediately removed. This exposed a fluff of freshly washed, frizzy gray hair with a comical circular impression from the hat, and Annie was barely able to stifle a giggle. Josie wore a rather flouncy crepe dress sprinkled with pink flowers, and a narrow-brimmed hat with a pink silk rose right in front. She smiled gently and left her hat on throughout the meal.

When they gather in the lobby to leave for the funeral, they are all dressed somberly. Annie has a sudden flashback to Carlo's funeral, and shudders. At least this time she doesn't need to camouflage herself. At Carlo's funeral she was still the main suspect, but refused to let that prevent her from going.

Judge's Chrysler speeds away toward the church, with Annie in the back seat between Charlie and Spofford-Braxton. Though it is a soft and roomy seat, Annie nevertheless tucks her skirt under her legs and draws her shawl tight around her shoulders, wondering whether she might be sitting next to the murderer. Spofford-Braxton has been quiet so far during the trip—but then he probably has a great deal to worry about between the rumored audit, the scandal surrounding Ethan's death, the possibility of a lawsuit, the restoration and addition of power in the castle, and a by-now agitated board of directors.

They seat themselves in one of the back pews. The church is filling up. Annie recognizes some of the faces in the crowd, including several senators and other notables, and notices the TV crew in a side alcove. The Hammonds are still hobnobbing with people of note, apparently. Spofford-Braxton, on her left, looks chagrined. More adverse publicity to reflect on the museum. Charlie takes the seat on Spofford's left, at the end of the pew, as he has been asked to do the eulogy. Josie sits down on Annie's right and pats her reassuringly on the arm. Judge looks around, nods to some people across the aisle, and waves discreetly to one of the state senators, who smiles back in recognition.

Annie immediately recognizes Eleanor Hammond Haskell when she appears—the Hammond features are distinct. A handsome woman, though she appears transplanted from a different era. No sunglasses here, no outward sign of mourning. A woman trained to keep her private emotions out of the public eye. Mrs. Haskell follows the casket, walking ramrod straight, her face pale and emotionless, accompanied only by the ushers. She steps into the front pew, where her only companion is the funeral director, and waits for the service to begin. Annie watches the people who have gathered, and she and Josie whisper and point out faces they recognize. As soon as the service starts, the atmosphere becomes too painfully reminiscent of Carlo's funeral, and Annie tries to tune it out. She follows the gloomy service only subconsciously, standing and sitting and mouthing any necessary responses automatically along with everyone else. When Charlie gets up to speak, Josie quietly opens her handbag to take out some tissues, and Annie's awareness returns.

"So young," Charlie says. "So full of promise. So like his Uncle Jack. Ethan was a brilliant young man assured of a successful future, following in the footsteps of his famous uncle and grandfather. My heart goes out to his mother, who now is the last remaining member of the Hammond clan. Ethan would undoubtedly have continued the bloodline, but now, with his death, this illustrious family has tragically reached its end."

Josie is dabbing her eyes with the entire wad of tissues. Annie feels that Charlie is carrying this particular line a bit far. A little consolation might be in order. She glances over at Mrs. Haskell, who sits stone-faced and tearless, her hands idly turning the pages of the hymnal. It hadn't occurred to Annie that Ethan was the last of the Hammond line, but she remembers reading somewhere that Jack and the other Hammond siblings died childless. Their cousin, Mrs. Haskell, is now the last leaf on the last branch of the family tree left alive.

"There is little one can say when such a young person is taken from us. Ethan was a wonderful addition at the Hammond Castle—a breath of life, a reminder of how it must have been when Jack lived there," Charlie says, casting a glance over to the pew where Spofford-Braxton, Annie, Josie, and Judge sit. Spofford-Braxton fidgets uneasily next to Annie, coughs drily, and pops a honey lozenge into his mouth.

"When Ethan was there, the whole world was visiting," Charlie continues. "London, Paris, Florence, all of Europe seemed to breeze in with him. When he moved a chair or opened a window, he seemed to be the reincarnation of Jack Hammond. Ethan was at home in the castle; he walked and lived there as though he owned the place. And of course, in a way he did. After all, it was a family home." Charlie pauses, touching the tip of his nose with a slight sniff and clearing his throat.

"We will all miss him—his gentle romps and escapades through the castle and grounds, the spirit of joy and adventure that he managed to impart in all of us, making us feel like a large and happy family." With a sad, pained smile, he turns to the grieving mother in the front pew. His face changes, becomes somber and mournful. "Mrs. Haskell, please accept our sincere and heartfelt grief at the loss of your gifted and enchanting son." Charlie bows and stands for a brief, heart-breaking moment turned to Mrs. Haskell, his face full of compassion, his eyes glimmering with tears. He stumbles slightly as he steps down from the pulpit, and walks slowly down the aisle. Spofford-Braxton moves over to make room and bumps into Annie.

"Sorry," he whispers.

"It's all right, Henry," Annie whispers back, while trying to scoot over toward Josie at the same time. Josie gives her a questioning glance before edging herself to the right, forcing Judge to constrain his generous physique in order not to spill over the edge of the pew.

After a final hymn, the casket is carried out, followed by Mrs. Haskell. The assembled guests squeeze in right behind her, as though competing to be the closest to her, eager to be seen on home TV screens as having turned up to ease her loneliness. Senators and other dignitaries solemnly press her hand before hurrying out into the rain, off to other duties.

Judge takes Mrs. Haskell's hand and does not let go of it. He says a few words of comfort, which earn him a faint smile, before he releases her hand. Josie steps up and promptly breaks into uncontrollable sobs, which unsettles Mrs. Haskell until she remembers having heard that Josie recently lost a member of her own family. This finally unleashes some of her emotions, and the tautly controlled features crumple in grief. The two women then draw to the side, where they spend a few minutes comforting each other.

• • •

CHAPTER THIRTY-TWO

"By strangers honor'd, and by strangers mourn'd"
(Alexander Pope, "Elegy to the Memory of an Unfortunate
Lady")

Josie and Judge sit down with Eleanor Haskell in the far end of the Haskell living room. Sherry is served by a butler, and platters of canapés are brought around by maids in black with little white aprons. The maids, like Mrs. Haskell, look as if they had stepped out of another time, hair charmingly curled under starched, winged caps. Charlie Field hands a glass of golden sherry to Annie and takes a sip of his own. They both accept a small tidbit, which neither of them bites into.

"Where's Spofford?" Annie asks, looking around.

"Back at the hotel. Said something about an incipient cold."

"I noticed he was popping cough drops," Annie says.

"Care for a stroll about the room?"

"Sure. Let's go over there," Annie says, motioning toward some bookshelves.

"Ever the librarian." Charlie is amused and escorts her gently by the arm toward the little library area. They both dispose of their canapés on a used napkin on a side table.

"Well," Charlie whispers, "how would you like to live in a place like this, paid for by a rich uncle's inventions?"

They both laugh, and Annie looks around, embarrassed to be mirthful at such a sad occasion.

On one of the bookshelves are photographs. In one, Mrs. Haskell as a little girl—she had been Eleanor Hammond then—sits in the lap of her famous grandfather, John Hays Hammond, Sr. There is a wedding picture of Mr. and Mrs. Haskell, where the likeness between the young woman and Ethan is striking.

"The Hammond genes were very strong, weren't they?" Annie says.

"Not strong enough, I guess," says Charlie. "They're all gone now, except for her." He points to the photo of Eleanor.

"I know. It is really too sad."

Annie studies the book spines on the shelf. She reaches over to pull one out, but catches herself. It probably wouldn't look right to be browsing books right now.

"Look at that," she says instead. "All the books you need if you wanted to know something about the Hammonds. *Wow.* Bet they have all the ones we're missing."

"What do you mean, missing?" Charlie asks.

"Somebody's been sneaking Hammond material out of the library." Annie bites her tongue, sorry that she mentioned it. She doesn't want to involve Charlie in the mystery of the missing Hammond files any more than in her looking into the past history of the Moonies. Now he'll probably go and talk to Duncan about it, and then Duncan will be caught in the middle. Charlie may be Duncan's closest friend, but he is also one of the library trustees—the only one who supported her when she needed it—and aside from getting irritated hearing about missing library materials, he might find her obsessive snooping unprofessional.

"First I've heard about it," Charlie says, looking mystified.

"Might just be a student. The high schoolers have to do an essay on American Inventors, and we were running low."

To change the subject, Annie looks away into the crowd before turning back to Charlie with a little conspiratorial smile. "Too bad Clare couldn't come, but I guess we can't all leave the library at the same time. I always feel a little lost in a crowd like this, when you don't know anyone," Annie says. Charlie gives her a curious look but does not comment. *No commitment yet,* she guesses. She leads the way out of the book corner and notices Josie wiping her eyes. It's time to get her away from here and back to the hotel. Annie takes Charlie by the arm and leads him over to the chintz sofa. Judge looks relieved at the sight of them.

"Annie, I was just looking for you. I think we'd better leave; we have a long ride ahead of us in the morning."

Mrs. Haskell nods with a sad smile.

"It was so kind of you all to come. It has meant an awful lot to me, almost like having family with me. You see, I'd so looked forward to Ethan getting married and having children. It was lonely for him, not having aunts and uncles and cousins. You are quite right, Mr. Field, the castle was like a home for him. I think it gave him a feeling of family."

Annie can tell by the trembling chin that Mrs. Haskell is about to cry again. Josie is aware of it, too, and puts her arm tightly around the woman's hunched back. Nothing remains of the self-controlled, emotionless family leader that walked behind the casket. Eleanor Haskell sits shrunken in her grief, a small, sad, old woman.

"Come now, Eleanor." Josie says quietly, "I'm so sorry that we have to leave you, but please do come and visit us in Rockport as soon as you feel up to it. We have a guest cottage at the back of the property, so you don't have to feel as if you're intruding—or you can stay in a guest room in the house with us. I'll give you a call as soon as we get back so we can set it up. I'd love your company—Judge is always busy, and I have a lot of time to myself. I could take you over to the castle, if you felt like it..."

At this, Mrs. Haskell starts crying in earnest. Josie shakes her head, angry at herself, feeling it is her fault. How insensitive of her to mention the place where Ethan had met his death. But Mrs. Haskell smiles through the tears.

"Don't mind me, Josie. I'd love to come and see you, and to visit the castle. I haven't been there since Uncle Jack and Aunt Irene were alive. I'm sure a lot has changed, but the building itself must be the same. I understand that some of the furniture and objects have been sold off, but it *was* rather cluttered back then. He was quite a collector, my Uncle Jack. And so generous. As I told Charlie, the house you are in was his wedding gift to us. Off you go now, I'll be fine," she says, rising to give Josie a gentle embrace, before sitting back alone.

Annie leads the way with Charlie and Judge following on either side of Josie, the tight little wedge pressing its way through the crowded room. Mrs. Haskell is still sitting alone in the sofa when Annie turns around at the door. The small, forgotten figure has been following their progress and now waves forlornly. Annie waves back, suddenly annoyed at the other so-called mourners who have obviously only come to be seen in the company of the rich and famous.

"I can't believe it. Not one of these people is bothering to notice that Mrs. Haskell is sitting there all alone," she says.

"Poor thing." Josie agrees. "She has a bad heart, too, she told me, but fortunately a pacemaker takes care of it. She had a near fatal heart attack after she lost her husband, but Ethan saw her through it. It was a long recovery, she said, and Ethan took a semester off from college to take care of her. Can you imagine? What a dear boy. This time, she's really alone."

"Josie, you have such a soft heart. I'm sure Eleanor will take you up on your invitation. Best thing in the world for her would be to come and visit you and Judge for a while," Charlie says, squeezing her arm.

"Quite right. I understand Eleanor still likes to ride. Well, we'll put her on old Napoleon and go for a canter down the lane," Judge says.

"Better make that a trot," Charlie says, laughing.

• • •

CHAPTER THIRTY-THREE

"... leave me here a little, while as yet 'tis early morn."
(Alfred, Lord Tennyson, "Locksley Hall")

Annie is back in Rockport and has gotten up before sunrise. On the way back from the funeral in Judge's car, she somehow expected to be going "home" to the Hannah Jumper House, and was shocked when Judge dropped her off at Duncan's house. Will she ever be able to think of it as home? Up before daylight, she walks down the street to her own house, after leaving a note for Duncan. Once the coffee is ready, she takes a tray out to the patio and sits down to watch the harbor come alive.

Gussy's Girls, a red lobster boat with a peculiar peaked front ("I built 'er to be able to take a whoppah," is Gussy's explanation) chugs out of the harbor a couple of hours before sunrise. Gussy the lobsterman bears no relationship to Gussie the dog, who is named after Augustus Finknottle of *Jeeves and Wooster* fame. Aside from *Gussy's Girls*, Gussy the lobsterman also owns a larger red fishing boat, the *Gretchen Marie*, named after his wife.

Gussy's Girls is the first boat of the day to leave harbor— "breaking glass," as the fishermen say. It cleaves the mirror surface, creating small wavelets that flutter to the shore before making their way back out again, crisscrossing new waves until the water surface puckers like seersucker. Soon the solar wind comes along, sending swaths of small ripples scudding across the harbor. Then the stirrings of humanity take over. The *Ocean Reporter*, an iron-tub workhorse of a trawler, starts up with a rumble that could wake the dead. All around the harbor fishermen stow their gear into little skiffs that lie tied up along the wharves and start poling out to their boats. Most of them use a single oar—some, like Gussy, stand poling in the back, like gondoliers in orange overalls. Gussy vigorously zigzags the oar, which is resting in a small slit in the aft board. Others stand in the very front and use the oar like a canoe paddle, one side at a time, with the aft of the skiff sticking up out of the water in a ridiculous fashion. None of them row the skiff in the conventional manner. If they actually do sit down and put the oars into the locks, they *backwater,* or row backwards—with the flat aft leading—presumably so they can see where they're going. "We're lobstermen, not seiners," they say in excuse—although some of them do a bit of fishing out on Jeffrey's Ledge or Stellwagen Bank during the few miserly hours allotted them by the government. These regulations are the reason the *Gretchen Marie* spends a lot of time lounging in the harbor these days. It used to be that fishermen would hand the business down to their sons, but that's no longer a certainty. One of the local lobster boats is actually named *Rising Son*—one can only hope that this optimism will pay off.

Early rising pleasure-sailors are transported to their yachts by the Sandy Bay Yacht Club launch. The "glass" is shattered for the day, and the water surface won't smooth out again until long past dusk, when the last delivery truck has vibrated off to the highway, the last "bleep-bleep" of a pneumatic air horn is heard calling the launch to come and give the yachtsmen a ride back to shore, and the last shop door on Bearskin Neck has been slammed shut for the evening.

Reluctantly, Annie gets up and goes inside. She picks up the phone and dials Sally's number.

•   •   •

CHAPTER THIRTY-FOUR

"With the color that paints the morning and
evening clouds that face the sun
I saw then the whole heaven suffused."
(Dante Alighieri, The Divine Comedy. Paradiso)

"Sally, what do you remember about the Moonies? I mean, about when they first came here?" Annie asks. She and Sally are walking on Wingaersheek Beach. They met just after sunrise and drove over to the beach at Loblolly Cove to go beach combing for starfish and shells and pieces of colored glass among the seaweed. The sea bled crimson from the edge of the shore out to Thacher Island while the red disk of the sun slowly edged its way up between the Twin Lights. The sky seemed unwilling to relinquish its glow, and they scrabbled their way out to Emerson's Point and sat down on the rocks. There the sun colored the granite boulders and ledges a deep rusty red, a stark change from their daylight pale buff complexion.

They spent the rest of the morning hiking in Dogtown, starting out along the trail that goes past Raccoon Ledges. The ledges are part of an old terminal moraine deposited by the great glacier that had once covered the Northeast. While in Dogtown, Annie decided it was time to harvest the cranberries in Briar Swamp before the skunks and raccoons got them all. Wearing rubber boots from the outset, knowing they'd sink deep into the wet sphagnum moss if they ventured out into the swamp, they gleaned a few cupfuls each. Then they sat in the unseasonably hot sun for a while on the wooden boardwalk that runs along the edge of the swamp.

When they got tired of Dogtown, they decided to go *ovah the bridge* to Wingaersheek Beach, and are now ambling on the high dunes behind the cabanas, where the sand is the whitest and finest of almost anywhere in the world and the view across the river over to the Annisquam Lighthouse, which some locals call the "Wigwam," is wide open.

"The Moonies? What do you mean, *remember?* I was just a kid when the Moonies came here. Anyway, why do you ask?" *Annie's always looking for the most peculiar information,* Sally thinks.

"Just wondering. You're older than I, so I thought maybe you'd remember."

"You just love to bring that fact up, don't you? Well, I do remember that the Gloucesterites were pretty hysterical about the Moonies moving in. A weird cult, brainwashing the kids, that kind of thing. But really, Annie, what's this all about? You have some library patron trying to start up trouble? Because I do remember *that,* the trouble. There was a lot of it, even violence, when the Moonies first came. I'm sure glad that's over. All we need is a religious war on Cape Ann. Bad enough the whole world is involved in religious warfare."

"I agree with you, Sal. I promise you that this isn't anything like that."

"*Aha.* It's got something to do with Ethan's murder, then, doesn't it?" Sally says, narrowing her eyes suspiciously. "If you're right, that is, and he *was* murdered. You've sure got a one-track mind, Annie." The wind catches Sally's curly black hair and whips her face with it.

Annie decides to drop the subject of the Moonies. "Come on, let's walk back down to the beach and find a place in the lee. Too bad the food stand isn't open, I'm starving."

"Hah!" Sally says. "I know you know I brought stuff. I noticed you glancing into the back seat."

Annie grins. "I didn't have to, Sal. I trust you implicitly. I know you always bring stuff. So, how about it? What did you bring?"

"Thermos of seafood chowder from Ellen's. Some biscuits I made myself. Stick of butter. Will that do?"

"That'll do great. Come on, what are you waiting for?" Annie giant-steps it down the steep, sandy dunes and over to the car. Sally catches up, sliding and laughing, and lifts the basket out of the back seat. They find a quiet place in a hollow between a pair of dunes that Annie has christened "the Maidenforms." The mugs of creamy chowder with biscuits and butter go down quickly. Stick-to-the-ribs food, but they'll walk it off. Tomorrow.

"I do know someone who knows a lot about the Moonies," Sally says, suddenly.

"Who?"

"Old Doc Ford. His son Jordy joined the Moonies, remember?"

"You're right. Jordy Fordy. Whatever happened to Jordy?"

"Don't know. He left town, though. Doc had some sort of breakdown after that. That's when he moved up into the woods."

"Ah, that explains it."

"Explains what?"

"Well, one day Dad got injured at the tool company. His hand got in the way of the drop forge, or something horrible like that. He was always getting hurt, they all did. Mom was working at the Story library across the street, and they ran for her. She picked Dad up to take him to the hospital, but he insisted that he just needed to go see Doc Ford. Well, when they got there, Doc was in his cups, and Mom dragged Dad away to the emergency room. And after that we didn't have Doc Ford for our family doctor any more. Must have been about that same time, then."

"Guess so. Poor old guy. His wife left him, too. Lives all by himself now—on what, I don't know. He stopped practicing. Probably lost his license."

"Is Doc Ford—eh, how do I put it—competent? I mean, would he remember?"

"Let's go find out," Sally suggests. "His place is over in Pigeon Cove, up near where Josie used to live before she moved in with Judge. We'll have to leave our car down on Granite Pier, though. He has a gate that he keeps locked." Which means Annie and Sally *will* get their walk in. Today.

The tide is coming in fast, and the seaweed-y, salty smell rivals that of the chowder. The storm is over, having deposited large mounds of sea wrack and dead crustaceans among the other flotsam on the beach. Annie picks up a sand dollar, scrubbed free of its skin by the sand and bleached by the sun to a perfect whiteness. She remembers—although it seems a long time ago now—picking sand dollars across the Annisquam River at Lighthouse Beach with Mandy, a classmate who had been terminally ill. Mandy had, in fact, died a few months later. Annie looks out across the river, then wraps the sand dollar carefully in a napkin and puts it in Sally's basket for safekeeping.

. . .

CHAPTER THIRTY-FIVE

"The shattered lobsterpot, the broken oar,
And the gear of foreign dead men. The sea has many voices."
(T. S. Eliot, Four Quartets. The Dry Salvages)

The sun is setting by the time they park the car on Granite Pier. With their backs to the sunset as they stand looking out over the ocean, the sky is a carnival glass bowl of bright orange washed with pink-streaked swirls of cloud. Annie squints toward the horizon. Once she stood on this pier and saw whales blow, far out beyond the great breakwater. There's nothing out there today except a massive barge hauled by a tug. *Garbage, probably. Where does it come from, and where does it go? Do we just trade ours for theirs?* Annie thinks. Closer to shore a couple of small lobster boats zigzag in Sandy Bay. When the men locate one of their buoys, they reach down and grab it with the gaff and haul in a string of traps. Neither boat is outfitted with a hydraulic winch. They're just small timers, like her father was, probably out there assessing their losses after the gale. The water is still choppy after the storm, and a number of lobster traps have washed up on the rocks at the base of the pier, the yellow or green wire mesh crushed and mangled. A fisherman's bright orange immersion suit bobs at the edge of the rocks, along with bits of wreckage. Tommy was lucky to get his traps hauled in time.

Annie and Sally trudge up the steep hill toward Doc Ford's gate. From the gate the dirt driveway winds through the woods for half a mile before they get to the cottage, which sits near a small quarry. Briar and burdock reach out across the road and grab at them, and cockleburs fasten themselves to their clothes. One side of the quarry is shallow, and the upper submerged ledges are visible through the clear, greenish water. Water lilies and pickerel weed grow there, attracting a swarm of flitting damselflies.

Annie and Sally arrive at the rundown cottage, hidden behind enormous lilacs fringed with brown seedpods. *Must be quite a sight in June,* Annie thinks. The shingles covering the cottage are weathered and thin, and the blue trim paint is flaking.

Sally knocks on the door. They hear shuffling steps, and the door opens a crack. Doc Ford, his white hair sticking up in tufts, squints at them suspiciously. He is smoking a pipe and puts his thumb over the bowl and sucks noisily to encourage the fire, then stands there waiting for them to state their errand.

"Hi, Doc," Sally says, "it's me, Sally Babson. Matt's wife. Remember me? And Annie Quitnot. Can we come in for a minute? We need your help with something."

"I'm not in business. Go away," he says gruffly.

"Oh, we're not looking for medical help, Doc. Please, can't we come in? It won't take long," Sally pleads. Annie already has a bad feeling about the whole thing. Just bringing up the subject of the Moonies will probably set Doc off on a tirade, judging by the mood he's in. But he grudgingly lets them pass and enter his hovel. He doesn't seem drunk at least, as he walks a straight line across the room.

Trash, newspapers, and dirty laundry cover the seating in the room, an old sofa and pair of club chairs that once must have been an elegant addition in a different setting. The sweet smell of pipe smoke mixes with other scents, more unpleasant. Sally takes a quick look around the room and walks over toward the kitchen, where a kettle is whistling shrilly.

"Can I pour your tea, Doc?" she says. Sally will take care of him now—it's what she does best, Annie knows. The woman should have been a nurse. Annie hears water running in the kitchen. Probably Sally washing out a mug. In a moment she enters with three steaming mugs on a tray. Annie pushes newspapers aside on the table to make room for the tray, and piles stuff from the chairs onto the floor so they will have a place to sit.

"Help yourselves, why don't you?" says Doc—belatedly or sarcastically, Annie isn't sure which.

They take a few sips in silence.

"So what is it you want, then?" Doc says, looking at Sally.

Annie decides to take over so that Sally won't be saddled with whatever anger and grief Doc will dish out when he finds out what they have come for.

"Information on the Moonies," she says, succinctly. They brace themselves for his reaction, but Doc sits perfectly still. Sparks from the wood stove crack like gunshots in the silence. A lone seagull screeches in the distance, and the wind hisses in the pines outside. Annie thinks that maybe Doc has forgotten they are there, and clears her throat softly. Doc looks at her, and she wonders what's going on behind those rheumy old eyes. *He must have moved up here to avoid just this,* she thinks, *talking about the Moonies and his lost son.*

"If you don't want to talk about it, we can leave," she suggests, giving him a way out.

"I don't know why in hell...pardon my language...you two ninnies want to come up here and ask me about those people," Doc rumbles.

Annie forges ahead. "Well, it's a long story, and I don't want to take up too much of your time to explain it. Sally and I are too young to remember much of how it was when the Moonies first arrived in Gloucester. We know what happened in your family back then—with Jordy, I mean—and we'd appreciate your perspective…"

Now Doc gets out of his chair, trembling with rage.

"Perspective?" he roars. "Perspective? My only child went off to college—a normal, good kid, good grades, a nice and quiet, well-behaved, typical American boy—and right off the bat, he got involved with some freaky group calling themselves…uh, CARP, I think it was, something fishy, I remember that. It stood for something about Research of Principles, mind you. These students, trainees in brainwashing if you ask me, got Jordy hooked on Moon's religion. You know, the Reverend Sun Myung Moon, the same character who got himself crowned the second messiah on Capitol Hill, in a big gala attended by Senators and other bigwigs!"

Annie and Sally sit quietly, afraid to stir. Doc harrumphs and starts walking about the room in agitation. Finally he sits down again and wipes his forehead.

"Well, anyway," he mumbles. He seems to have decided to get it all off his chest, as he continues with his tale. "Pretty soon Jordy joined the 'Moon Children,' which is what they're called officially. 'Moonies' is more of a derogatory term that some of them don't like, although they coined it themselves, and Moon uses it all the time in his sermons and speeches.

"After a while Jordy started working for Moon. First he was selling flowers down by the rotary—that's one of their favorite fundraising methods, you know, selling flowers and trinkets. That made it tough for other, honest folks who'd been selling flowers there for years. People would stop and honk and shout abuse at them, even after they put up big signs that said they weren't Moonies, so in the end most of them gave up and the Moonies got a monopoly on the spot. I have to admit that it was a painful embarrassment for the family to see Jordy sitting there, beside those big buckets of carnations or whatever they could get cheap wholesale, but I think Jordy almost enjoyed seeing us cringe when we drove by." Doc looks out through the window. In the distance, a flock of Canada geese fly by, squawking loudly.

"Later on he worked on their fishing boats. The Moonies had expanded their business from lobstering into bottom fishing by then. He worked hard—and all for a bed and a couple of meals a day. It all went to Moon, you know—the *Messiah*, no less. The Father of all Mankind. Moon liked it here, liked the Cape Ann coastline. Thought it would be a nice place to live."

"Well, they did move in, didn't they?" Sally asks.

"Sure did. People in Gloucester got really afraid that Moon was trying to build some sort of religious colony, that we'd have another Jonestown here." Doc shakes his head and sucks hard on his pipe, which has gone out. He refills it with tobacco and tamps it down well before relighting it. "Moon went to jail for tax evasion and conspiracy to obstruct justice, but when he got out, he still had his money and his church, didn't he, and his followers loved him all the more for having 'suffered.' Heck. Some martyr." Doc shakes his head and puffs on his pipe for a while, trying to deal with this thought. Sally casts a glance at Annie while sipping her tea.

"Anyway," he continues, "back at the time, I gave Jordy an ultimatum: quit the Moonies and go back to school, or move out. He moved out. He was young and impressionable, easily led as kids are at that age, and soon he got in with a bad crowd. Got into drugs, too—but I guess I can't blame that on the Moonies, even though I saw a report in a paper recently that said Moon's buying up land in South America— Paraguay, I think it was. The reporter suggested Moon is trying to corner a piece of the narcotics trade. Drug money would certainly fuel his campaigns and help him with church membership, which I understand is sagging these days." Doc Ford has calmed down a little and sits back in his chair, taking a sip of tepid tea. Annie remains quiet, not wanting to disturb Doc's train of thought.

"Then one day Jordy was gone." Doc's face has gone blank. "Suppose it was partly my own fault. I should never have handed him that ultimatum. I went and grilled the kids he was staying with, and finally one of them told me that Jordy had said he was moving to California. That's the last I know of him. I tried to locate him, but the cops said it's too easy for people who don't want to be found to stay hidden. And he wasn't a minor anymore, they pointed out. They tried to tell me, 'He's probably okay. He'll show up on your door-step when he runs out of money.' Never happened, of course. Could be dead of an overdose, or anything. Oh, heck…" His voice cracks.

"I'm so sorry, Doc. I didn't mean to bring up such awful memories." Annie thinks they should probably leave, but decides to change the subject and ask one more question.

"How about these days? Do you know if the Moonies are still active in Gloucester? I mean, there are still rumors of them buying up land that comes up for sale there, especially along the waterfront. Are they recruiting new members? Are their businesses successful?"

"Now, what's your name again…Annie? You'd have to go talk to somebody else about that. Talk to the fishermen, they'd know. Don't bother going to the realtors. If Moon wanted to buy something, he'd use a middle man, like some shady lawyer, that's how he operates."

"Of course. Thank you so much for talking to us Doc, and I'm really sorry we brought this up. I know it must be painful for you to talk about it," Annie says, rising. Sally brings the mugs out to the kitchen and rinses them out. Annie knows she'd better go and grab Sally quickly, before she starts cleaning the whole house.

"Quitnot, eh?" Doc asks, as he walks them to the door. "You must be Roger and Mairead's kid. I remember you now...skinny, with long red braids, right? Your dad used to work down at the forge. Your folks still alive?"

Annie shakes her head. "Long gone, Doc. We moved out of the Cove when the tool company closed, and I live downtown now, in the old Hannah Jumper House. I work at the library, just like Mom used to. Well, Sally, we'd better hurry. I promised to help Duncan with some paperwork, and I haven't even thought about what to make for supper. Thanks so much for the tea, Doc, and for talking to us."

Sally looks around Doc's messy living room with a frown of regret. Annie takes her by the arm and steers her through the door. Sally is just too kind for her own good, sometimes. Doc waves them off and starts to rekindle his pipe, sucking away so hard his nostrils flatten.

• • •

CHAPTER THIRTY-SIX

*"Yes, this is the ancestor of that terrible American dish
called Pork and Beans with Frankfurters."
(Jeff Smith, The Frugal Gourmet)*

Duncan is in for an unexpected treat tonight. Leftover soup. She'll just have to think of a good name for it, so she can fool him. Annie lets the unlikely mixture stew together while she changes out of her sweat suit, which has gotten itchier by the minute what with cockleburs and catbrier thorns pricking her skin. She'll have to spend some time picking the suit clean later.

When her husband returns, Annie snuggles a bit to make Duncan feel welcome home. She stops short of raising his hopes for some sort of pre-prandials that they might both enjoy, and he looks at her a little curiously.

"Later," she assures him. "Dinner's just about ready."

"Mm. Smells good. What is it?"

"Cassoulet," she replies, thankfully coming up with a name just in time. *Well, it's close enough to a cassoulet, isn't it?* A slice of bacon to grease the pan, then she'd added leftover cut up pork chops, leftover carrots, leftover stewed tomatoes, a couple of leftover chopped breakfast sausages, and a handy can of white beans from the cupboard. Sprinkled it with garlic powder and Herbes de Provence, and popped in a couple of cloves. Simmered a while, and—presto. On the side, a crunchy chopped salad and thin rounds of baguette—toasted, since the bread was a couple of days old.

"Wife, you're a great cook," Duncan says over a spoonful. "And a liar, besides. I'm sure this took more than half an hour."

"Well, I guess you're right, dearest." *If you include the time it took to cook the first time,* she thinks.

"Dearest, hm." He raises his eyebrows. "Sounds a bit Jane Austenish."

"Just trying it out. How about 'luv,' then?"

"Too Cockney."

"Sweetums?"

"Ugh. Keep going."

"Leave me with some ideas to try next time?"

"Okay, dear."

Now it's Annie's turn to grimace. "Wow. That one's kind of stodgy. Sounds as if we've been married fifty years."

"We'll have to work on this, I guess. Right now I'd like to work on another aspect of marriage," Duncan says, rising and approaching rapidly.

"Wait, wait...I said I'd stop by the Camerons' after supper. I won't be long, Dunc, I promise. Can you hold it right there?"

Duncan stiffens his pose, arms held out for her, one foot in the air ready for the next step. After a moment he lets out a breath and puts his foot down.

"Don't think so. I'll place myself at the ready, though, say...on the couch, for when you get back?"

"Better not be asleep."

In the car she considers other terms of endearment. *Cara,* she thinks, I like *cara.* She has never been called anything she loved better. But *cara* was what Carlo had called her, and it can never be used again. She sighs. How about *honey,* or *sweetheart,* then? Hm.

• • •

CHAPTER THIRTY-SEVEN

"Some circumstantial evidence is very strong,
as when you find a trout in the milk."
(Henry Thoreau, Journal)

"How 'bout this, Annie?" Tommy has already had a look at the contents of the plastic trash bag Annie got from the Coast Guard, and pulls a piece of wood out of it. He holds it up like a trophy. Annie does not think it looks very significant. It is jagged and splintered at both ends, and looks like any piece of flotsam you can pick up on the beach after a storm.

"Yes, well. Very interesting. A piece of wood. It *could* be from the boat, I suppose." Annie is not too impressed. Tommy turns it over, showing her the other side. There the wood is black with white letters painted on. The letters spell *IONE.*

"Ione? A woman's name, maybe?" Annie guesses. She doesn't recognize the name as the name of any boat she is familiar with. Certainly not from Rockport, she knows the names of all the boats, seeing them through her living room window every day. Could be from Gloucester, Ipswich, Essex, or any of the other nearby harbor towns, though. Tommy smiles enigmatically, but keeps silent. Why is he smiling? Then it hits her.

"My God," she gasps. *"PIONEER!* Don't tell me the boat was the Pioneer! Could it be?"

"Nope, 'fraid not. Not the raht kind of boat atall. Not big enough. I sawr it through the windahs as it was comin' taw'ds us, ya know. But I figguh'd the name could'a been meant as some kahnd of message. And wait, heah's the clinchah," he says, and pulls a heavy-looking metal object out of the bag.

"What on earth is that?" Annie asks, perplexed.

"I'm not a hunnerd percent shoah, but I think it's a Gyrad. Ya know, Hammond's radio control invention."

"You really think so? If it is, it could mean that the boat *was* remotely controlled, just as I thought—but I have no idea what a Gyrad should look like. The name must be a combination of *gy*-roscope and *rad*-io, don't you think? Does that thing look like it might be? Are you sure that's what it is?"

"No, I'm not," he admits, "so you'll have to look into it. Ask Spoffohd, he'll know."

"Oh, no, I couldn't," Annie says.

Tommy gives her a doubtful look. "Uh-oh. Spoffie's on yoah list of suspecks? I don' believe it," he says, laughing.

"Well," she says defensively, "you got any better ideas?"

Tommy shakes his head, unwilling to get drawn in. "Anyway, Annie, these two ah the only things in the bag that seemed interestin'. The rest is pretty nondescript, but take the lot. Now, I'd offah yaw some coffee, but since ya din' bring hubby, I assume y'ah in some hurry to get back. Wouldn' wanna guess what could be so impahtant that ya have to rush home, but off with ya, then. Annette had to go out, anyways, so we'll make it anothah tahm."

"Thanks, Tommy. I did tell Dunc I'd be right back. You won't tell him about this, will you?"

"Scout's honah. But I bet he knows."

"Nah. Can I call you tomorrow?"

"Shoah. Been thinking about puttin' some traps back in, but I think I'll give it anothah cupla days. Some of the guys ah still out theah untanglin' them strings. I maht have to go out just for a bit, to keep an eye on things. When the ropes get tangled and ya have to cut 'em, ya have to be shoah to tie 'em back togethah prop'ly. Some people ahn't to cahful 'bout that, and all they'll haul in will be a cut length o' rope."

• • •

CHAPTER THIRTY-EIGHT

*"Hide thyself as it were for a little moment,
until the indignation be overpast."*
(Bible, Isaiah 26:20)

Lorraine Davis appears at the Main Desk, and Annie hunkers down in the video section around the corner, unable to cope with the impossible woman. Ben, who is shelving books, casts a surprised glance down at the crouching reference librarian as he walks by with his trolley. Annie shakes her head vigorously and puts a finger to her lips. *Don't give me away.* Ben nods and smiles, and Annie notices something glistening below his lip. Probably just had a drink of water at the bubbler. The pages can't seem to pass it without stopping for a slurp. Ben whistles softly and walks on. After a while Annie peeks around the corner to make sure Mrs. Davis is gone.

"Did she return all her books?" Annie asks Marie.

"Yes. Complained that someone had scribbled in one of them with a ballpoint pen. Now, could you possibly imagine who that might be? Couldn't be that Timmy of hers, who is such a good boy, could it?" Marie says.

"She didn't return any of the *other* stuff, by any chance?" Annie checks the trolley for her missing materials. Not that she expects to find them.

"No. And she didn't go over to the vertical file, either. And Hedwig isn't here, so the Rockport Room is closed. But watch out," she says in a hushed voice, "Mrs. Davis is still in the library. I saw her follow Ben over to Nonfiction." As they speak, Mrs. Davis appears, stalking briskly past the Main Desk. She seems exited, doesn't even take notice of them, and charges up the stairs with admirable speed for a woman of her proportions.

"Uh-oh," Annie says, "now what?" But she has work to do, and whatever it is that has gotten Mrs. Davis excited has to wait until later. Annie spends the next several hours immersed in reference questions, crisscross phone calls, and assembling selections of current bestsellers and staff choices to go on the "Recommended Reading" shelf. At lunchtime she goes down into the dungeon and pulls a yogurt out of the fridge. Instead of sitting down at the round table, which is piled high with outdated *National Geographics*, which are probably the most commonly donated items in the library, she brings the yogurt with her into the Rockport Room. This is a serious no-no, but Eagle-Eye Hedwig isn't here and Annie plans to be careful.

She puts the yogurt down on top of the microfiche reader and walks over to the biography shelf. The Hammond biography has still not been returned. Next she goes over to the bank of files. Now the Hammond file is not only empty, it seems to have disappeared altogether. A little agitated, she checks to see if it might just have been misfiled, but it is not to be found.

Perplexed, she walks over to the card file. Not everything in the Rockport Room has been catalogued on the computer yet—it is happening at a slow pace, mostly done by volunteers—so, like many small libraries, they are still relying on the old card file system down here. Annie has a premonition as she pulls out the "H" drawer. The cards are gone. Not a single listing relating to *Hammond, John Hays, Jr.* remains. She shuts the drawer. *This is going too far,* she thinks.

Deep in thought, she walks over to the microfiche reader and turns it on. Time is fleeting, and she tries to focus on the task at hand. She pulls out the drawer labeled "Local Newspapers," where she locates the microfiche cards from the seventies and eighties, looking for any reference to the Moonies. A pretty good index, prepared by some long-ago volunteer, guides her. Right away she hits pay dirt.

Immediately after the sale of the Cardinal Cushing Villa, she learns, the mayor of Gloucester had cabled the Vatican, addressing Pope Paul II personally. The mayor asked the pope to help reverse the sisters' sale of the Cushing Villa to the Moonies. A reply telegram soon arrived from the Vatican's Sacred Congregation for Religious and Secular Institutes. The sale of the Villa had been investigated, it said, but could not be invalidated.

"We regret this unfortunate occurrence and hope that as little harm as possible will be done to the population, especially the youth of Gloucester," the statement further read. *Poor Doc Ford. In his case, harm has certainly been done.* The mayor had also appealed to Humberto Cardinal Medeiros for help—but if the pope himself was powerless, what could the poor cardinal do except express his deep regrets?

The door to the Rockport Room opens and Charlie Field walks in, smiling when he notices Annie. She knocks the yogurt cup off the top of the microfiche reader while hurrying to switch it off. *Drat, caught again.* The cup hits the edge of the table and turns upside down before continuing on its way downward, splattering creamy pink raspberry yogurt over the low wooden cabinet that holds the microfiche cards. Luckily she has closed the drawers.

"Oops, let me help you with that," Charlie says. "Didn't mean to startle you, Annie. Marie said you were down in the dungeon having lunch, and when I didn't find you there I remembered what a workaholic you are, so I looked in here. You seem very engrossed in your work. But, my dear Annie, you should really take time out for lunch, no need to work through it. Too conscientious, as usual," he continues, walking closer. Annie rises and looks under the microfiche stand.

"Good grief, what a mess," she says, looking disgusted.

"I'll get some paper towels," Charlie volunteers, and Annie nods eagerly. It will give her time to restore the microfiches to their drawer. She makes sure to put them back in chronological order, and shuts the drawers just as Charlie returns with a roll of paper towels and a bowl of hot water.

"So what are you working on so diligently, Annie?" Charlie asks, while she wipes the cabinet and scrubs the carpet clean.

"Oh, somebody was looking for an old obit," she says, bending down to brush some yogurt spatters off her shoes to hide the fib. "Well, I'd better get back upstairs. Thanks for the help, Charlie."

Charlie nods and walks her to the door. "I was just up in the office talking to Duncan," he says, "when that Davis woman came charging in. She started raving about our page— Ben, right? I can never keep Ben and his brother Brad apart in my mind. Anyway, she said something about Ben's pierced lip? Had you noticed?"

Now Annie understands what it was that she saw sparkling below Ben's lip. Charlie doesn't wait for a reply. "She went on and on about how she'd never hire someone like that—after all, she has an 'appearance code,' in her business, how come the library doesn't? And furthermore, her son Timmy is certainly better qualified for the page position than Ben is, she said—better grades, highly motivated, and planning on going on to college. Timmy also has supportive and college educated parents who are well respected in the community, etc., etc.—so how come we chose someone like Ben over him?" Charlie shakes his head.

"What did Duncan say?" Annie asks. *How could Lorraine Davis do this to Ben, her son's buddy? And to Sally, who was supposedly a friend of hers? Well, it's typical of the woman.*

"Don't know. I left."

"What do *you* think, then?" Annie asks. It is probably an inappropriate question, but Charlie is a friend, and she is not at her desk now.

"I grew up in the big city, Annie. Piercings and tattoos don't prejudice me against people, especially kids. Ben's a smart boy, open and friendly, not afraid of working hard. Deals well with patrons, I've watched him. Very helpful. In the interview we had with Timmy Davis on the other hand, that boy came off as smug and superior. I think we made the right choice. This isn't *Hahvad,* after all."

"Thanks, Charlie. It's a good thing we've got you. But, oh dear, now I really have to run. I'm very late. Don't want anyone to think I get special privileges just because I'm married to the boss," she says.

Charlie laughs. "I'll take care of the mess, don't worry," he says, returning to collect the soiled paper towels and bowl of water. "I promise not to let Eagle-Eye Hedwig find any evidence of your most recent infraction of the rules. You just run along."

• • •

CHAPTER THIRTY-NINE

"Patience is a flower that grows not in every garden."
(Old proverb)

"Now that we're married, are you and I still supposed to each have a turn at library coffee night?" Annie asks.

Annie and Duncan are slouched on opposite corners of the couch in the living room, sharing the day's paper. Now and then they have to switch, when an article is continued in another section. Duncan looks up from the paper while pondering her question.

"Well now. Hm. Yes, I think we should. It would seem cheap to do otherwise, don't you think? And after all, it's not that big a deal to get ready for."

"Okay then. I think it's your turn this week," Annie says, turning back to her article. Duncan rustles his papers a bit before crumpling a page into a ball and tossing it at Annie.

"Hey," she says, "I hope that's not the ending of my article."

It is the first evening in what seems like a long time that they have spent relaxing at home together. In fact, the first since the wedding. And yet, while enjoying it, Annie feels impatience crawling under her skin. She wants to go over to the computer and finish her search on the Moonies. She wants to go back to Hammond Castle and look for information on the Gyrad in order to check if what Tommy fished out for her at Norman's Woe could be Hammond's probably most famous invention (avoiding Spoffie while she does it, of course.) Annie has made an admirable effort not to bring up any subject tonight that might touch on the murder of Ethan, feeling that bonding with her new husband must be given ample opportunity. They read and read, and then read some more, and Annie is beginning to squirm. Impatience is slowly winning out over her sense of conjugal obligation.

"Charlie told me that Lorraine Davis charged into your office today with some complaint about Ben," she says, suddenly remembering.

"That she did," he says, putting down the paper. "Apparently Ben has had his lower lip pierced. He has a small sparkling stone there, I checked. I didn't make any comment to him about it, though. Just a typical teenage impulse, I'm sure. Give it a couple of weeks and it'll be gone. I hear it can be very irritating—just drinking out of a cup is supposed to be a challenge. As for Mrs. Davis, I think she was trying to suggest I should let Ben go and then hire her son Timmy instead. I smiled very politely and said that wasn't possible, and then to change the subject I asked how her son was doing with his essay and which inventor he had decided to write about."

Annie sits up straight. "Who?" she asks—hoping, naturally, that he will say "Hammond."

"Alexander Graham Bell."

Annie hisses, disappointed. It sounds as if someone let the air out of a balloon.

"Curious thing, though," Duncan says. Annie waits. "Apparently, she said, Bell had a hand in getting Hammond started in his field. And Bell came to stay in Rockport, Mrs. Davis thinks. It seems Timmy wanted to include this fact in his essay. I didn't ask her how she found out, though," he adds.

"Oh, that's mentioned in at least one of the Bell biographies. The family stayed in a house in Pigeon Cove, that greenish-gray one, I think, on the left side going up Powsel Hill. There's a marker on it, or used to be, anyway. I think that's where he got the news that his newborn son had died. Or else that's where the wife was, and he was abroad and had to hurry home. Something like that."

"Maybe you ought to check it out, and then call Mrs. Davis and give her that information?" Duncan suggests.

"And maybe not." Annie frowns. "I've given Lorraine Davis enough information for Timmy's homework and assignments to earn him a doctorate. Besides, she's the one who does all the research for his essays. She should sign her name on the papers and get her own doctorate."

"Now, Annie. I know it goes against your sense of justice, but it might be a good move. Politically, I mean. Public relations are important in a small town library, you know."

Annie makes a face.

"Besides," Duncan continues, "it might give you an opportunity to ask how Mrs. Davis discovered that there was a connection between Bell and Hammond. If you take my meaning." He won't tell Annie directly to trick the woman into mentioning any missing books and papers—if indeed she has any knowledge of them, which he doubts, anyway. But Annie's eyes sparkle suddenly, and he knows she will call Mrs. Davis first thing in the morning.

· · ·

CHAPTER FORTY

"This is one of those cases
in which the imagination is baffled by the facts."
(Remark made by Winston Churchill in the House of Commons
following the parachute descent in Scotland of Rudolf Hess)

However, first thing in the morning Annie drives over to the castle. She is early, the museum is not open yet, and she parks the car in the lot and goes for a stroll on the castle grounds. The wind is coming up strong from the water, which today shows dark marine blue between the stone arches. Fall is sharp in the air, and the leaves are turning. Beech, birch, and hickory leaves are already yellow, and in wet areas the swamp maples are on fire in flames of orange, gold, and red. The tupelos have started turning scarlet in their peculiar fashion, one random leaf at a time. Annie shivers and walks through the formal part of the castle garden. The flowers lie prostrate, bloomed out and covered with sour-smelling leaves from the ancient, tall trees that cast such a lovely, dappled shade in the summer. Farther down the hill, near the water, the trees are stunted, crouching and bent over like old crones leaning away from the cruel winds.

She hurries back up to the road to get out of the wind and decides to walk over in the direction of the Cardinal's Villa. She won't be able to enter the grounds, of course. A great storm fence was erected around the property in the early days to keep curious (or irate) Gloucesterites from looking in. People have long since stopped honking and jeering when they drive by, a common pastime back then. Coming around the corner not far from the property, Annie sees a bicyclist approaching and crossing the street, slowing down before turning in through the entrance gate. She can hardly believe her eyes, but there is no mistaking that spiked hair. It is Vinnie. What on earth would Vinnie be doing on Moonie property? Slightly alarmed, she hurries forward to the gate.

Down in the yard Vinnie leans his bike up against a tree and walks down the path toward the villa. There is no one else around, so she follows him, dashing from tree to tree, keeping an eye on the black-clad figure. Vinnie enters the house through a side door, and Annie creeps closer. She waits, and then sees him through a first floor window, talking to an older woman. The woman puts her arm around his shoulders and they stand talking, heads close together. After a while a man joins them, and then the three disappear together. Annie skulks around outside the building, anxiously keeping an eye out for anyone who might be watching the grounds. Standing partly concealed behind a great blue spruce, she hops up and down, trying to catch a glimpse of Vinnie in one of the many other windows. Lights are on in parts of the mansion, but she sees no other people. When she hears a door slam, she hides behind some shrubs. After a few minutes she steps back out. A man standing on the lawn catches sight of her and walks up, frowning slightly.

"Can I help you? Are you looking for someone?" He is soft-spoken, polite. The face is weathered, which makes it hard to determine his age. Balding, dressed in jeans and a gray sweatshirt, he stops a few feet away from her.

"Oh, I thought I saw someone I know walking in here," Annie says.

"Why don't you come inside then, maybe we can find out," he says.

"Oh no, that's all right. I was probably mistaken, anyway," she says.

The man looks dubious. "We don't kidnap people, if that's what you're afraid of," he says, with a cold smile.

"Of course not," Annie says quickly. "It's only that, well, I'm on my way somewhere, and I'm in a bit of a rush now. But thanks anyway." She gives the man a nervous smile and starts to walk around him. He steps out of her way and watches as she hurries down the driveway. When she reaches the gate she turns around and, seeing him still standing there, gives him a small wave. He waves back, his face blank.

Annie returns to the castle, a little shaken and deep in thought. Vinnie? Could Vinnie be somehow involved in the mystery? What would *he* have had against Ethan? Jealousy of someone guaranteed a successful future? Annie has briefly toyed with the idea of Vinnie as Spofford-Braxton's accomplice, since he seems to be so familiar with Hammond's inventions. But if Vinnie is a Moonie, could he have been working on *their* behalf? She shudders, remembering seeing him in the workshop, restoring items for the museum. How knowledgeable is he? Might he have gotten the Gyrad working in order to crash the *Pioneer*, for instance? With his tattoos and spiked hair, and the language, Vinnie seems such an ordinary teenager. Could there be another side to him? What *is* his connection to the Moonies?

. . .

"Well, you're a frequent visitor these days," Ruth says when Annie gets inside the Castle.

"I know. Our students are doing an essay on inventors at the moment, so I'm arming myself with some up-close-and-personal facts. Are you open yet? Just wanted to have a look in the inventions room," Annie says.

"I'll come with you and turn on the lights. You'll have it all to yourself for another half hour, and then we'll be open. Want a cup of coffee? Just making some. I'll bring you a cup when it's ready."

"Oh, don't bother, I'll come and pick it up in a few minutes. You've got plenty to do, I'm sure."

"Well, Vinnie is actually supposed to be here to help this morning, but he hasn't showed up yet," Ruth says, looking at her watch. Annie hesitates but can't make herself mention the fact that she saw Vinnie enter the Moonie property and go straight into the Villa.

Annie spends a few minutes looking around before remembering where she saw the copy of the U.S. Patent Office paper, with drawings, specifications, and claims of the Gyrad patent application. The patent was issued on June 20, 1922. The first time Hammond applied for it was in 1913. Nine years. You have to be patient to be an inventor.

"System for the radio control of moving bodies," it says, and then the drawings follow. Annie takes her own rusty gadget out of her backpack, trying to compare it to the drawings. There are too many little numbers and arrows in the drawing, referring to a page containing explanations. Once she is able to focus in on the details, she begins to see some similarities, but also differences. Hers does not appear to be the same as that in the drawings. Maybe it's an earlier version? Or a later one? Knowing how many patents Edison took out for what was basically one single invention, she remembers Edison's advice to Hammond: *Patent everything!* In other words, every time you change something even a little bit, you must patent it again. Annie feels no wiser and puts her Gyrad back in the bag just as Ruth arrives with a tray holding a cup of coffee and a plate of donuts. She puts it down on a side table.

"Here you go. I'll be running back, since we're open and people are coming in. Vinnie just arrived, but he's helping Henry with something. Are you all set in here? Need anything? Any questions?"

"Oh no, thank you Ruth. I'll just look around for a little longer before I leave."

She spends a few minutes looking at the photographs of Hammond. She feels she is somehow letting him down. The handsome face gazes at her, serene, trusting. *"You will find the answer,"* he seems to say.

"I'm doing my best," she mumbles. Time to go or she'll be late again.

•   •   •

CHAPTER FORTY-ONE

*"There is nothing so easy but that it becomes difficult
when you do it reluctantly."*
(Publius Terentius Afer, The Self-Tormentor)

"Josie called," Duncan says when she arrives and walks into his office, flushed from running from the house to the library. With the shortage of staff parking, they have agreed not to drive the few blocks to work.

"Oh, dear," Annie says, stung by guilt. She hasn't talked to Josie and Judge since they came back from the funeral. Usually the four of them get together for dinner or coffee frequently, but Annie has been preoccupied lately.

"Give her a call. She asked if we'd like to come over later, either for dinner or dessert, whatever suited. Do you have anything planned for dinner? Otherwise we could bring takeout, so they don't have to fuss," Duncan suggests.

Annie hasn't given dinner the slightest thought yet, and is quite amenable to this idea. "Sounds good to me, Dunc. Would be nice to spend an evening with friends for a change." Duncan nods emphatically, and Annie's feelings of guilt double. She had better back off on her crime investigation for a while, and pay more attention to Duncan—and to her job at the reference desk, for that matter. She starts by giving her husband a new-wifely kiss, which is observed by Stuart who just walks in the door.

"Well, pardon me," Stuart says, turning on his foot. Before he is out the door, Annie stops him.

"It's okay, Stu, I was just leaving," she says, smiling benignly.

"And a good thing, too," Duncan says, doing a Groucho Marx-thing with his eyebrows and leering at her as she walks out the door.

"Well, Stuart, what can I do for you today?" she hears Duncan say as she walks toward the stairs.

When Annie gets to her desk she calls Lorraine Davis.

"Hi, Lorraine. This is Annie Quitnot. Duncan said you were looking for information on the connection between Alexander Graham Bell and Jack Hammond. Is that right?"

"Oh. Hello, Annie. Yes, it is, although I didn't actually expect you to call me."

"Well, here I am. What do you have, so far?"

"Just a notice I read—forget where, though—that Bell had been staying in Rockport. Thought maybe the two had gotten together then."

"Aha. But you don't remember the source, you say?"

"Sorry, no. Returned all the books to the library already, unfortunately." Lorraine sounds more snippy than sorry. Has she actually returned *all* the books?

"Do you recall whether this was in one of the Bell biographies, or one on Hammond?" Annie asks, trying to make a leading question sound casual.

"One on Bell. Didn't know you had any on Hammond. Didn't see any on the shelf." Lorraine says. No way to tell whether she is evasive or telling the truth. *Oh, well.*

"I see. Well, Lorraine, Bell and his wife did stay in Rockport for a while, in Pigeon Cove. I think there's still a sign on the house where they stayed—it's a greenish-gray house, just past the tool company, up on the left. His wife gave birth to a baby boy there, Edward, but he only lived a few hours.

Soon after that Mr. and Mrs. Bell sailed for England. But this was in 1881, and Hammond didn't move into the Castle until 1929. Somewhere in between those dates, though, Hammond worked with Bell for three years in the U.S. Patent Office. So they certainly did know each other. Bell apparently was very helpful to Hammond, who was much younger, of course."

"Why Annie, thank you so much. That will make Timmy's paper so much more interesting. You know, the local angle. Nice of you to call. Well, you must be busy, so I won't take up any more of your time. Good-bye."

Annie hears a click. Lorraine has hung up. Whoa—what was that now, the royal brush-off? For a moment, Lorraine Davis had almost managed to sound gracious.

"You're quite welcome, Lorraine. Well, I'll see you soon, I'm sure. Bye, now," she says into the dead receiver.

Next Annie tends to the day's stack of reference questions. By lunchtime it has been reduced by more than half, and Annie decides to spend a few minutes of her break on a personal search. She clicks on one of the "people search" sites and punches in "Jordan Ford." After a few tries, she has located three possible phone numbers in the vicinity of L.A. She jots them down for later. Then she walks upstairs to discuss dinner plans with Duncan.

"How about this: you call Josie and tell her we're bringing dinner and wine, and then all she has to do is provide coffee after. I'll order dinner, to be picked up...say, around seven? That'll give us time to go home and freshen up after work," Duncan suggests. *And make a few phone calls,* Annie thinks.

"Good plan," she says.

• • •

CHAPTER FORTY-TWO

*"To let friendship die away by negligence and silence, is certainly
not wise. It is voluntarily to throw away one of the greatest
comforts of this weary pilgrimage."*
(Boswell, Life of Johnson)

After a generous buffet from the Fish Shack that includes
clam chowder (and a bowl of haddock chowder for
Duncan, who eyes clams with a certain amount of suspicion),
lobster rolls (which meet with Duncan's lazy-man's approval),
and a heaping platter of fried clams (*with* the bellies, of
course, there's just no other way to have them, Annie says, as
Duncan makes a face), they sit back in Judge's living room.
The windows look out over stables and paddocks and the
little guest cottage in the back, where Judge's granddaughter
Dot lived until recently. The country lane continues past the
cottage into the South Woods, which lie in darkness now, the
sun having set a few hours ago. The moon, on the other hand,
is nearly full and casts a white light over the outbuildings and
the rustic wooden fences that surround the paddocks.

"That was divine," Josie says. "Anyone ready for coffee
yet?"

They all groan. Maybe later.

"Well, what have you two been up to?" Duncan asks.

"Not much, to tell the truth," Judge replies. "Sheik of
Araby was down with a lame leg—I was afraid he'd broken

it, but we had it X-rayed, and it appears to be all right. The other horses seem more accepting of him now, strangely enough. Sheik's such a dominant fellow—I suppose they feel less intimidated since his injury. The foal is growing well; she'll make a good riding horse some day. Good temperament, you can tell. Otherwise, well, Josie's been busy pruning the garden. With winter coming, it was high time to tame some of the shrubbery around here."

"Yes, I noticed," Annie says. "I'm glad you don't prune and trim like Judge, though," she says, turning to Josie. "He just makes big, round balls out of everything—forsythia, bridal veil, holly. Why do men do that? I like bushes to have a wild form."

"Aren't you generalizing a bit, m'love?" Duncan says. "I like a wild form myself, now and then," he adds. Judge lets out one of his belly laughs, and Annie realizes with a pang how much she has missed these evenings, and the friendship of Judge and Josie.

"Oh, I mustn't forget," Josie says. "I spoke to Eleanor Haskell, and she'll be coming up for a visit. She's arriving on Saturday and will stay here with us for a few days, maybe a week. So make sure to set some time aside to come and visit then."

"Actually," Judge says, turning to Josie, "I just spoke to Spofford-Braxton. I haven't even had time to tell you this, Josie. He called just before these two arrived. He was calling about something else, but when I told him Eleanor was coming he suggested we bring her over to the castle for sherry on Saturday evening—after hours, so she won't have to risk 'parading her grief in front in front of tourists,' as he put it." Judge turns to Duncan. "Would you two like to come along? It might make it easier for her to have a little distraction available."

Duncan does not look overly enthusiastic but nods anyway. "Of course, Judge. We'd be glad to, wouldn't we, Annie?" he says, looking at Annie, who tries not to look overly enthusiastic, either. Another chance to snoop around in the castle, and maybe feel Spoffie out in the process, is perfectly fine with her.

"Of course, we'd love to. But now, Josie, how about if I help you make some coffee? All this food is making me logy," Annie says.

Duncan sees through her little diversion, of course—knowing that Annie is more than happy for a chance to visit the castle—but smiles indulgently. He might as well accept the fact that he is married to a terrier, who won't let go of one old slipper until she is offered a more interesting one.

· · ·

CHAPTER FORTY-THREE

"The days may come, the days may go,
But still the hands of memory weave
The blissful dreams of long ago."
(George Cooper, "Sweet Genevieve")

When they get home Annie makes her phone calls to California while Duncan is in the shower. On the third try, she is successful.

"Hello, may I speak to Jordan Ford, please?"

"That's my dad, but he's not home. He's in Alaska, won't be back for a couple of weeks," a young, female voice replies.

"How about Mrs. Ford?" Annie tries.

"She's not home either. She's in Seattle."

"Who's home with *you,* then?" Annie can't help asking. How can people leave their kids alone like that? She thinks she hears a chuckle.

"Nobody. I'm in college. I take care of myself. Who is this, anyway?"

"Oh, I'm sorry! My name is Annie Quitnot, and I'm calling from Massachusetts. I went to school with your dad, if I have the right Jordan Ford, and I was just wondering how he was doing."

"Then...you're calling all the way from Rockport?"

Annie feels triumphant. She has obviously found Jordy.

"Yes, I am. I was talking to your grandfather the other day, that's when I got the idea to call."

"My *grandfather?* He's alive?"

"Sure."

"How come we've never heard from him?"

"Well, he didn't have Jordy's number," Annie says carefully. "I had to spend some time looking it up. What's Jordy up to, anyway?"

"He's fishing, up in Alaska, as I said. Goes out on one of the big crab boats. When he's through he'll be meeting Mom in Seattle, and then they'll come home together."

"Who's he working for, one of those big international companies?" Annie asks, on a fishing trip of her own, trying to find out whether Jordan is still a Moonie.

"Alaska Crab Fisheries. Some of the big ones you may know of are owned by the Moonies, but Dad doesn't work for them," she says.

"I see. What's your name, if you don't mind telling me?" Annie asks.

"Libby. Anyway, speaking of the Moonies, did you know Dad when he was a Moonie?" she asks, sounding curious. Annie wishes she could see Libby's face.

"No, Libby, I didn't. Your dad's a few years older than I, and I didn't know him all that well, really, I just remember him from school. He was a good basketball player. I used to go and watch the games. And Doc Ford, your grandfather, was our family doctor until…well, until he retired," she says.

"Is he okay? Grandfather, I mean."

"Well, that depends what you mean by okay. Can I be honest with you?" And when Libby says yes, Annie goes on to describe her visit to the grandfather, and to tell Libby some of what Doc Ford had said about Jordy.

When she's finished, there's a long silence. Then Libby says, "Dad never told me any of this. He just told us that he didn't get along with his parents and moved away from home. He did tell us that he had joined the Moonies for a while after they offered him a job. Then he came out here and started over, and never looked back. You mean my grandparents were divorced? I bet Dad doesn't know that. I don't know why he never got in touch with his dad. I thought my grandparents were dead. We're a pretty happy family, Mom and Dad and I. My parents are happy together. I wonder what Dad would feel if I told him all this."

"Well, Libby, you'll have to think about it. I wouldn't want to cause any unhappiness to anyone. Anytime you want to call me, though, you go right ahead."

She gives Libby her address and phone number, and her grandfather's, too, in case Libby should ever get a notion to contact him.

"Thanks for calling me, Annie. Somehow it feels really good knowing that I have a grandpa somewhere out there. Mom was an only child, and her folks were gone before I was born. We don't have any relatives out here except an old aunt of my mother's."

Duncan steps out of the shower and goes upstairs to the bedroom. Annie hangs up the phone, and when Duncan comes back down he is wearing his checkered flannel robe, which is ancient and frayed and has a belt that doesn't match. Annie makes a mental note to get him a new one for Christmas.

Well, she's made contact. Now it's all up to Jordy.

• • •

CHAPTER FORTY-FOUR

"Don't tell her everything you know,
but tell her one thing and keep another thing hidden."
(Homer, The Odyssey, XI, 441)

Unable to sleep, Annie gets out of bed in the middle of the night. All it takes is just one glass of wine and she is wide awake, and she's had a couple. To make matters worse, Judge's wine glasses are of the old-fashioned, large goblet variety. She slips out of bed carefully, trying not to wake Duncan, and goes downstairs to the computer. Might as well finish the couple of searches she has bookmarked. She has managed to find a few references on the Internet regarding the local uproar in Gloucester after the Moonies' purchase of the Cardinal Cushing Villa. When she gets into the first one, she learns about a debacle initiated by the city council.

After the pope's and the cardinal's inability to reverse the sale of the Villa, the Gloucester city council had offered a resolution in which citizens were asked to refuse to sell property to Moon's Unification Church, especially along the waterfront, "thereby protecting the future of our children from encroachment by the Rev. Moon and his followers in trying to control Gloucester's waterfront property, which would prevent the situation which happened in the state of California." (Referring, of course, to the Jones sect in California, and later the mass suicide at Jonestown, Guyana.) The resolution had been met with everything from passionate approval to ridicule and warnings of a "Hitlerian scenario," she reads in the report.

She feels a hand on her back and turns around to find Duncan.

"Duncan, you scared me!" Annie says.

"And how do you think I felt, waking up and finding my wife gone from my side? Sorry, didn't mean to scare you, though. Now, Annie my dear, what do I have to do to stop you from pursuing this, day and night?" He says it gently and smiles to show that he may be exasperated, but not offended or angry.

"Divorce me?" she suggests, with a little smile of her own.

"Bit dramatic. Fire you, maybe."

"Now, there's a thought."

"I have a different thought. How about if we tackle this together, like married people should? I am just as interested in seeing this mystery solved as you are, honey."

Honey? Annie cringes, but lets it pass.

"What do you say? Want to tell me what you have so far?" he continues.

So Annie tells him (with a little judicious editing) what she has discovered. She informs him that now, not only are the Hammond biographies and files missing, the complete set of cards relating to Hammond have also been pulled from the local history card file. It's as if the library's material on Hammond never existed. She goes on to describe the Coast Guard's diving finds (airily avoiding to mention how they were acquired) and the visit to Doc Ford. Then she tells him about seeing Vinnie entering through the gates of the Cardinal Cushing Villa, and the salient points of what she has learned of the history of the Moonies and their long interest in buying up Gloucester property. Without going into her visit to his property, she mentions that Spofford-Braxton lives on Eastern Point.

Duncan listens patiently to it all. When Annie gets to the Moonies, he becomes thoughtful, pursing his lips. He doesn't want to tell her the reason for this, which is that Charlie has come to him wondering what Annie's sudden interest in the Moonies was. Duncan was rather perplexed himself when Charlie brought it up.

Charlie discovered her interest when he found the microfiche card Annie had forgotten in the reader in her great hurry to get back to her desk. Duncan explained to Charlie that Annie was trying to solve Ethan's murder, and that possibly one of her thoughts might be that the Moonies could be involved.

Charlie laughed uproariously before suggesting that Duncan rein his wife in, redirect her, and make her put that kind of effort into her "real job." "Speaking as a trustee," he had said, "I think it would be better if you could keep her out of these things. Her reputation already took a hit with the Carlo thing—no, Duncan, hear me out. I don't mean the murder itself, but you know how people are in small towns, the prurient interest in secret love affairs and such. And now I'll speak as a friend: take her off somewhere for a few days— or, if you can't take the time yourself, send her off with her friends for a girl's weekend out. But, by God, man, you've got to get her under control!"

Charlie's advice is probably quite sensible, but Duncan knows it would do no good whatsoever to tell Annie any of this. However, maybe a weekend with her friends would do her good. It will have to be the weekend after the coming one, though, since they have promised to go to the castle on Saturday night with Judge and Josie and Eleanor Haskell.

"Come on, Annie, the bed feels lonely without you," Duncan says.

"Poor bed! Isn't there anything you can do to make it feel better?"

Duncan steps forward and pushes the "off" button on the computer with his toe.

"Look what you just did! You didn't shut it down properly! In the morning we'll have to sit and wait for it to go through the whole scanning process and passwords and all. I was going to shut down any minute anyway!" she says, banging his chest with her fists.

"Come now, wife. Time for bed and..." he says, without finishing the sentence.

"And what? I hope that's not an empty promise," she says.

• • •

CHAPTER FORTY-FIVE

"Bluid is thicker than water."
(Sir Walter Scott, "The Lord of the Isles")

When Annie gets out of work on Thursday, she hurries back to the castle, hoping to get there before they close. No one is in the shop, so she lets herself in and walks around looking for Vinnie. When she gets to the courtyard, she hears his voice from the bridge.

"Hiya," he says, waving to her.

The yellow tape is gone, and the courtyard looks normal except for the fact that the pool is still without water. Annie walks around it. Dead weeds cling to the edges of the pool, and the bottom is streaked with some white residue, probably from the water-purifying chemical, she thinks. She joins Vinnie on the bridge, and they cross it and go into the Gothic Bedroom.

"So, Vinnie, what are you up to?"

"Cleaning. Just finished dusting the cardinal, as a matter of fact. Thought maybe he could use, like, some polish, too, but Henry says that's a no-no."

A life-sized bronze bust of Cardinal Cushing sits by the bed in the Gothic Bedroom, keeping an eye on whoever sleeps there—would have kept an eye on Duncan and Annie, as a matter of fact, had they spent their wedding night there. Annie pats the cardinal on the biretta. Poor Cardinal.

He must have been quite unhappy with the appellation of the mansion next door as the "Cardinal Cushing Villa." The cardinal was a modest man, not given to vacationing by the seaside. Unfortunately senility set in, and despite what some people believe, he didn't have anything to do with the sale of the Villa.

"Vinnie," Annie says, hesitating, wondering whether she is making a mistake in asking the question, "what were you doing at the cardinal's Villa? I was out for a walk and happened to see you turn in there."

Vinnie looks at her, stricken, she doesn't know by what feeling—guilt, anxiety, fear? She can't read his face. He avoids looking at her and does not answer right away. Then he raises his eyes to hers, giving her a look that is both pleading and determined.

"Miss Quitnot, please, you can't tell anyone," he says, almost in a whisper, looking around as if to check if someone is listening.

"Tell them what, Vinnie?"

"I…that is…my folks, I mean my biological parents, they're Moonies. I go to see them sometimes at the Morning Garden—that's what the Moonies call the Villa—even though I'm not supposed to. My foster parents don't want me to have any contact with them. But when I turn eighteen I'll be able to do what I want," he says, a little obstinately.

"You were taken away from your parents because they are Moonies?"

"No, no. That wouldn't be legal. But my parents weren't able to take care of me and my sister, so we were farmed out. My sister is younger; she's staying in another foster family in the western part of the state, so I don't get to see her. My parents are good people—just, you know, misled."

"So you are not a Moonie yourself?"

"No. My foster parents are Episcopalians. They used to make me go to their church. I don't go to church a lot anymore, though. But they wouldn't like it if they knew I had contact with my parents. My mom wants to leave the Moonies, but my dad says they wouldn't make it out in the world on their own. Mom's blind. Born that way. Dad's sort of a loser. He's a fisherman, like my grandpa was. My great grandpa and his brothers came from the Azores. All fishermen. Dad used to have his own boat. When fishing went downhill he started to drink, and then he lost the boat. He's okay now, the Moonies cured him of the drinking. I'd like to help my parents out, once I'm through school."

Annie, feeling ashamed about her earlier suspicions, squeezes her eyes shut so they won't sting. "So the Moonies let you come and go there?" she asks.

"They don't mind. They think I'll join them one day. I don't say one way or another."

Annie has suddenly noticed that Vinnie isn't using his regular teenage speak. "I promise I won't say a word, Vinnie." Annie gives Cardinal Cushing's head another pat, as if to prove her sincerity. Cardinal Cushing looks serene, just as Hammond had a while ago. She thinks for a moment, and then makes up her mind.

"Listen, Vinnie, you know a lot about Hammond's inventions, right? Could you have a look at something for me?"

Vinnie checks the window overlooking the courtyard to see if anyone is looking for him yet. "Sure. Looks like I need to do some more dusting here," he says, waving the feather duster about aimlessly. Annie pulls what she suspects might be a Gyrad out of her bag, and Vinnie's eyes widen with interest.

"Wow, where'd you get that?" he says.

"Long story," Annie says. "Could you tell if this is one of Hammond's inventions? Like a Gyrad? I've tried to check it against some of the drawings in the Invention Room, but I can't tell."

"Lemme have a look. Man, what happened to this poor thing? Looks like it's taken a beating." He takes the gadget and turns it around, studies it from every angle. It does not appear to Annie as though he has seen it before. He seems curious about it, though, seems to try to figure it out. He rubs one of the edges, spits on his finger, and rubs some more. He brings it under a light and bends close to it. Shakes his head.

"Nope. Don't think so. See here? There are initials here, E.F., and a Patent Application Date, which is almost unreadable. Nineteen seventeen, I think. It might be part of something *like* a Gyrad, but I've seen Hammond's. It's quite different, really. Ethan and I had a good look at the one Hammond designed. In fact, we were working on it for a while, just cleaning it a bit. It might still be out in the work-shop, actually."

Vinnie looks suddenly sad. He stares out through the window and down at the pool, and shakes his head.

"Ethan was real smart, you know. Could have become an inventor just like his uncle, I bet. He taught me a lot about his uncle's inventions, how they worked and stuff. In fact, he said he'd like to put out a book on them some day. Said he was talkin' to a publisher about it." Hefting the gadget, he returns to the subject. "Anyway, this one's different, but it might do the same job. So where'd you find it?"

Annie hedges. "I can't tell you that, Vinnie."

"What are you gonna do with it? I mean, when you're through with it, can I have another look? I'd like to figure out if it would work."

"Oh, I'm pretty sure it works, Vinnie," she says.

"Oh, man," Vinnie says. "How d'ya get a hold of this, anyway? I'd really love to have it—when you're finished with it. I mean if you don't, like, have a use for it, you know."

"Well, Vinnie, we'll have to see. It's closing time here, and I've got to hurry back home and cook dinner for my husband. But thanks for your expertise! And I promise not to mention your visits next door. That's your business. Hope it all works out okay in the end."

Annie is almost glad to hear Vinnie's teenage jargon return. But the last few minutes have proved that there is more to him than she previously realized.

• • •

CHAPTER FORTY-SIX

"Knowledge puffeth up, but charity edifieth."
(Bible, 1 Corinthians 8:1)

When she gets back home, Duncan is busy baking librarian tea bread, using (without asking permission) a cupful of Annie's Dogtown cranberries. He gives her a guilty look.

"Oops, caught red-handed," he says. "Only figuratively, of course, cranberries aren't that juicy," he adds.

"That's what they're for, silly, for your tea bread," she says, popping a berry in her mouth, grimacing at the crunchy tartness.

Now then, what to make for supper? With the librarians coming she doesn't want to stink up the house; otherwise she could reheat the leftover fried clams that Josie insisted they take home with them. She would have heated them in the oven, naturally, not in the microwave, where they would get soggy. Annie decides to leave the clams in the freezer and make a salad instead. She slices cheddar cheese, smoked cold mackerel (only slightly fragrant in comparison with the clams), and hard-boiled eggs to go on top. Tiny grape tomatoes, kalamata olives, and some dill from the pot on the windowsill finish the dish. Good enough. Lovely, in fact. But no wine tonight. She needs a good night's sleep.

A stiff, chill wind coming in from the northeast heralds another storm. Duncan starts a fire to raise the temperature in the living room a little. Annie hopes Tommy hasn't put his lobster traps back out yet. The shoreline is going to be covered with lobster traps this fall, with one surprise storm after another. And the price of lobster will skyrocket. Augustus comes shuffling into the living room, giving them one of his looks: *Thought you'd light a fire and lounge about in here without me, huh?* He takes a position in front of his favorite leather chair, the one nearest the fireplace, and waits. Duncan looks at Annie, who bursts out laughing.

"It's your furniture!"

"What's mine is yours, my dove."

"Oh. So now I'm a candy bar."

"You told me to keep trying."

Gussie is getting impatient with all this needless chatter. Duncan picks him up and puts him in the chair, fluffing the pillows behind his back a little.

"Oh boy. How come you don't fluff *my* pillows?" Annie says.

"Watch out, here I come. I'll fluff your pillows, all right."

Annie screeches with delight as Duncan starts fluffing her pillows, and they miss the knock on the door. Duncan reddens slightly when Marie, Jean, Maureen, and Geri start clearing their throats behind him.

"Oh, welcome, welcome, have a seat everyone," he says, rushing about, moving chairs into a more or less circular grouping. Gussie sighs deeply before sliding off his chair and padding off to the kitchen. The oven is still giving off some little warmth from the earlier baking, and Duncan thoughtfully puts a braided mat down on the floor in front of the stove for Augustus before bringing a large coffee tray into the living room.

The librarians go through their usual routine. Annie jots down a long list of holiday reading recommendations. Afterwards they go over upcoming meetings and discuss library and town preparations for the holidays—decorations, displays, and events. Nothing religious, of course, as far as the library is concerned. The town still puts on a Christmas Pageant, with the manger placed on the Congregational Church lawn. A young girl of the town, whose identity is kept secret until the start of the pageant, is chosen each year to act as Mary. The Pageant is an old tradition, and so far it has not been stopped. Santa Claus, whom no one seems to object to, arrives by lobster boat in early December, and is transported to the huge Christmas tree in Dock Square—until recently by horse and cart, but these days atop a fire engine with lights flashing and sirens blaring. Santa pulls a switch to light the tree, and carol singing follows. Sometimes local politicians have a few words to say after the tree-lighting, which is when people start meandering across the street to the Fish Shack for some free hot cocoa. The cocoa is always appreciated, after all that singing and huffing and puffing in the cold air.

Stuart has not showed up for library coffee tonight. Perhaps he has just forgotten. He is not greatly missed. His caustic remarks about patrons—children in particular—and snide comments in response to any book suggestion not his own always put a damper on an otherwise pleasant evening. The congenial members that meet tonight seem to have covered most everything and get up to have seconds of coffee and cranberry bread, spreading some by now nicely softened butter on the bread.

"Anything new about those missing Hammond items?" Marie asks. Annie has avoided talking about this, being sensitive to how Duncan feels about it. Now she looks at him for guidance.

"No, nothing yet," he says simply, without bothering to mention the further development of the cards gone missing.

"Oh, well, maybe they'll turn up," Maureen says optimistically. Maureen has a charming Pollyanna attitude about everything, which is probably why she has arrived at her advanced age vivacious and fit as a fiddle, still able to work and serve shut-ins who are far younger than she.

There is a knock on the door. It is Stuart, looking grim and irritable.

"Just came from the library. I noticed the light was on upstairs, so I went in to check—thought maybe Esa or one of the pages had left it on. Didn't see anyone there, so I turned the light out and went downstairs. The doors were all locked, and there were no signs of a break-in. As I was leaving, Officer Hale turned up at the back door—the police had received a report of lights on in the library, he said. I told him I'd checked everything out, but he insisted on having a look for himself. Which is why I'm late. By the way, your computer was left on, Annie," Stuart says, with evident glee. The unwritten rule in the library is to turn off the computer before going home for the day, or else expect to find it messed up in the morning. Annie has learned from experience that when her computer is left on, patrons will feel free to use it if she is not at her desk—and will even tell their children to. (*There, Johnnie, why don't you play on the computer while Mommy finds a book?*)

"Really?" she says now. "I'm sure I turned it off before I left."

"You seemed to be in a hurry leaving work. Maybe you forgot," Stuart says. "I was coming down the stairs just as you ran out the front door." He is enjoying this immensely, pointing out her imperfections publicly, especially in front of Duncan. Anyone else would just have turned her computer off and left it at that.

"Well, I had an errand to do before getting ready for tonight," Annie says, a little defensively. Stuart's faultfinding always smarts, especially since he takes such pleasure in it. Now he smiles, gratified at her discomposure.

"Whatever you say," he says, looking away from her, having made his point. "Are we all done here?"

"More or less. Just social hour left. Like a cup of coffee, Stuart?" Duncan points to the coffee tray. Stuart declines and leaves as quickly as he came.

"Isn't he a pleasant fellow," Geri says sarcastically. "Well, if we're all set, I think I'll leave, too," she says, which starts a general exodus. Annie and Duncan carry the dishes out to the kitchen. Gussie opens one eye a crack, annoyed at being wakened out of his warm stupor. Duncan makes it up to him with a small treat before turning out the light.

"Now, let's go upstairs and fluff some more pillows," Duncan says.

• • •

CHAPTER FORTY-SEVEN

"...nothing can reincarnate their spirit except to walk through rooms in which they have lived and through the scenes that were the background of their lives."
(John Hays Hammond, Jr., from an unpublished letter, 1929,)

Judge calls early Saturday morning. Duncan has just left for work, and Annie takes the call.

"Got another call from Henry. He said why don't we make a party of it tonight? It might make it easier on Eleanor, he thinks. Invite some of the people who were there for the wedding, he suggested. Say, a dozen or so, all told. He'll arrange something to nibble on. I know it's last-minute, but why don't you ask some of your friends—Sally and Matt, Tommy and what's-her-name, and Charlie of course—Eleanor found him so kind and sympathetic—and maybe a couple of your other library friends, if you like. Henry said Vinnie has promised to help. How does that sound to you?"

Annie is delighted. "That sounds great, Judge. I was a little concerned about Eleanor coming to the castle at night—dark and chilly, voices echoing and all that—and so close to her loss, seeing the place where Ethan died. A group to soften it a little sounds good to me. I'll get right on it."

"See you tonight then, girl," Judge says.

I'm getting called a lot of things lately, but "girl"? Annie thinks.

• • •

Annie needn't worry. Spofford-Braxton has a fire going in the fireplace, and a small chamber group is playing in the Great Hall. The windows rattle a little with the half gale blowing outside, and the moon casts a cold light through the leaded glass panes. The light from the fire and the many candles about the room makes a warmer impression, and the group of people filing in, combined with the music, creates a mellow atmosphere.

"Oh, how lovely," Eleanor says. "How thoughtful of you, Henry. What is that piece of music they are playing?"

"Gluck's 'Dance of the Blessed Spirits,' I believe," he says. Annie is sure that Spofford-Braxton knows very well what it is, since he has selected the music program himself. "Come, have a glass of sherry and a bite of something, if you feel like it. Then we can walk around, and maybe you'll tell us all something about your visits here with your Uncle Jack," Spofford continues, leading them into the center of the room.

They help themselves at a great tavern table laid out with platters of crudités and dips and tiny open sandwiches. Carved wooden boards hold crackers and cheese, and a large crystal bowl is filled with cut fresh fruit and berries to be spooned into dainty glass cups and topped with sweet whipped cream. Vinnie, in a white shirt and with his hair combed neatly, though ludicrously parted in the middle, serves at the table and walks around offering seconds and picking up discarded plates and glasses. He gives Annie a nervous smile, but she nods reassuringly. She won't give his secret away.

Annie has been able to reach and invite Charlie, Clare, and Marie from the library contingent. The Babsons, Sally and Matt, have also come, riding together with Tommy and Annette Cameron. Sally, sipping cream sherry and nibbling on a cracker, is casting an anxious eye up toward the courtyard where she had so recently and in vain tried to resuscitate Ethan.

"Feel free to bring your drinks along," Spofford says, gesturing for them to gather around and follow him. Spofford is taking them on one of his grand tours, starting in the courtyard. The pool has been cleaned and filled since the electricians quickly finished their work, urged on by the anxious curator. Eleanor stops to look at the placid surface of the water as they walk by. Josie stands by her, ready if needed.

"Uncle Jack let me swim in the pool when I was a girl," Eleanor says. He used to stand up on the bridge and shout, 'Watch out for the fish! He might bite your toe!' He actually kept fish in it sometimes, you see. My father told me he went swimming in the pool with Greta Garbo once. *Imagine.*" She sighs. "It seems impossible that this is where…" She can't quite finish the sentence. Josie takes her by the arm and leads her resolutely into the library. The lights are on, glowing softly on the backs of the books that cover the walls in the round tower room. The ropes that usually keep tourists away from the furniture have been removed, and people seat themselves about the room.

"How about a demonstration of you-know-what, Henry?" Charlie suggests, and Spofford-Braxton places himself on one side of the room and starts speaking very softly to Clare, who is standing next to him. Eleanor, sitting on the opposite side of the room, smiles.

"I hear you perfectly, Henry. I remember when Uncle Jack explained it to me. It's the shape of the ceiling. A cupola. It makes the sound bounce, like an echo." Now they all have to try it out to see if it's just a trick, but they find that it really works.

As Spofford-Braxton continues leading the tour, they walk up and down narrow staircases, through secret passages and up to the clerestory, where they view the Great Hall from above. The storm is strengthening outside, and chill drafts come whistling in through cracks in walls and windows, muted by the pleasant music that follows them wherever they go.

When they enter the Gothic Bedroom, Eleanor sits down in the corner love seat, which was designed by her uncle and built from old confessionals.

"This was always my favorite room," she says. "Uncle Jack used to let me sleep here. He'd make this love seat into a bed for me. And in the morning he'd turn on the rain out in the courtyard."

"Turn on the rain?" Geri says, looking confused.

"Artificial," Spofford-Braxton explains. "Another of Hammond's little arrangements, a fine spray from narrow pipes across the glass ceiling of the courtyard. The system has been out of order for a while, so we don't turn it on. Makes a mess, but we're working on having it fixed," he assures them.

"It was lovely, wasn't it, Henry? Soft rain, even when the sun was shining outside! I remember the rainbows!" Eleanor laughed at the memory. "Then he'd bring me hot cocoa and muffins that he had baked himself."

"Well, Eleanor...if you'd like, you could sleep in here again tonight," Spofford-Braxton offers. "Just like old times. I don't promise hot cocoa and home-baked muffins in the morning, but I could probably manage some tea with toast and jam. You'd have to sleep in the poster bed, of course; this little love seat would be a bit cramped for you now. And you two could sleep in the Colonial Bedroom, on the other side of this little passageway," he says to Judge and Josie. "I know I still owe the bridal couple a night at the castle, but I'm afraid we don't have any more beds made up, so that will have to wait. What do you think? I'll be staying in a small, private room downstairs, so you wouldn't be alone in the castle."

"Oh, I'd love it," Eleanor says excitedly before Judge or anyone else has a chance to voice a possible objection.

"And, Henry, why don't you let the two love birds sleep in the library?" Eleanor adds. "They're young; they can sleep on the sofa. It would be such fun, all of us waking up together in the morning!" she cries. Spofford-Braxton ponders this for a moment, looking at Duncan and Annie.

"I don't know—oh, what about Augustus?" Annie says. Duncan hesitates, too, but more at the thought of the two of them fighting for space on the narrow brocade sofa that he remembers seeing in the library. However, it seems this would mean a lot to Eleanor—and what harm could one night's discomfort do?

"Augustus will be fine. He had his dinner, and we'll be back home in the morning. He won't even know we're gone," Duncan assures Annie. She nods.

"Well, now, let's all go down to the Hall for a little night-cap, or maybe a cup of coffee for the designated drivers," Spofford-Braxton says. "Meanwhile, I'll have Vinnie bring some pillows and blankets for Annie and Duncan, and turn the covers back in the bedrooms. The sheets are clean; we change them often so the place won't smell musty. We'll open the windows out to the courtyard, too; that way you'll get the benefit of the rising heat. Although it's quite pleasant in here tonight, I think."

They all walk across the bridge and through the courtyard to the Great Hall. Spofford has a word with the musicians who nod, agreeing to play on until the guests are ready to leave.

• • •

Eleanor is the first to retire, and Josie accompanies her up to the Gothic Bedroom. They sit and sip a glass of sherry while Eleanor reminisces about Uncle Jack and Aunt Irene, and about Ethan.

"I'm so glad I came here, and so grateful for Charlie's words. I can still feel Ethan's spirit here. And it's true, this does feel like home. There's no other place I can think of where I've felt so close to my family since I moved from my parents' home and into the one Uncle Jack bought for us. This place holds so many wonderful memories from my childhood— weekend picnics, holiday get-togethers, and summer visits. I'm glad Ethan got to experience it, too," she says, wiping a wayward tear and taking another sip of her sherry. Josie opens the window wider, so they can hear the music wafting up from the Great Hall.

"Well, Eleanor, I'll go back down now. Knock on our door in the morning as soon as you're dressed, and we'll go down together for tea. Is there anything you need before I go? A glass of warm milk?" Josie says.

"Oh, I don't think I'll be needing anything. I'm having a hard time keeping my eyes open already. Not used to drinking wine these days, and besides, I always fall asleep as soon as my head hits the pillow. But thanks for the thought. Until tomorrow, then, dear Josie."

Later, when Josie returns to check on her, Eleanor is fast asleep. Charlie offers to lend Eleanor his cell phone, in case she should wake up and feel lonely or anxious.

"Going up to Maine for the rest of the weekend to do a spot of leaf-peeping. I'll be in the mountains, and I don't get any reception there anyway, so a cell phone is useless to me. I've got my bag stowed in the car, so I can start from here and be up there to meet my friends in the morning. Anyway, it might be a comfort for her to have it."

He pulls out the phone, and Vinnie brings it up and quietly puts it down on the little bedside table, just under the light where Eleanor would be sure to see it. A little before midnight the last guests say their good nights, and silence settles over the castle. The Babsons and the Camerons leave together, and Clare is driving Marie back home. Spofford-Braxton finally closes the door behind Charlie, the last guest to leave, after asking him if he's sure he can't join them for tea in the morning.

"Would have loved to, but unfortunately I already made those plans with my old friends," Charlie says. "But thanks, Henry—how about a rain check? The evening was a great success, and I think it did poor Eleanor a lot of good. Closure, as they say, although I abhor those stale clichés."

The musicians pack up their instruments and leave after being profusely thanked, and probably well remunerated, by the curator. Vinnie stays for a while to help clean up, but when Duncan goes looking for him later to see if he'd like a ride home, Vinnie has already left.

• • •

CHAPTER FORTY-EIGHT

"Grief fills the room up of my absent child.
Lies in his bed, walks up and down with me,
Puts on his pretty looks, repeats his words,
Remembers me of all his gracious parts. Stuffs out his vacant
garments with his form."
(Shakespeare, King John)

The wind is howling outside, and waves crash majestically over the Dog Bar Breakwater. Just as in olden times, sailors and fishermen in small boats and large still stand to lose their lives off the New England coast, despite inventions by Hammond and those who followed him. The sea is getting greedier, eating away at the shoreline, climbing up onto the land, a little higher each year. The storms are becoming wilder, in what may be a natural cycle or a result of man's mismanagement and ignorance.

On the mainland side of Gloucester Bay the castle sleeps, its hulk of solid rock invisible in the dark, as the moon is resting comfortably behind fat, billowing storm clouds. The light from Eastern Point Lighthouse across the bay flashes its white signal every six seconds, which in ordinary weather can be seen from a distance of thirteen nautical miles; but tonight the visibility is sharply cut by the rain and mist. The foghorn blares, perhaps even less effectively. In the howling onshore wind, the horn can be easily heard inland, but hardly far out at sea. Sea gulls huddle on the castle lawn, sheltered from the wind by rocks and shrubbery, disturbed only by the driving rain and the sound of the horn.

She is fast asleep, unaware of the roaring storm outside and deaf to the whistling wind. Ethan's image is etched on the inside of her lids—indelible, yet she does not want to risk losing it, does not want to open her eyes, does not want to hear the phone that is ringing on the bedside table. She reaches for it blindly, holding onto the vision of Ethan, her darling son. The light surrounding Ethan pulsates, then begins to fade but remains the vision she takes with her into eternity as the phone slides out of her hand, coming to rest by her neck.

• • •

CHAPTER FORTY-NINE

"I see thy glory like a shooting star
Fall to the base earth from the firmament."
(Shakespeare, Richard II)

Josie knocks on the door for the third time. Still no answer. She opens it just a crack and peers in. Eleanor is still fast asleep. *Poor thing, she must be exhausted,* Josie thinks. Just then she sees Annie through the courtyard window, coming to knock at the other door. Annie is less timid than Josie, and walks into the room when there is no answer.

"Mrs. Haskell? Eleanor? Are you still asleep? Tea is served, Henry asked me to come get you." Annie walks over to the bed and gently pats the satin quilt near the foot end, putting her hand on one of the small hills outlining Eleanor Haskell's feet. The little lamp on the bedside table is on, casting its light on a half empty glass of sherry and a small Bible with a rosary draped across it. Cardinal Cushing, recently dusted, stands mutely watching the sleeping woman. Josie steps into the room, stopping just inside the door.

"She's a sound sleeper, she told me," she whispers.

Annie walks up beside the bed, taking the hand that rests on the quilt between her two. She pulls her hands back quickly.

"Oh, no," she says. "Josie, get Judge. Hurry."

• • •

"Her heart," Doctor Farber says. "Some hours ago, I would say. Seems to have gone peacefully," he adds gently, with the bedside manner of an old-time family doctor on a house visit.

"Oh, but how could it have happened?" says Josie, too stunned and distraught to cry, still refusing to accept the unacceptable and believe the unbelievable. "She got a pacemaker a few years ago, after a bad heart attack. I thought that was supposed to prevent something like this from happening. What if there was something wrong with it?"

Dr. Farber frowns slightly.

"With the pacemaker? Unlikely. Pacemaker failure causing death is very rare," he says. Judge takes him aside, and when Farber hears about the ongoing investigation into the recent death of Eleanor Haskell's son, the physician agrees that the cause of the woman's death should be looked into further. Dr. Farber assures Judge that the pacemaker also will be examined for possible malfunction.

Spofford-Braxton, who collapses on a bench in the kitchen when Duncan hurries down to bring him the ill tidings, soon recovers enough to take some action. Having probably resigned himself to the likelihood that his tenure at the castle now must be nearing its end, he alerts the police. In an effort to avert unnecessary publicity, he suggests to the desk sergeant that arriving at high speed with blaring sirens will not be necessary, since death has already been established by a licensed physician. This part of the message must have gone astray however, for soon they all hear the scream of sirens as a cavalcade of police and emergency vehicles pull into the museum parking lot, followed closely by a reporter from the local paper.

"Oh, no, not again," Annie says.

• • •

CHAPTER FIFTY

"O magic sleep! O comfortable bird,
That broodest o'er the troubled sea of the mind,
Till it is hush'd and smooth!"
(John Keats, "Endymion")

"**A**nnie, when are you coming to bed?"

"Never."

"We have to get up and go to work in five hours."

"You sleep, then. I can't."

It has been a long day. Annie usually finds off-season Sunday afternoons at the library a pleasant change. The tempo is laid back; patrons come in to read the papers and chat or argue about town goings on. Students sit with their noses in books for a last-minute cramming before a test, or run around desperate for easy answers to tough questions. Occasional tourists come in to use the bathrooms. *There are too few year-round public restrooms in Rockport, especially on the Neck,* they complain. Then they stay for a while, enchanted by the friendly library, getting pointers from the librarians about sights they may have missed.

But today Annie didn't make it to the library, her heart too sick and her brain too addled. Duncan called Penny to sub at the Main Desk, and Jean took the reference desk for the day. Jean armed herself with a stack of local pamphlets, maps, and restaurant menus and told Marie and Penny to send any tourists her way. While Duncan sat at his desk trying to concentrate on the library budget, an annual challenge, his brain was as addled as Annie's.

When Annie finally crawls into bed, she lies stiff and unmoving, feeling very cold, on her side of the bed. *Is there no end to this? Here I am, a newlywed, lying next to my loving husband, and I feel nothing. Nothing. Emptiness, that's all.* She tries to lie still and breathe slowly and quietly, as though she is asleep. Duncan, who is not fooled, finally reaches over and rolls her into his warmth, and something between a sigh and a sob escapes her.

•   •   •

CHAPTER FIFTY-ONE

"Mordre wol out, certeyn, it wol nat faille."
(Chaucer, The Prioress' Tale)

When the *Cape Ann Chronicle* comes out on Monday morning, Duncan and Annie know that they must call the trustees immediately. Matthews and Swernow seem none too pleased that further scandal is to be connected with the library. *"Another Death at Hammond Castle"* is the headline. The article refers back to Ethan's death, "still under investigation," during the wedding of two Rockport librarians—named, naturally—which is now followed by the death of yet another Hammond family member, Eleanor Hammond Haskell. And by some coincidence, the two librarians have again been present. The paper then cannot avoid the opportunity to also mention the Carlo Valenti murder which took place earlier in the year, when Annie Quitnot was a suspect, though later exonerated.

Charlie has not yet returned from Maine, and Duncan leaves a message for him to call as soon as he returns. They have Charlie's cell phone number, but Annie remembers that he has loaned his phone to Eleanor Haskell—*for all the good it did her,* she thinks. Annie decides to call Spofford-Braxton to see if he has found it.

"Hello, Annie," he says, sounding hoarse and generally dreadful. Maybe he's been dipping into the sherry. Not that she would blame him.

"Henry, how are you today? No better than we, I am sure. Did you see the paper yet?"

"Unfortunately. I'm sorry this has gotten you into the news again," he says—a little tersely, she thinks, as though he is intimating that her presence really might have caused the whole sorry mess. "Duncan must be upset. However, since Charlie was there, too, at least you two should have no trouble with *your* board of trustees."

Annie frowns. Is he suggesting that he is having trouble with *his* board of trustees?

"I sure hope you're right, Henry. The other trustees didn't seem too happy when Duncan called them, and we haven't been able to reach Charlie yet. Actually, I'm calling to see if you happened to find Charlie's cell phone. It was left for Eleanor on her night table in case she might need it. I didn't notice it by her bed, or I would have picked it up," Annie says.

"I'm sorry Annie, I haven't run across it. They've had the room closed off. The whole museum was closed off yesterday. Doesn't much matter anymore. Season's over. We're closing anyway," he says, dully, "probably forever."

"Oh, Henry, don't say that. Maybe they'll confirm that Eleanor died of natural causes and determine that Ethan's death was an accident." Annie finds herself fervently wishing that this could be true. Suddenly she feels guilty. Could she have caused the situation they are in by embarking on some crazed mission of her own, driven by a personal obsession with murder? Why did she so rashly assume that it *was* murder? She begins to shake. Maybe Carlo's murder has made her paranoid. Maybe when the fog lifts, broad daylight will show her a complete fool.

"With the way things have been going lately, I doubt it." Spofford's voice is wavering, almost tremulous. Annie hopes he is not about to start crying. She'd better either hang up or change the subject. A sense of pity tells her to stay on the line.

"While I think of it, Henry, have you seen Vinnie?" Annie asks.

"Vinnie? No, haven't seen him since Saturday night. But then, I wasn't expecting to. As I said, the season is over. I'm sure he has another job lined up for the winter. He'll do anything rather than stay home, it seems. I was hoping to call him in to help prepare the museum for the off season. The usual clean up, moving artifacts out of the light and away from leaky windows, that sort of thing. But I don't know now. Maybe it'll be someone else's responsibility."

"Well, I'm sure everything will sort itself out, one way or another," she says. *What a stupid, trite thing to say.*

"I don't know, Annie. It all seems so unbelievable. I don't know what to think any more. As for the phone, I'll go and have a look. Maybe they're finished up there. If I find it, I'll drop it by. I need to get out of here, anyway," the curator says, still sounding resigned and depressed.

"Stop by at our house for coffee later, Henry, whether you find the phone or not. We should be home around seven," Annie says, feeling sorry for him—even guilty, worried that she may have pushed things too far. If she hadn't kept prodding, maybe it would have been all over now, just two unfortunate accidents, with Ethan and Eleanor peacefully on the way to their eternal rest.

· · ·

CHAPTER FIFTY-TWO

"Remember me when I am gone away,
Gone far away into the silent land."
(Christina Rossetti, "Remember")

In the afternoon Duncan gets a call from Judge, who asks if Annie could get him a copy of Ethan's obituary in the Washington Gazette, and maybe Nathan Haskell's, too, Nathan being Eleanor's husband. Newspapers usually keep that kind of information in their archives.

After trying in vain to chase down Eleanor Haskell's lawyer, Judge has gotten in touch with the funeral home to see what they can do to help get arrangements started, as there is no family left to organize this. That's when the subject of an obituary came up. Judge left a message at the church where they so recently buried Ethan, assuming that would be where Eleanor would also be laid to rest. Then he decided to call Charlie before remembering that he went away for the weekend, and called Spofford-Braxton instead. Together they decided that, despite the upsetting circumstances, there ought to be an obituary in the local paper as well. There should be enough information in the family obituaries to borrow from, and they would include the connection to the Hammond family, of course.

"Sure, Duncan. I'll give the paper a call," Annie says. "I'll have the information faxed here."

She looks up the number and dials.

"Obits, please."

"I don't know if anyone is at the desk. Just a moment, please."

Annie gets put on hold, and waits. Out of the corner of her eye she sees Mrs. Ridley who, next to Lorraine Davis, is one of Annie's least favorite library patrons. *Trapped.* Mrs. Ridley glances her way and then, with a malicious smile, comes walking over.

"So, Ms. Quitnot," (she purposely pronounces it Mizzz), "I see you're in the news again! Why am I not surprised? I can hardly believe they took you back to begin with. Mr. Langmuir must be feeling a bit rueful, I daresay. Doubly so, you might even say."

Annie keeps her mouth closed and points silently to the receiver. Then she puts her hand over it and whispers:

"On a long-distance call, Mrs. Ridley. Sorry."

Mrs. Ridley snaps her neck and walks off. Annie feels her jaws tighten and opens her mouth wide to relax them. Mrs. Ridley, of this Annie is sure, had a lot to do with her suspension after Carlo's murder earlier in the year by loudly voicing her objection to the presence of an "accused murderer" in the library.

"Hello, this is Mary. Can I help you?" The *Washington Gazette* is back on the line.

"Hi Mary, this is Annie Quitnot. I'm calling from the Rockport Library—that's Rockport, *Massachusetts,*" she emphasizes. Annie states her needs, saying she's sorry she doesn't have the exact dates, but she is preparing an obituary for Mrs. Eleanor Haskell, Nathan's wife and Ethan's mother.

"No prob. I'll look them up by name." Annie can hear Mary humming under her breath while searching on her computer, clicking away rapidly. Must be wearing a wireless headset.

"Oh, is that Mrs. Eleanor *Hammond* Haskell? I see here that we actually have an obit prepared for her already. It's common with prominent people, you know. Would you like a copy of that? As far as I know, we haven't even received a notice that she passed away. If you give me the date, we'll run the obit here, too."

"Certainly. Oh, and Mary, while I have you on the line," Annie says on a sudden impulse, "we've lost our library file on Jack Hammond, that's *John Hays Hammond, Jr.,* and I'm trying to restore some of the material. How far back does your archive go?"

"Oh, all the way," Mary laughs. "But for the really old stuff, someone has to go down to the morgue and look it up on microfiche."

"I see. Good old microfiche. Will it all ever be computerized? Well, I'll go through my notes—handwritten notes on paper, you know—and see if I can come up with dates of the things I used to have. Patents and stuff like that I can get online, that's no problem. I do remember one article from the *Gazette* right off the top of my head, though. It was on an inside page, the year was 1922, and it was in June or July. Hammond had just received an important patent sometime at the end of June, and there was a picture of him on the page, too."

"Wow. I don't know, Annie. That may be a tall order. We're kind of busy here today. I'll see if I can put someone on it, though. Meanwhile, I'll fax you the obits. Okay?"

"Thanks a million, Mary. And I'll call you back when I have some more specific dates."

"Sure. Ask for me when you call, and I'll put you onto someone who can help you out."

Annie prints "Washington Gazette, MARY, obits" and the phone number on a card, which she puts it in her rolodex. Maybe she should have told Mary of the circumstances surrounding Eleanor Haskell's death. Well, she'll have to check with Duncan first. Speak of the devil—the intercom button from the director's office is blinking.

"Hi, Dunc, what's up?"

"That was *my* question. You've been on the phone for quite a while, rosebud."

"So, now I'm a sled, huh?"

Duncan is silent—speechless, maybe? Annie makes a face and relents, feeling a little guilty. "Okay, okay. Sweet one, Dunc, but I'm a little bit past the bud stage, I think... Anyway, I've been on the phone with the *Washington Gazette*. They're faxing the info on the obit."

"Sounds like a foreign language. Love that jargon stuff."

"Sorry. That's what happens when you are on the phone with a big-city person. Aren't you glad you live in a small town where people are patient, understanding, and kind, and give you a little slack when you don't quite measure up?" Annie is still smarting at the thought of Mrs. Ridley's comments.

"Ahh. She came to see you then."

"I'm sure I don't know who you're talking about."

"Don't listen to her. I don't."

Annie decides it's time to change the topic. "I'm going home to make us a sandwich for supper. Henry may be coming over for coffee around seven. See you in a little bit?"

"You bet, my chickadee. Why don't you come up and see me sometime?"

"Hey, if I'm the chickadee, that's supposed to be my line."

"Well, we can practice our lines later, when I get home."

She'd forgotten to ask Duncan whether she should call back and give the *Washington Gazette* the details about Eleanor Haskell's death. Well, she'll talk to him about it when he gets home. He'll probably say no, anyway.

• • •

CHAPTER FIFTY-THREE

"Life is the art of drawing sufficient conclusions from insufficient premises."
(Samuel Butler, Notebooks)

Duncan, in case I don't run into you on the way, your sandwich is in the fridge. You must have gotten tied up. Not Mrs. R. again, I hope? Just going down to the library to check if the fax came. I'll be back before Henry comes. Love, A.

Annie sticks the note on the mirror in the hall, where they usually leave messages for each other. When she gets close to the library, she can see that the lights are out in the director's office, so she must have missed Duncan. Maybe he stopped to pick up the paper. *Funny,* she thinks, *we get all the daily papers at the library and yet we still feel the need to have one of our own, one to read at home, slumped in a chair along with our evening coffee.*

Annie lets herself into the library by the back door and walks over to the fax machine. There is a curl of paper there, indicating a fax has been received. She rips it off and unrolls it partly, until she sees the obituaries. Then she walks over to her desk but decides she doesn't want the big lights on, inviting people to call the cops. Instead she goes down to the dungeon, where she turns on the small light fixture that hangs over the round table. The light will hardly be visible from the outside, as the windows are shielded by the Garden Club's healthy specimens of mums.

She grabs a bottle of juice in the little fridge—Duncan sees to it personally that water and juice are always available for the staff—and sits down at the table. Reading Eleanor Haskell's obituary suddenly makes her death very real. *How sad,* Annie thinks, *not to have a single family member left to note one's passing.* She unrolls the fax to find Ethan's—which she can't bear to read at all—and Nathan Haskell's. She unrolls the paper further and finds that Mary has managed to include the article Annie mentioned from the archives. *How nice of her.* Annie takes the fax upstairs and separates the obituaries from the newspaper article. She brings the article over to the copier and inserts the library key. Fax paper is notoriously bad, and will deteriorate right in front of your eyes, so she will make a good copy for her files. Annie puts some archival copy paper in the tray and presses the start button. When she checks the copy to make sure it is legible, she notices the headline beneath the Hammond article. She remembers it from the castle, but there the article itself had been cut off. She reads it now, out of curiosity. It is a time capsule, and she is transported to a different place, in a different time.

"Suicide of Local Inventor." She remembers the headline, remembers thinking how ironic it had seemed to see it there, right next to Hammond's success story. "A local man, Elias Field, was yesterday found dead in his small workshop, apparently by suicide. Mr. Field was discovered by his grief-stricken wife, who immediately summoned their physician. Dr. Edward Wetherbee determined that Mr. Field had been dead for some hours. An empty cup was found near the body, which was later determined to have contained rat poison. Mrs. Field would only say that her husband lately had been depressed, and had for several days been in extremis upon learning that an important patent had been denied him. Mr. Field leaves behind his wife and three small children."

The blood drains slowly from Annie's face. Her hands feel so cold, and her legs, even though she tries to will them to walk, seem rooted to the floor. *Oh, but it can't be, it just can't.* But her brain keeps going at light speed, entirely of its own volition; she can't stop it. She tries to cover her eyes, yet she sees before her the device that was brought up by the Coast Guard, the device with the initials *"E.F."* Elias Field. A *suicide.* Charlie Field's grandfather had committed suicide after a "business failure." Hammond had received a patent for his Gyrad, the system for radio control of moving bodies, at the same time that Elias Field had been denied his.

There is someone at the door, someone with a key. *Please, make it be Duncan,* she prays. But it is Charlie; she sees him through the glass pane. Annie still cannot move and can only hope that he will go by her in the dark, but he turns on the lights as soon as he steps inside the door. She is momentarily blinded and blinks in terror, like a mole surprised by daylight.

"Why, Annie," he says, looking startled, "what on earth were you doing here in the dark?"

"I...was just leaving," she says, her throat so dry the voice comes out in a croak. "I only stopped in to pick something up."

"I see. Me too, actually. I just came in to make a copy," Charlie says, smiling, and walks over to the machine. "I see someone left the copier on. Well, that's convenient. Do you happen to have the key handy, Annie?"

Annie opens the drawer and pulls out the key again, and hands it to Charlie. When he turns to the copier, she quickly reaches over to the desk and grabs the copy she has made and stuffs it into her bag. But it won't do any good. When Charlie lifts the lid she sees that she has left the original fax in the copier.

Charlie stays bent over the copier for an eternity. When he turns to her, his face is sad, as terribly, mournfully sad as when he turned to Eleanor at the end of his eulogy for Ethan.

"Oh, my dearest Annie," he says.

"Charlie," she whispers.

• • •

CHAPTER FIFTY-FOUR

"Extreme fear can neither fight nor fly."
(Shakespeare, Rape of Lucrece)

Someone else is at the door. Dusk has settled outside, but it is not dark enough yet for the timed lights to be on. Annie, from her vantage point behind the circulation desk, cannot make out who is outside. But Charlie can. He moves toward her, and she stares at him, paralyzed. Suddenly she is able to move again, and she quickly pulls the gate between the counters closed and latches it before he can reach it. The outer door opens, and in the light Annie sees Duncan and just behind him, Henry Spofford-Braxton. As they rush forward to the inner door, Charlie manages to wrench the gate open, breaking the latch. He steps behind her, putting one arm around her shoulders. She feels a hard object against her back.

"If only you hadn't been so stubborn, Annie," Charlie says softly, almost plaintively.

Duncan and Henry burst into the library, but as they start to move toward Annie she screams.

"Don't move, he has a gun pointed at me!"

Duncan spreads his arms wide, covering Henry. "Stay where you are, Henry. Charlie, I beg you. Don't do this. She has done you no harm. Let her go."

"Sorry, old friend. Can't be helped now. Out of my way, Duncan." Charlie moves forward, kicking at Annie's heels to force her ahead of him.

"Why, Charlie? Why?" Henry calls out. "What did Ethan ever do to you? And Eleanor, a lonely old woman..." Duncan tries to silence Henry, but he steps out, trying to prevent Charlie from passing them. Charlie gives Annie a violent shove forward and she nearly falls into Henry's arms, but Charlie pulls her away and puts his back against the door so he can open it without letting go of her. As he pulls Annie through the door, the outer door opens.

Before Charlie has a chance to turn around, a gun is pressed against the back of his neck.

"Freeze," Officer Hale says.

•   •   •

CHAPTER FIFTY-FIVE

"Man is neither angel nor beast;
and the misfortune is that he who would act
the angel acts the beast."
(Blaise Pascal, Pensees)

Officer Hale is backed up by Officer Elwell, whose large, trustworthy frame looms right behind him. Officer Elwell is busy calling for reinforcements, and a few moments later sirens wail and flashes of blue light flicker all around the library walls. Within minutes Charlie is handcuffed and manhandled out to the cruiser, which takes off immediately.

"Oh, Billy, thank you," Annie says, in a near whisper. Duncan is there, one arm around her waist, holding her upright.

"Good thing that wasn't a real gun," Billy says. The gun had turned out to be the library copier key, and Charlie had been "disarmed" without incident. "And a good thing that some observant citizen called in and reported that the lights were on in the library. But Annie, how did this all start? Why did Field attack you? Was he...uh...I mean, did he try to, eh...make advances?" Billy has reddened slightly. Normally, he has no difficulty with this kind of questioning, as it has become routine; but he knows Annie and had been involved in the sometimes steamy questioning in the Carlo Valenti case, which makes things a little touchy. But Annie can only stare at him.

"Advances? Oh, God."

"He's the murderer, don't you see, the murderer!" Henry shouts, exasperated.

"Murderer?" Billy swivels around. "Who's been murdered?"

It takes Duncan to explain, in as few words as he can, what their suspicions are. Officer Hale makes a quick call to the station. Annie, Duncan, and Henry are immediately requested to come in and talk to the chief. When they get into the cruiser, Officer Hale turns to Annie.

"I do wish you'd let the local police handle violent crimes around here, Annie," he says. *Good,* she thinks, *he's calling me "Annie," not "Miss Quitnot," which is what he calls me when I'm is in trouble.*

"The chief will want to talk to you all of course, both about the incident at the library tonight and about your theory."

Annie rolls her eyes in the dark. She can just hear the chief's voice calling it a "theory," dismissively, as though the accusation obviously has no merit whatsoever—especially against the upstanding Rockport Library trustee that they have just put in the keeping cell. No doubt the chief is already envisioning an embarrassing situation. He is probably swiveling in his chair, imagining some of the possible headlines.

"After that I'm sure you'll be free to go," Billy continues. "Chief Murphy may, of course, want to get in touch with you again in the morning. Try to stay out of trouble until then, Annie," he says, and a little exasperation creeps into his voice.

"I promise, Billy," Annie says meekly. She has no strength left to be her feisty self.

Chief Murphy shakes his head while listening to Annie's elaborate unwinding of the plot, as she has it figured. She also suggests that the chief call and inform Judge Bradley of the situation, which somehow doesn't surprise him. Nothing will surprise him now, after hearing Annie's *theory*. The chief tries to hide a sigh. He knows he'll have to do it, Judge Bradley being a town bigwig. But the story, like everything else having to do with Ms. Quitnot, seems wholly unbelievable. A fantastic tale, certainly a figment of her vivid imagination. Had Mr. Field by any chance confessed to her, he asks.

"No, not exactly, not in so many words," she has to admit. Chief Murphy nods sagely.

After the police have taken Annie's, Duncan's, and Henry's statements (separately, so that they can be compared later, of course), they are allowed to go home. Duncan starts a pot of coffee while Annie goes to change and wash her face and hands. She feels dirty. She is not sure whether this is because she has just betrayed Charlie or because his touch has made her feel soiled. *Oh, my God. Dear, sweet Charlie. How could this have happened?* she thinks.

· · ·

CHAPTER FIFTY-SIX

"We have just enough religion to make us hate,
but not enough to make us love one another."
(Jonathan Swift, Thoughts on Various Subjects)

Another sleepless night is in store. Annie cannot stop fretting. Carefully, she crawls out of bed and tiptoes downstairs to the study. Elbows on the desk, head in her hands, she sits by the computer. The chief listened to her story, called it "fantastic." And then he said, "Where is the proof? There's not a shred of evidence in what you are telling me. We'll keep Mr. Field overnight for accosting you, naturally, but beyond that—well, it'll be up to you. Will you be pressing charges, Ms. Quitnot?" *Pressing charges?* As if "accosting" her was the only crime they believed Charlie could possibly be guilty of.

She turns the computer on and, to pass the time, goes back to her searches of the early Moonie days in Gloucester. Oh, if only it had been the Moonies! She feels guilty at the thought and turns her attention to the screen.

Moon has moved on to bigger and better things, it seems, and has not set foot in Gloucester in a long time. Presumably, he has been too busy subjugating. The coronation, of course, helped put him back into the limelight. The billionaire "Savior of Humanity, Messiah, Returning Lord and True Parent," is still out to conquer the world, according to reports.

He intends for all religions to be "reconciled," blended into one faith, *under him.*

When Moon is finished reconciling and has everyone under the umbrella of the Unification Church, it is said that he aims to replace the United States Constitution with his "Godism."

"My dream is to organize a Christian political party including all the Protestant denominations, Catholic, and all the religious sects. We can embrace the religious world in one arm and the political world in the other... The whole world is in my hand, and I will conquer and subjugate the world," Moon is reported to have said in a speech outlining Godism, his ideal theocratic government.

"The separation between religion and politics is what Satan likes most," he states frequently, as a lead-in to his campaign for a global theocracy. However, religion has lately taken a back seat to politics for Reverend Moon, who seems to be more interested in influence peddling and buying people and property on a global scale, while his empire morphs from cult to conglomerate.

Aside from the notables who appeared at his coronation, he has won mainstream acceptance and support from "the highest level in the land." Not to mention the mega-funds he has received from many organizations, including the Faith-Based Initiatives program. Many religious and political organizations in turn have been bailed out of financial difficulties (for instance, Moon is said to have lent the money-squandering Jerry Falwell 3.5 million to rescue his struggling Liberty University).

Scores of politicians and ultra right-wing organizations have accepted donations from Moon, and are beholden to him in return. Money laundering, influence-peddling—such as funding Korea-gate and Ollie North and the Iran-Contra gang—were scandals that Moon apparently overcame by simply spreading more cash around.

Annie returns to Moon's current influence on the local arena. The fear that gripped Gloucester in the early Moonie days, and the near-frenzied attempts to stop the Unification Church from taking over the town and turning it into a Korean-speaking Moon-land, have long since abated. A recent article reports that the long-ago proposed resolution to ban anyone in Gloucester from having anything to do with the Moonies, including selling them property, was quickly retracted when city councilors realized that it would be unconstitutional, and would breed hatred and discrimination.

The number of Unification Church members still living in Gloucester has decreased, most of those remaining working in what's left of the Moonie-owned fish and lobster industry. Moon's one hundred thousand dollar tuna-fishing tournaments are history, as is his armada of large fishing boats. Some people in town note that the remaining members are hardworking local folk and that the Moonie businesses pay taxes on their properties and contribute to the local economy. Other than that, you don't hear much talk about the Moonies anymore. Moon himself has definitely moved on to bigger and better fishing-grounds.

Annie shudders slightly. It's getting chilly in the alcove, but she feels too edgy to go back to bed. She'd only toss and turn and wake poor Duncan. Five more minutes, then she'll make a cup of tea and go lie down on the couch.

She clicks on another hit, which states that when Reverend Moon was sent to jail, Senator Orrin Hatch of Utah came to his defense. "The prosecution of Reverend Moon has sent the wrong message. The federal government accused a newcomer to our shores of criminal and intentional wrongdoing for conduct commonly practiced by other religious leaders, namely the holding of church funds in bank accounts in their own names."

The last article she reads is from a local source. It states that, at the time when the initial resolution was proposed, a lone city councilor in Gloucester, Abdullah Khambaty, argued against it. Khambaty was in India during the struggle for independence from Britain. The article quotes him: "Have you ever seen one million people being killed within a three-month period because their beliefs were different from others? Have you read about Northern Ireland? India and Pakistan? The Crusades and the Holy War? If this order is approved, what will happen to the city? Today it's the Moonies. Tomorrow it will be something else."

Annie pulls her robe closer around herself, feeling chilled. She remembers other words, from another time—those of Pastor Niemuller:

"They came for the Jews, and I said nothing, for I wasn't a Jew..." she mumbles aloud to herself.

"Amen."

Annie whips around in her chair. Again, she hasn't heard Duncan, who has arrived quietly and is now standing behind her, reading over her shoulder.

"How long have you been standing there?"

"Long enough, I hope," Duncan says, massaging her back lightly.

"Oh yes. I'm all done," she says.

• • •

CHAPTER FIFTY-SEVEN

"We sit around in a ring and suppose,
But the Secret sits in the middle, and knows."
(Robert Frost, "The Secret Sits")

"By the way, what made you come looking for me at the library?" Annie asks as she crawls under the covers.

"Well, when Henry brought Charlie's phone...oh God, the phone." Duncan sits up in bed. "I completely forgot. It was very curious. Henry handed it to me, and I just checked to see if the battery had gone dead, and then I noticed that there was a call received on it, but the caller number was blocked."

"Well, so what?" Annie rolls over and unwillingly gets up on one elbow.

"It was made that night," Duncan continues, "*after* the party. At three o'clock in the morning, to be exact. I suppose it could be one of Charlie's friends trying to reach him," he suggests. He lies down again, putting his head on the pillow before, very reluctantly, he whispers. "You know, I started thinking...what if it was...Charlie? But why would *Charlie* have called *her,* and at three o'clock in the morning? Doesn't that seem odd to you, for him to call and wake her? God forgive me, but what if he wanted to call Eleanor and scare her, trying to cause her to have another heart attack? I couldn't think of a single reason why. In my wildest dreams, I would never have suspected that it might be Charlie. My dear old friend Charlie. Of course, I still think the idea is pretty far-fetched. I mean, there was no guarantee that scaring her would work, especially since she had a pacemaker." Annie sits up straight in bed, then tosses the bedwear aside.

"Oh, God." Annie is out of bed now, scuttling back and forth, pulling on her jeans and trying to tuck in her nightie, then giving up and putting on a shirt, letting the nightie hang out underneath. "I'll bet you anything it's a digital phone. *That's* how he did it, Duncan. Another remote control murder, don't you see? Oh, the wicked, deadly irony. Digital cell phones can cause the pulses to become irregular, or even stop the pacemaker from delivering pulses altogether if you hold the phone close to the pacemaker and don't remove it right away—especially if you've already had a significant heart attack and depend heavily on the pacemaker. I looked it up for someone in the library once. People with pacemakers shouldn't own or use a digital phone, and Eleanor would have held it to her ear…she was probably half asleep, and maybe she fell back and dropped the phone onto herself, not aware of what was happening even if she had known about the danger. Oh, Duncan, you have to call the chief. And call Judge, too, to make sure that he's been told. I think the chief was just humoring me when he said he'd call Judge."

"But Annie, we're just speculating…" Duncan says anxiously, sorry he voiced this ludicrous idea.

"Dunc, at least we have to make them trace the call!"

Duncan sits up and looks at her pleadingly. "Come on, wife, it's the middle of the night. I can just imagine Chief Murphy if we sprang this idea on him now. Annie, I promise we will call him first thing. But right now, my beloved, it's three o'clock in the morning, so get out of that amazing outfit and come back to bed."

• • •

CHAPTER FIFTY-EIGHT

"What a chimera then is a man! What a novelty! What a monster,
what a chaos, what a contradiction, what a prodigy! Judge of all
things, feeble earthworm, depository of truth, a sink of uncertainty
and error, the glory and the shame of the universe."
(Blaise Pascal, Pensées)

When Duncan calls Judge Bradley in the morning to tell
him of Annie's new hypothesis, Judge immediately
says he'll stop by and pick up the cell phone. Armed with
this piece of evidence, he drives over to the Rockport Police
Headquarters and talks to Chief Murphy, explaining in detail
how the crime could have been committed. Needless to say,
Chief Murphy is highly dubious. His eyebrows rise higher
with every word of this new theory. However, the number is
traced and indeed turns out to be Charlie Field's home number. Armed with that fact, the chief agrees to try the theory
on "Library Trustee Field," as the chief still respectfully calls
him. To Chief Murphy's amazement, on being faced with the
cell phone and Annie's theory, Charles Field suddenly and
unexpectedly confesses. In fact, he seems eager, even pleased
to do so.

Later, when Judge comes back to tell them about it, he
says Charlie appeared proud and quite satisfied during his
lengthy confession. He had waited for this for a long time,
he said, ever since his father died and his mother told him

261

how Jack Hammond had robbed his grandfather of the famous patent and the Field family fortune that would have resulted from it. Standing in the castle's Renaissance Dining room window, Charlie used his grandfather's remote control gadget to set in process the sinking of the *Pioneer* with the "Uncle Jack" dummy on board. It was an act full of symbolism, but easily accomplished. That was how he "killed" Jack Hammond. Annie now recollects seeing what she assumed was one of Hammond's inventions casually resting on the windowsill in the dining room.

Ethan's death, on the other hand, took some planning. Charlie borrowed one of Hammond's lesser-known ideas to accomplish this, one which Jack originally had used to turn his dorm room lights out automatically, using a sensor and a circuit breaker, should the door be opened by a monitor coming to check. (Though, to his chagrin later, when this clever idea became widely popular, it turned out that Hammond had neglected to patent it.) Charlie had also managed to add a large quantity of salt to the pool water to ensure a positive result. Annie remembers seeing the whitish residue on the pool floor, after it had been drained, without understanding its significance.

Then came the murder of Eleanor Hammond Haskell— well, that was easy. As soon as Charlie heard about Eleanor's severe heart condition and the pacemaker (while they were at the reception in her house after the funeral), he knew how he would accomplish that killing. Remotely, of course.

When Ethan came to him some time ago with the proposition of publishing a book about his uncle's patents and inventions, that was the moment he had begun planning, Charlie said. He was speaking softly, smiling as though he found the whole chain of events amusing, seemingly expecting them all to see how brilliantly clever and reasonable it all was and to agree that justice had finally been done. He erased the Hammond family from this earth—even removed every trace of them from the library, he confessed with some exuberance, erasing all computer records in the system and removing books, files, and any other evidence he could find in the library of the existence of Jack Hammond, and burning it all in his fireplace.

"Of course!" Annie says. "That's how it was done. Charlie had access to everything in the library. It never occurred to me to think of that, of the filching being done by one of us. How simple." *Oh, dear. A thousand pardons, Lorraine...*" Of course, I don't think Charlie is computer savvy enough to erase the records in the whole system. I'm sure a lot can be restored. But the card files and the hard copy material, well, we've lost that."

Annie rubs her eyes. She could use a week's sleep but figures it will take a few more nights of tossing and turning before the cobwebs have been cleared.

"I don't know what to say." Duncan slumps in his chair. "I'm all torn apart. What a horrible thing. The poor man just went over the edge. I wish he would have come to me. We were such close friends, yet I never had an inkling...Could I have helped him? Who knows. Probably not. I knew Charlie's business was failing—he told me recently that he filed for bankruptcy. It may explain some of the anger he must have felt, but it doesn't excuse these terrible black deeds, of course. I can see the symbolism in doing the dummy in. But killing Ethan? Or Eleanor? The family tragedy that led to it all, well, people survive tragedies and go on with life." Duncan looks gray and distraught.

"Do you remember how, in his eulogy, Charlie referred to Ethan being the end of the Hammond line? His death would be a powerful revenge, don't you see? Charlie must have grown up with so much resentment about all the tragedies in his family, blaming them all on Hammond," Annie says.

"But what about Eleanor? That poor woman never did him any harm." Duncan puts his head in his hands.

"I remember when we were at her home after Ethan's funeral, Duncan. Charlie was looking around at the rather opulent surroundings, and he said, 'How would you like to live in a home like this, paid for by a rich uncle's inventions?' and we both laughed."

"Having just lost everything, I suppose Charlie must have felt it to be a great injustice," Duncan says, nodding slowly.

"Oh, Duncan. Maybe the real tragedy is that Hammond *didn't* cheat Charlie's grandfather," Annie says quietly. Judge and Duncan look at her, waiting for an explanation. "Charlie was obviously convinced that he did, but the truth is that Jack Hammond actually filed his patent application four years before Elias Field did. Hammond applied in 1913, according to the Patent Office papers. Field did not apply until 1917— at least according to the date on Field's contraption. Maybe Elias didn't know that. After all, the Gyrad patent wasn't granted until 1922. Elias might even have copied Hammond's invention, for all we know…but what difference does any of it make now, anyway? And also, the patent for the Gyrad alone wouldn't have amounted to a great fortune. It was the sum total of all of them, together with Hammond family money, of course, that made him a rich man." Annie says. "But oh, if Charlie had only asked me to research it…"

• • •

CHAPTER FIFTY-NINE

"Through our own recovered innocence
we discern the innocence of our neighbors."
(Henry Thoreau, Walden)

Duncan has made his share of phone calls, and Annie takes over. She must call Henry first, of course, and tell him the news. Annie is still nagged by guilt feelings for having suspected Henry of killing Ethan to protect his own position at the castle. That suspicion had been far more serious than the petty and, she must admit, utterly biased one she had harbored against Lorraine Davis for file-snatching.

"Oh, Annie, all I can say is, I'm relieved that it's over," Henry says when she is finished, and Annie imagines all the worried wrinkles in his face smoothing out. "Still, it is incomprehensible to me. *Charlie Field, of all people.* We've lost a friend—well, you and Duncan have, most especially, but I had become quite fond of Charlie, too. Such a sympathetic man. Oh, dear. But the loss of the Hammond family members, now that is too staggering to comprehend," Henry says.

"Now, my dear Annie," he continues," while I have you on the line, I must tell you about something else. A very curious thing, I must say. Vinnie stopped by this morning to explain his sudden absence here. Apparently—and this is a long story, I'm afraid—he has been meeting with his biological parents all along, without the knowledge of the foster parents, who had explicitly forbidden the contact..."

"Oh, I know a little about that, Henry. I mean, Vinnie told me he saw them now and then. So, what is going on right now? Is he all right?" She hopes she hasn't created a problem for Vinnie.

"He's fine, fine. He went and told the foster parents everything, and as it turned out, they were quite moved by the way Vinnie cares about his folks—who apparently are living in some pitiful circumstances, which Vinnie did not go into—and they were also impressed by how he wants to help his folks out when he gets through with school. So they're allowing the contact. And Vinnie has assured the foster parents that he's not about to become a Moonie, he said. I don't know what *that* has to do with anything—I mean, Vinnie is a little odd, to be sure, but a Moonie? What a strange notion—but there you are."

"So, he's still working at the museum, then?"

"He'll be back working here as soon as we reopen in the spring, which is a relief. So, things are slowly going back to normal. I had a bit of a snafu with my board of trustees recently over an audit that turned out to be routine, and everything has been sorted out. So I'm going on a little vacation, just for a week or two, to visit old friends in Virginia."

Annie sighs inaudibly, relieved.

"That sounds lovely, Henry. And I take it that Hammond Castle is safe and sound for another season, then, with no harm to it from all that happened. That's good news. Bon voyage, Henry, and let's all get together when you come back!" She can't make herself mention his castle on Eastern Point, or of coming face-to-face with the ominous-looking character there. Her guilt feelings over having believed Henry capable of murder are strong enough to defeat her curiosity about that encounter.

A little anxious, Annie next calls Clare—dear, sweet Clare (wasn't that just how she had thought of Charlie: "dear, sweet Charlie...") whose bad luck with men has suddenly erupted into the truly disastrous. Clare's voice seems soft and distant when she answers. Oh, she has heard the news. Duncan called to inform Marie, and Marie called the other librarians, without suspecting the powerful effect this would have on Clare.

"It's okay, Annie, really," Clare says finally. "I thought, before your wedding, that something was going to happen between Charlie and me. But instead there was that terrible event with Ethan, and after that, well...I haven't seen Charlie since, not once, and he's never called me. Now I can see why, of course," she says with sudden bitterness.

"Oh, Clare, I'm so sorry. Let's get together and have a girls' night out sometime soon, you and Sally and I. I don't mean one of those cry-your-heart-out events—just a fun time, like we used to in the old days. We'll go to the Museum of Fine Arts or the Isabella Stewart Gardner, and then go take in a play, or something."

"Love to. Thanks, Annie."

• • •

CHAPTER SIXTY

"That is my home of love: if I have rang'd,
Like him that travels, I return again."
(Shakespeare, "Sonnet 109")

It is Friday and the library is closed, after what seems like an endless week. Annie goes down to the Hannah Jumper House to start preparing it for the second part of their "trial balloon." Soon they will move out of Duncan's house and back into hers for a month.

First of all she turns on the heat. The ocean air has had free rein to creep in through cracks and leaky windows (oh, she has to remember to call Ned Mazzarini to replace a couple of windows up in the bedroom—Duncan would definitely have something to say about them) and permeate the house with humidity, and Annie wants to remove every reason against choosing her home as their permanent domain. How she has missed it! Every door handle, every molding, every surface she passes gets a loving caress. What can she do to make Duncan accept it? She spends the morning dusting and cleaning, oiling the old darkened wall paneling, cleaning out the fireplace and laying in some handsome birch logs. She even cleans the refrigerator, a dreaded chore. The food in the freezer appears surreal to her, fishcakes and muffins and Dogtown blueberries from before the wedding and the horrendous events of the last few weeks, remnants from what seems another lifetime.

Around lunchtime Duncan shows up. He looks around the place and laughs.

"Trying to pretty the place up, huh?"

Annie heats a couple of the fishcakes for lunch, and starts a pot of coffee in her beloved old gurgling coffee maker. She microwaves two bowlfuls of blueberries with a sprinkling of sugar, and puts a dab of still frozen Cool Whip on top.

"Dessert," she says. They take the bowls and a couple of mugs of coffee and sit down by the picture window in the living room and look out over the harbor. Only the workboats are left in the water now, bobbing vigorously on the chop. All pleasure craft have been moved to their winter quarters, where they have been heat-sealed in plastic and hoisted up into their snug little condo dwellings. T Wharf, usually wall-to-wall with parked cars, is empty but for a couple of trucks. Out at the end of the wharf a group of warmly dressed people are milling around, taking pictures of each other with Motif #1 in the background. Annie suddenly recognizes old Doc Ford. And could that tall, middle-aged man be Jordy? Then the people with them must be the wife and the daughter, what was her name? Libby.

"Annie, you're supposed to get the spoon to the mouth before you empty it, I believe. You've got blueberries running all down your chin, darling," Duncan says.

Annie starts to cry.

"What is it? Oh, I guess *'darling'* won't work either?"

"Oh, no, Duncan, 'darling' is just wonderful. Please call me darling anytime. It's perfect," Annie says, trying to wipe her tears but getting blueberries all over her cheeks instead. Duncan assumes she is just having a delayed emotional reaction to recent events, and scoots closer to her, putting an arm around her. *If I hadn't suspected the Moonies,* Annie thinks, *Jordy might never have seen his dad again. And Libby might never have met her grandfather.*

They sit for a while, watching as the midday light begins to mellow, each trying to sort out any unanswered questions. Annie has told Duncan about Vinnie, of course, of how his foster parents have given their blessings to Vinnie's open relationship with his parents. She is still curious about Henry Spofford-Braxton, though.

"What do you know about Spoffie, Duncan?" she asks.

Duncan smiles. "I was waiting for you to ask, my dear. I imagine you did a bit of checking him out? Drive by his house, maybe? Well, according to Judge, Henry lives in a sort of castle on Eastern Point. Years ago, Henry's wife died in a car accident, and their young son nearly died, too. Severe head trauma. He survived, but with seriously reduced mental capacity.

"There was a rather large financial settlement, I guess," he continues, "and that's when Henry bought the property. He felt the boy would be safe there. Hired a nurse at first to take care of him. School was out of the question—the boy was violent as a child, I guess, and not educable. Apparently he is quite talented in some ways, though."

"Let me guess: stone cutting, carpentry, gardening, that sort of thing?" she says. Duncan does not seem surprised. He has already come to accept that his wife has certain talents, too. "I talked to Henry," Annie adds. "He's going on a little vacation, he told me. I said that when he gets back, we should all get together. We ought to have him over for dinner, don't you think? I'd love to hear some more about Hammond so I can recreate the files for the library, and he has great stories about him."

"I'm sure he'd be glad to help, Annie. Henry went to Oxford, too, you know. We were actually there at the same time, but I didn't know him then." Duncan says.

"Well, you both have a British accent still, although I notice yours less and less. That's the way it always is,

I guess. I never noticed my mother's Irish accent until people mentioned it to me." Annie laughs.

After a while they get up and stretch their legs. Annie goes over to the corner of the living room and unlocks the door to the little studio apartment that she rents out to an artist couple every summer. The apartment is attached to the main house by a doors-width, and has its own front door right on the sidewalk. The place will need a little airing out before she prepares it for the winter. Duncan follows her into it.

"Well, now. I didn't realize it was so spacious in here," he says. "It looks like a little shed from the outside. This would make a very nice study. Yes, indeed. But I know you can't disappoint your tenants, of course."

Annie looks at him, a ray of hope in her eyes. "Hm. It just so happens I heard from them recently. It made me kind of sad, actually. They've just retired, and one of them is ailing in some way, and they have decided to move to Florida. So they won't be coming back," she says.

Duncan takes a more serious look around. "Now, that might just make all the difference, darling, don't you see? If we sold my house—and I'm not saying yet that we will, mind you—but *if* we did, then we could afford *not* to rent this out...and look at this place! I could build bookshelves all around, and then this room might just hold all my books and everything I really need...and as for the rest of your house, we could trade some of my furniture for some of yours, so we'd both have something we are used to. But, oh dear, the kitchen..."

"Not a problem, Dunc, really." Annie rushes to interrupt him. "I won't be using the alcove for my bedroom anymore, so we could incorporate that into the kitchen. I think that would make it roomy enough, don't you?" she says hopefully. "I actually thought of doing that once, long ago," she says, without adding that this was before Carlo moved out and left his ghost behind. She had felt desperately lonely after that, in the large bedroom upstairs, and moved down to the cozy little alcove. No risk of feeling lonely now. And she is no longer afraid of Carlo's ghost.

Duncan takes another walk around the studio, surreptitiously measuring the floor with his paces.

"Well, we'll see, darling," he says, before they step back into Annie's living room. In there, her old Shakespeare volumes crowd the shelves, the leather backs freshly buffed, gold leaf titles gleaming softly.

"Yes, indeed, we'll see," he says again, taking her hand and giving her a light kiss on the cheek.

"That's it? That's all I get, a peck on the cheek?"

"Come here, you," he says, pulling her close.

• • •

ABOUT THE AUTHOR

Gunilla Caulfield was born and educated in Stockholm, Sweden, before immigrating to the United States. After ten years as an art dealer in Boston she moved to Rockport, a small fishing town and art colony on Cape Ann, *"That Other Cape,"* as they say on Cape Cod. She served as reference librarian at the Rockport Public Library, which is fictionally depicted in her mysteries. Along with husband Thomas and a steadily growing clan, she divides her time between Rockport, Massachusetts, and Bridgton, Maine.

Future works by the author include a new novel as well as additional mystery sequels with Annie Quitnot as sleuth, and a book of Christmas stories.

• • •

AFTERWORD

This book is a work of fiction, and all active characters and locations are either the products of my imagination or else are used fictitiously.

John Hays Hammond, Jr., is a historical character, as is his famous father, John Hays Hammond, Sr. The active Hammond family characters in this book are invented. There are no members of the illustrious family left, as John Hays Hammond Jr. and the remaining members of his generation died childless.

In case the reader of this book is blessed with a curious nature and starts looking into Hammond and his inventions: the murderer's motive is based on a fictional event. As for the Moonies—well, they are an integral part of Gloucester history, and have been reported on widely since their arrival on the island. I will leave it to historians to sort out fact from fiction.

Hammond Castle, the real life home of John Hays Hammond, Jr., is now a museum. It is located on the western shore of Gloucester Harbor, and well worth a visit.

Gunilla Caulfield

. . .

32592225R00160

Made in the USA
Middletown, DE
10 June 2016